GRIMMISS ISLAND™

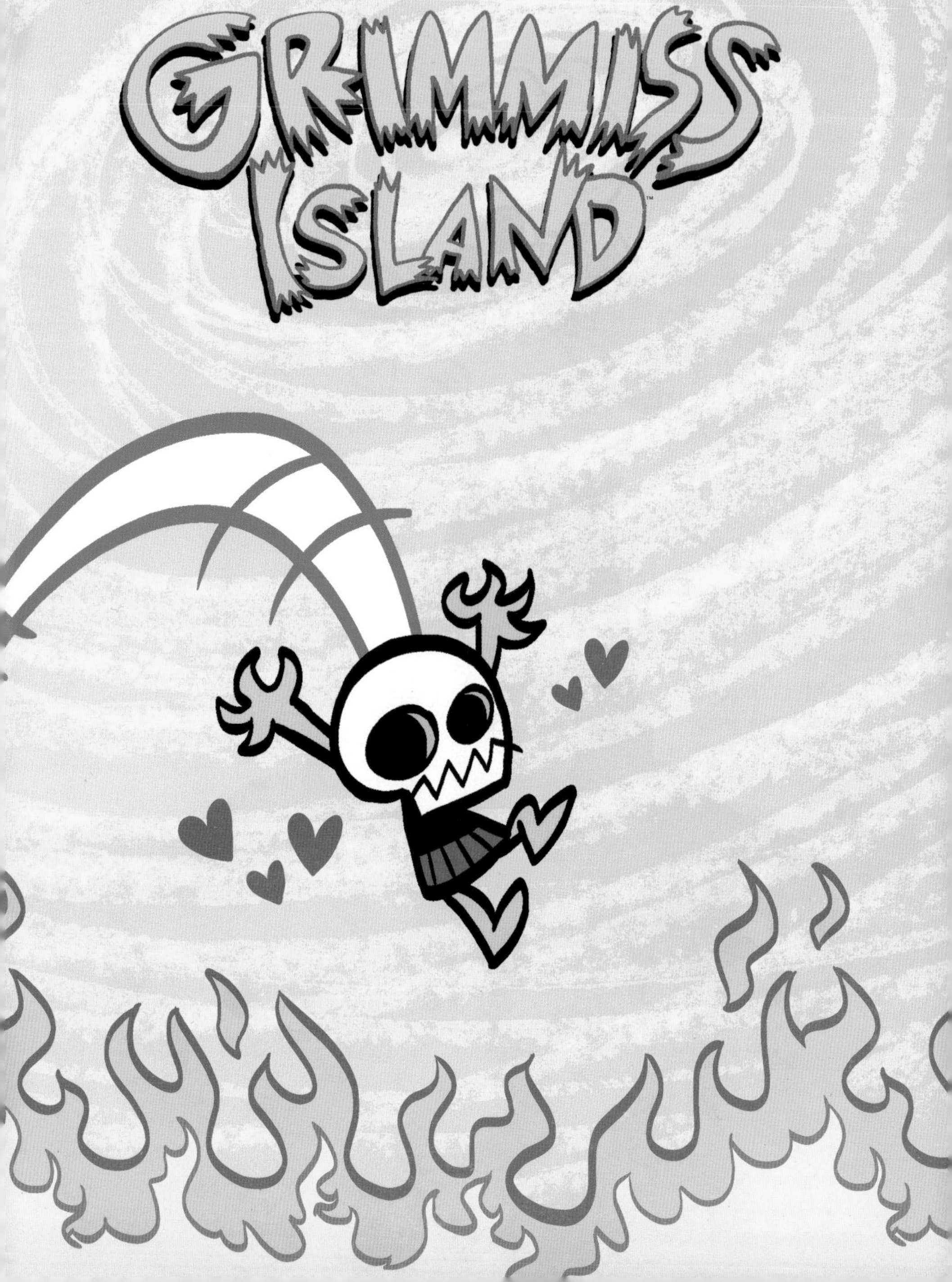

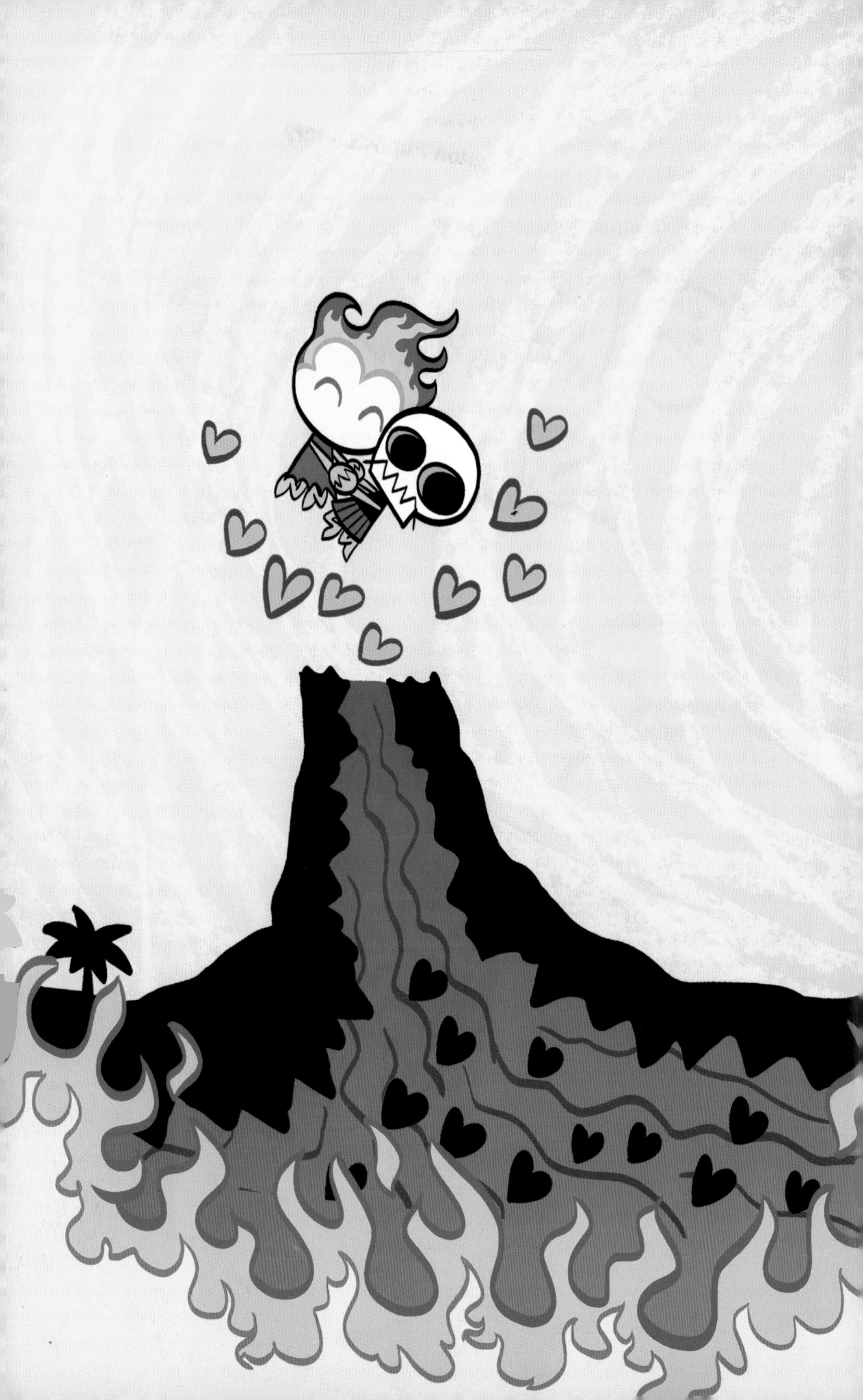

GRIMMISS ISLAND

ART BALTAZAR & FRANCO

WRITER & ARTIST   WRITER

Dark Horse Books

President and Publisher **MIKE RICHARDSON**
Editor **BRENDAN WRIGHT**
Assistant Editor **JEMIAH JEFFERSON**
Designer **KAT LARSON**
Digital Art Technician **CHRISTINA McKENZIE**

Published by
Dark Horse Books
A division of Dark Horse Comics. Inc.
10956 SE Main Street
Milwaukie. OR 97222

First edition: October 2015
ISBN 978-1-61655-768-3

GRIMMISS ISLAND

This volume collects issues #1–#4
of the Dark Horse Comics series *Grimmiss Island*.

1 3 5 7 9 10 8 6 4 2
Printed in China

NEIL HANKERSON Executive Vice President • TOM WEDDLE Chief Financial Officer • RANDY
STRADLEY Vice President of Publishing • MICHAEL MARTENS Vice President of Book Trade
Sales • SCOTT ALLIE Editor in Chief • MATT PARKINSON Vice President of Marketing
DAVID SCROGGY Vice President of Product Development • DALE LaFOUNTAIN Vice President
of Information Technology • DARLENE VOGEL Senior Director of Print. Design. and Production
KEN LIZZI General Counsel • DAVEY ESTRADA Editorial Director • CHRIS WARNER Senior
Books Editor • CARY GRAZZINI Director of Print and Development • LIA RIBACCHI Art
Director • CARA NIECE Director of Scheduling • TIM WIESCH Director of International Licensing
MARK BERNARDI Director of Digital Publishing

CHAPTER ONE

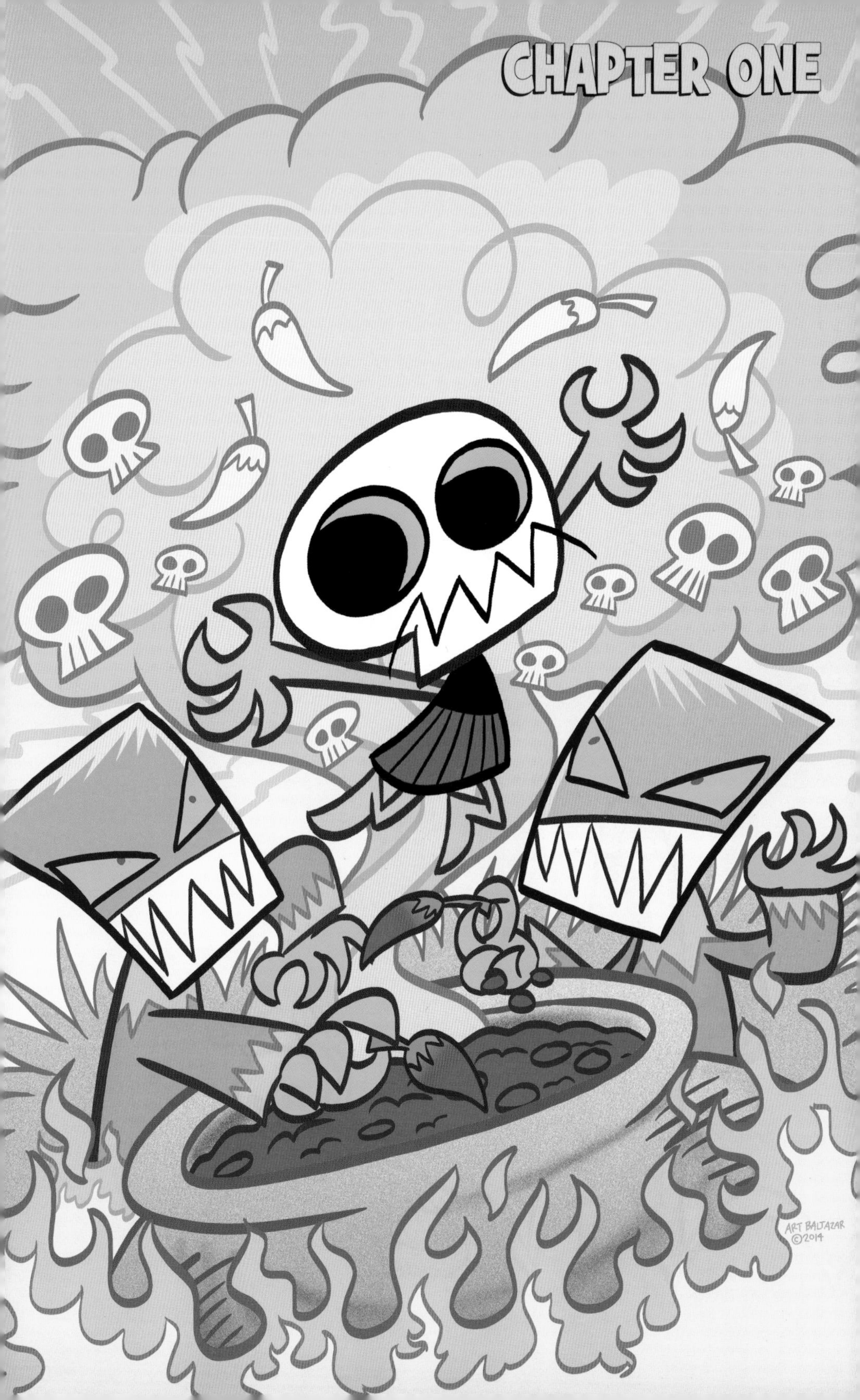
ART BALTAZAR
©2014

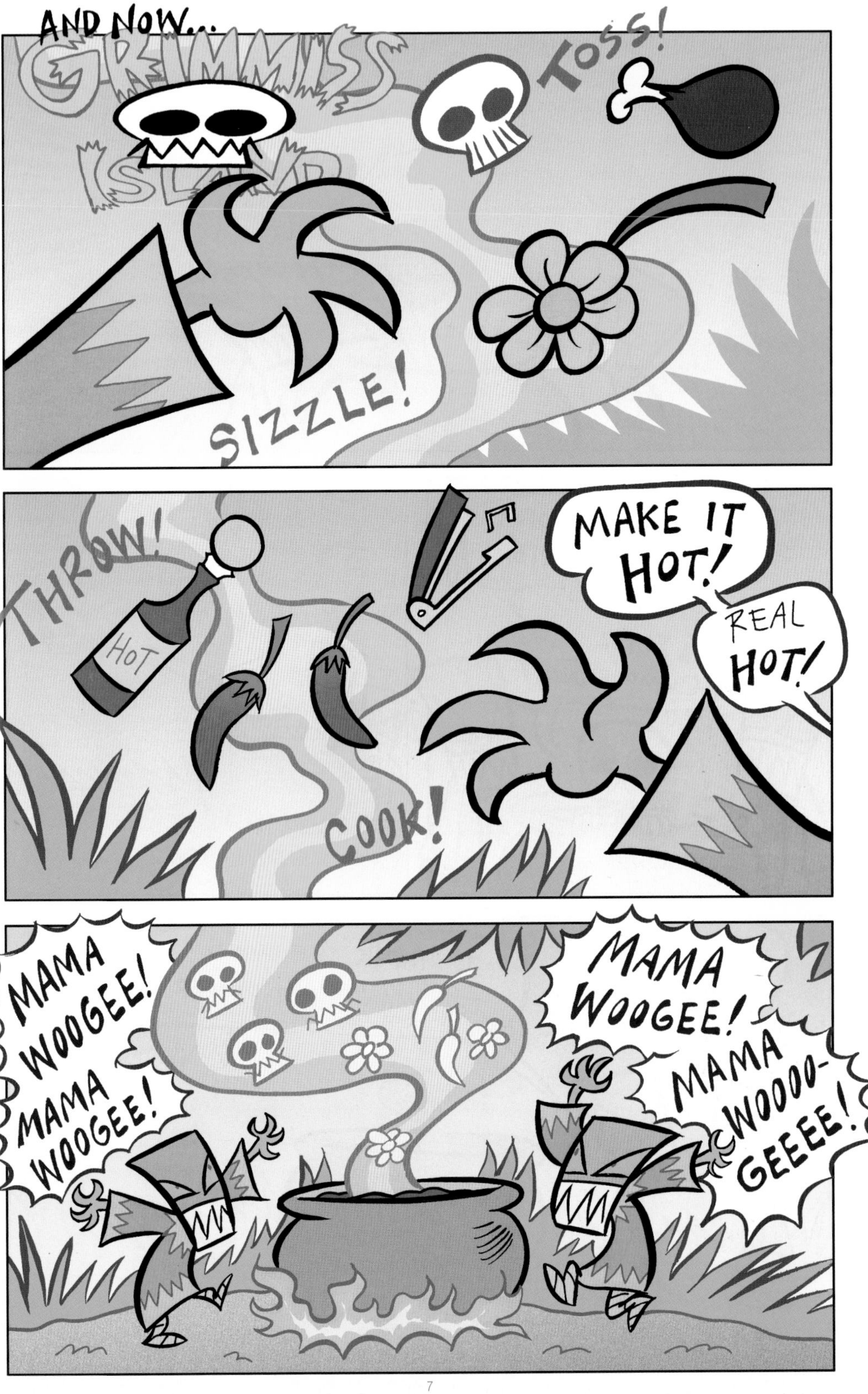
AND NOW...
GRIMMISS ISLAND
TOSS!
SIZZLE!
THROW!
HOT
MAKE IT HOT!
REAL HOT!
COOK!
MAMA WOOGEE!
MAMA WOOGEE!
MAMA WOOGEE!
MAMA WOOOO-GEEEE!

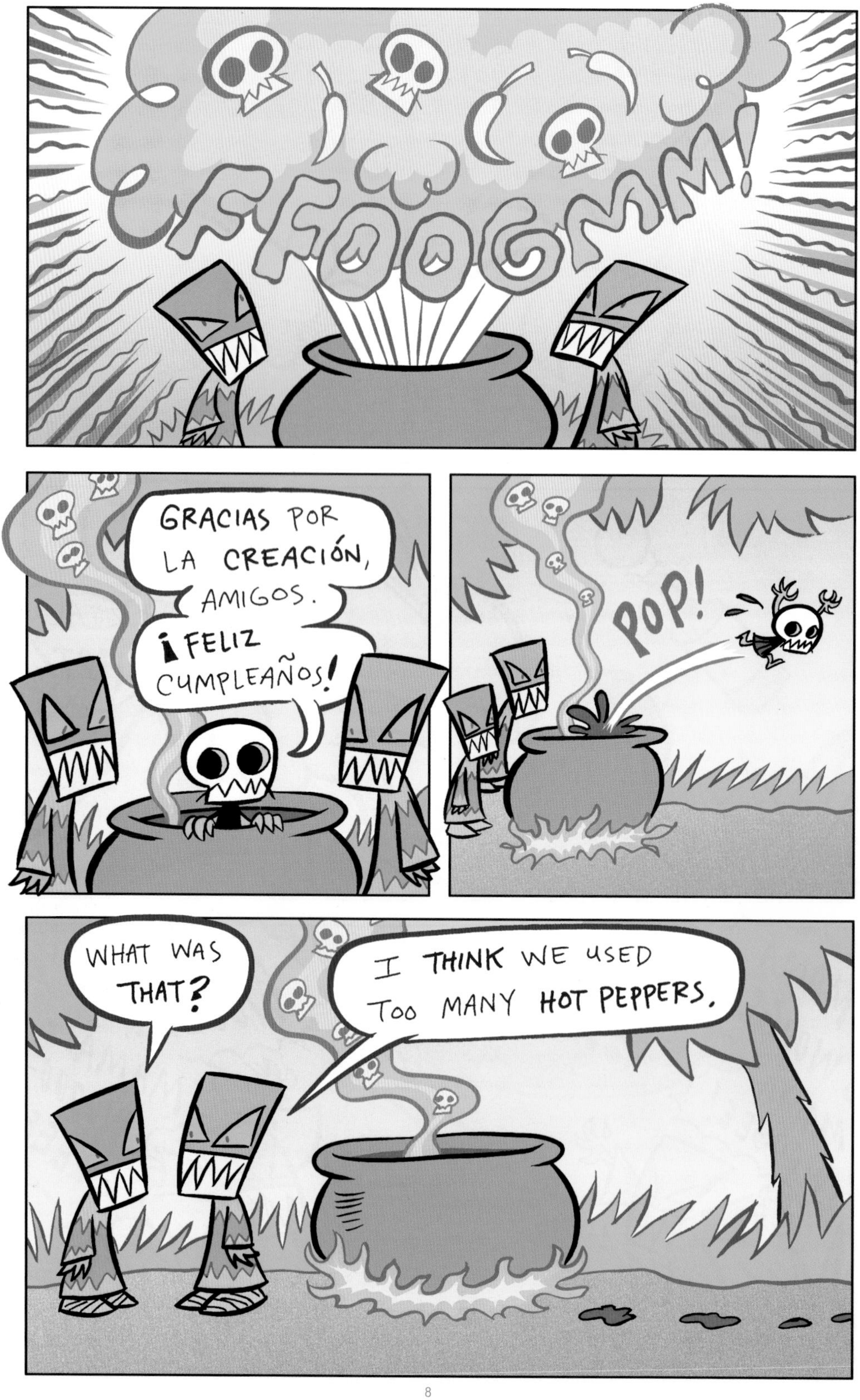
FFOOGMM!
GRACIAS POR LA CREACIÓN, AMIGOS.
¡FELIZ CUMPLEAÑOS!
POP!
WHAT WAS THAT?
I THINK WE USED TOO MANY HOT PEPPERS.

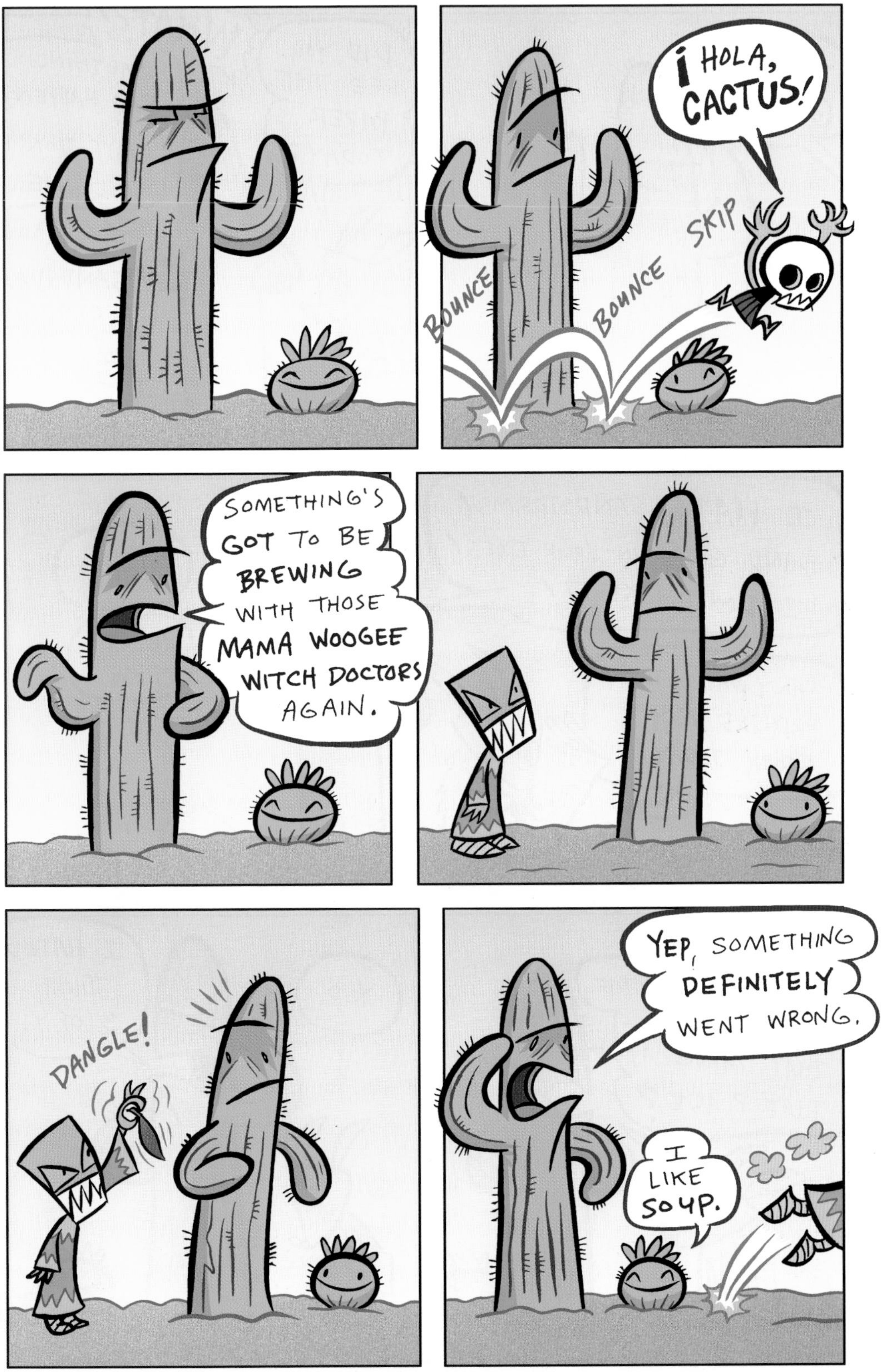
¡HOLA, CACTUS!
BOUNCE
BOUNCE
SKIP
SOMETHING'S GOT TO BE BREWING WITH THOSE MAMA WOOGEE WITCH DOCTORS AGAIN.
DANGLE!
YEP, SOMETHING DEFINITELY WENT WRONG.
I LIKE SOUP.

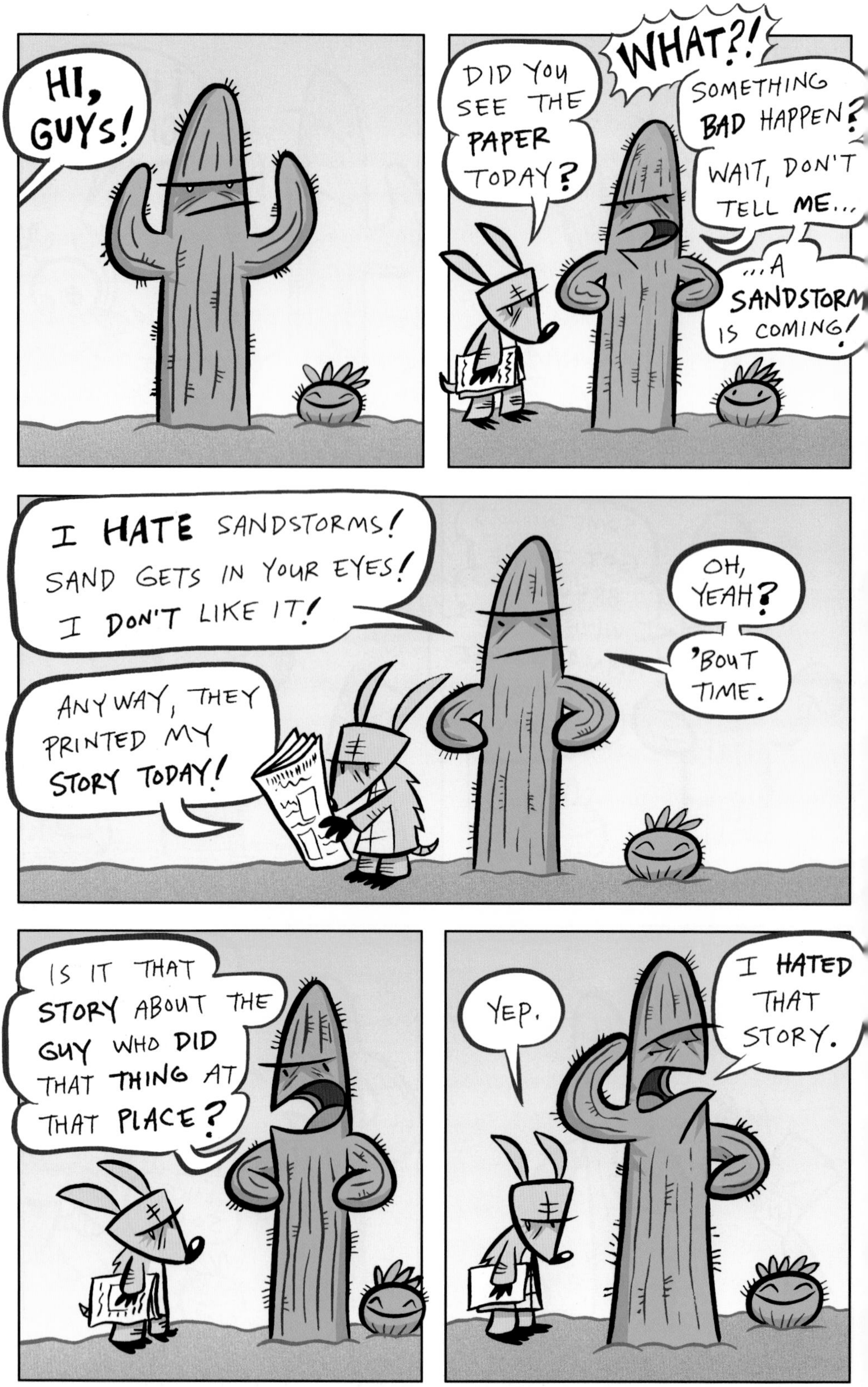
HI, GUYS!
DID YOU SEE THE PAPER TODAY?
WHAT?!
SOMETHING BAD HAPPEN?
WAIT, DON'T TELL ME...
...A SANDSTORM IS COMING!
I HATE SANDSTORMS! SAND GETS IN YOUR EYES! I DON'T LIKE IT!
ANYWAY, THEY PRINTED MY STORY TODAY!
OH, YEAH?
'BOUT TIME.
IS IT THAT STORY ABOUT THE GUY WHO DID THAT THING AT THAT PLACE?
YEP.
I HATED THAT STORY.

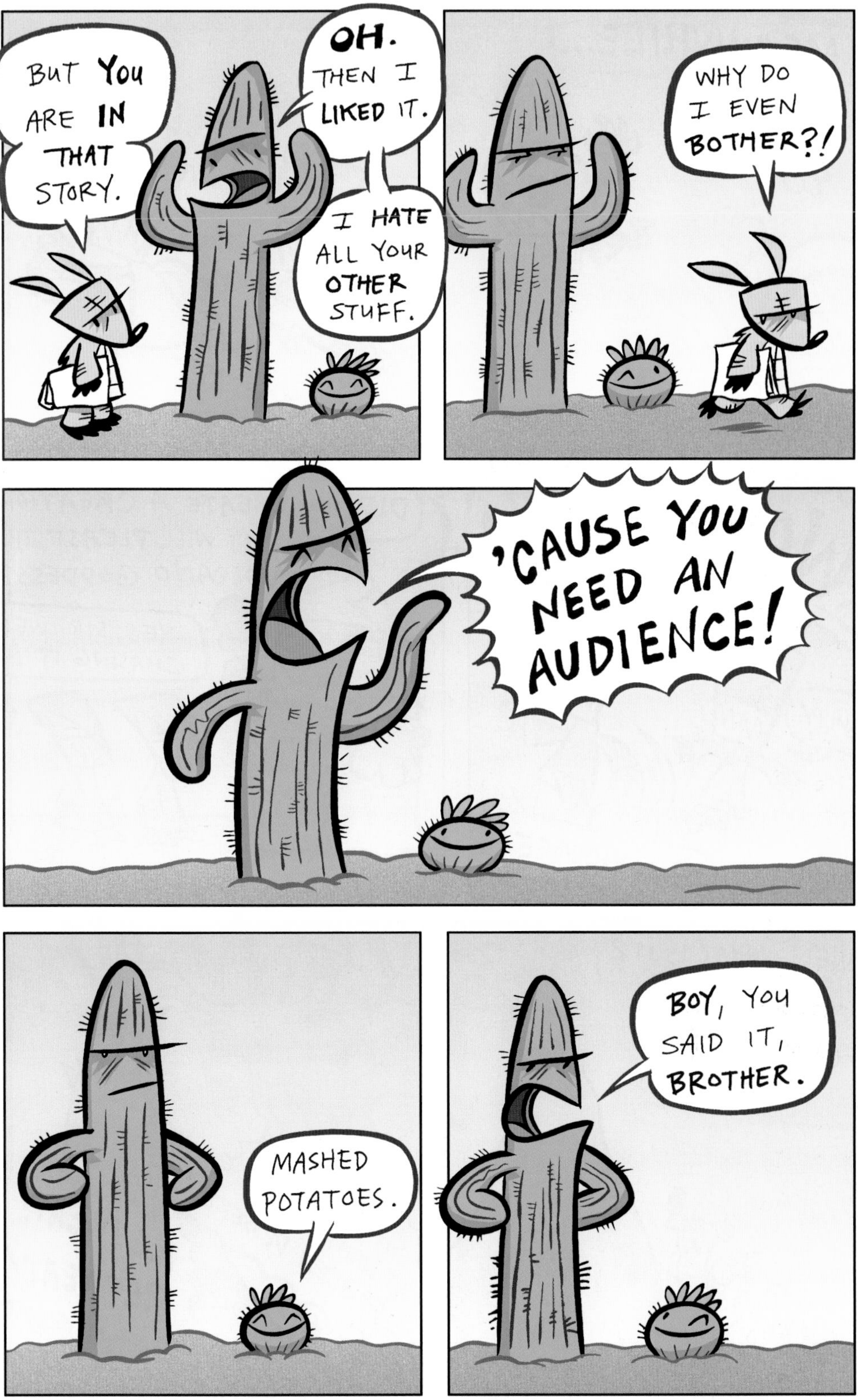
BUT YOU ARE IN THAT STORY.
OH. THEN I LIKED IT.
I HATE ALL YOUR OTHER STUFF.
WHY DO I EVEN BOTHER?!
'CAUSE YOU NEED AN AUDIENCE!
MASHED POTATOES.
BOY, YOU SAID IT, BROTHER.

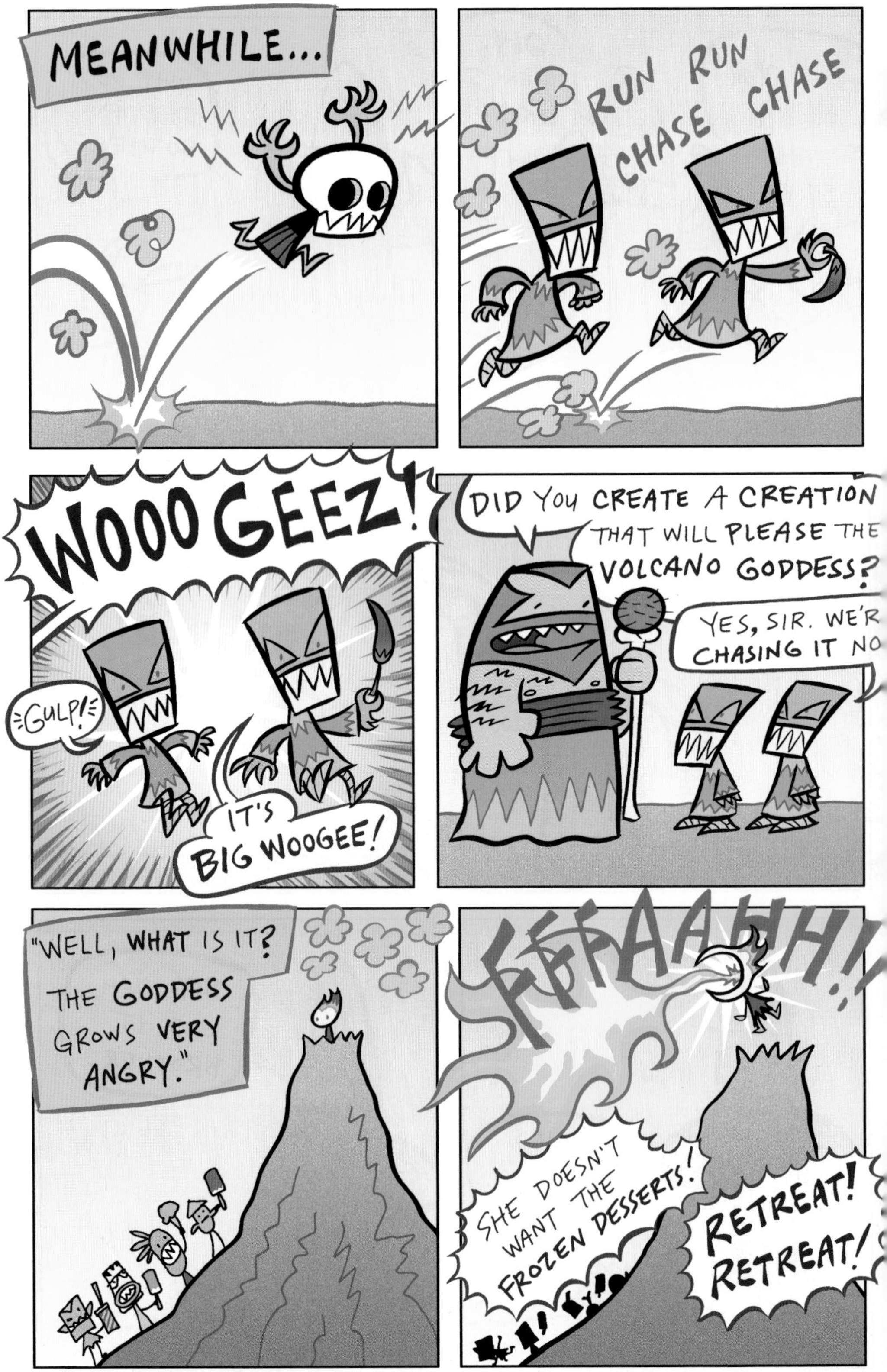
MEANWHILE...
RUN RUN
CHASE CHASE
WOOO GEEZ!
GULP!
IT'S BIG WOOGEE!
DID YOU CREATE A CREATION THAT WILL PLEASE THE VOLCANO GODDESS?
YES, SIR. WE'R
CHASING IT NO
"WELL, WHAT IS IT? THE GODDESS GROWS VERY ANGRY."
FFRAAHH!!
SHE DOESN'T WANT THE FROZEN DESSERTS!
RETREAT! RETREAT!

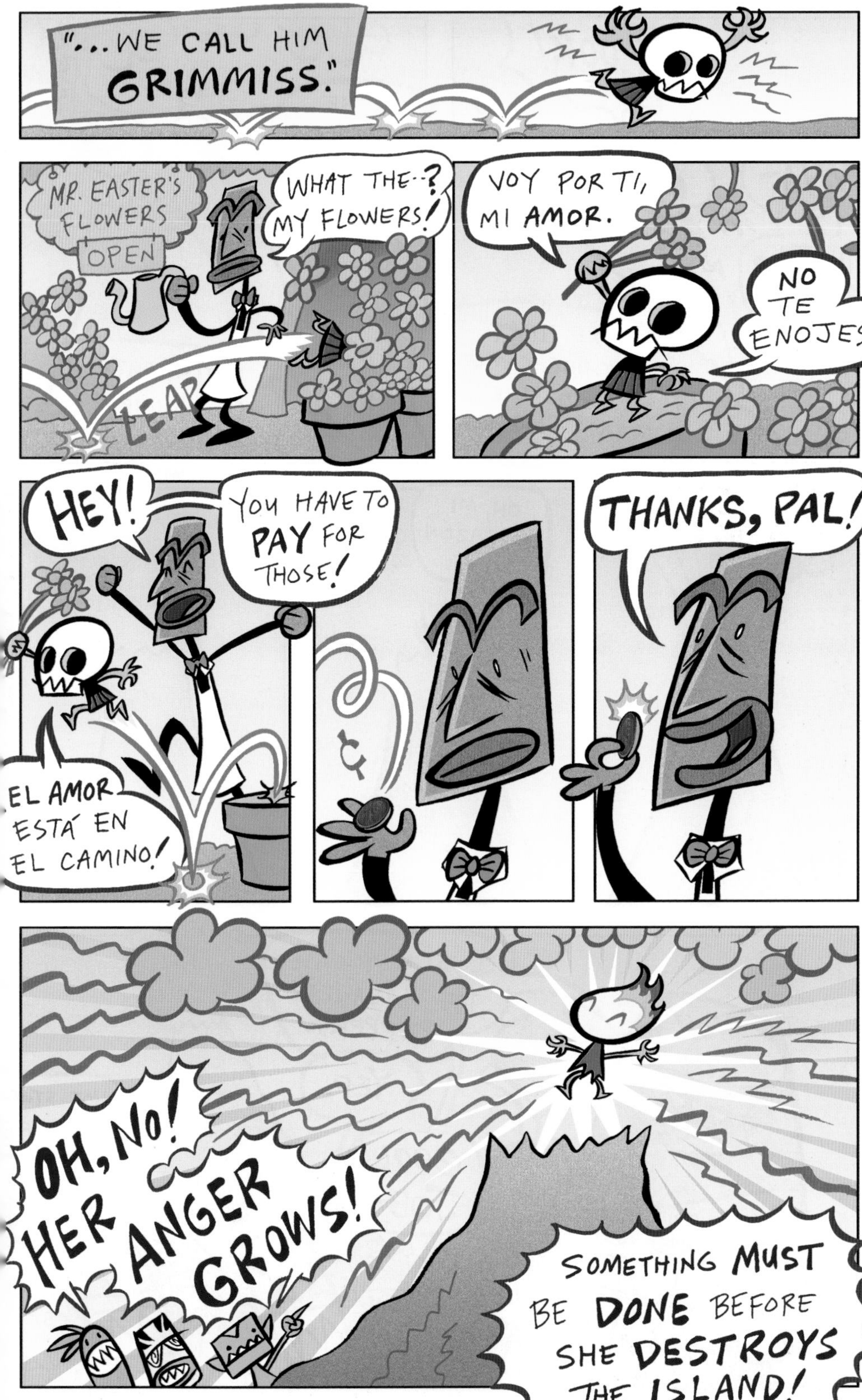
"...WE CALL HIM GRIMMISS."
MR. EASTER'S FLOWERS
OPEN
LEAP
WHAT THE--? MY FLOWERS!
VOY POR TI, MI AMOR.
NO TE ENOJES.
HEY!
YOU HAVE TO PAY FOR THOSE!
EL AMOR ESTÁ EN EL CAMINO!
¢
THANKS, PAL!
OH, NO! HER ANGER GROWS!
SOMETHING MUST BE DONE BEFORE SHE DESTROYS THE ISLAND!

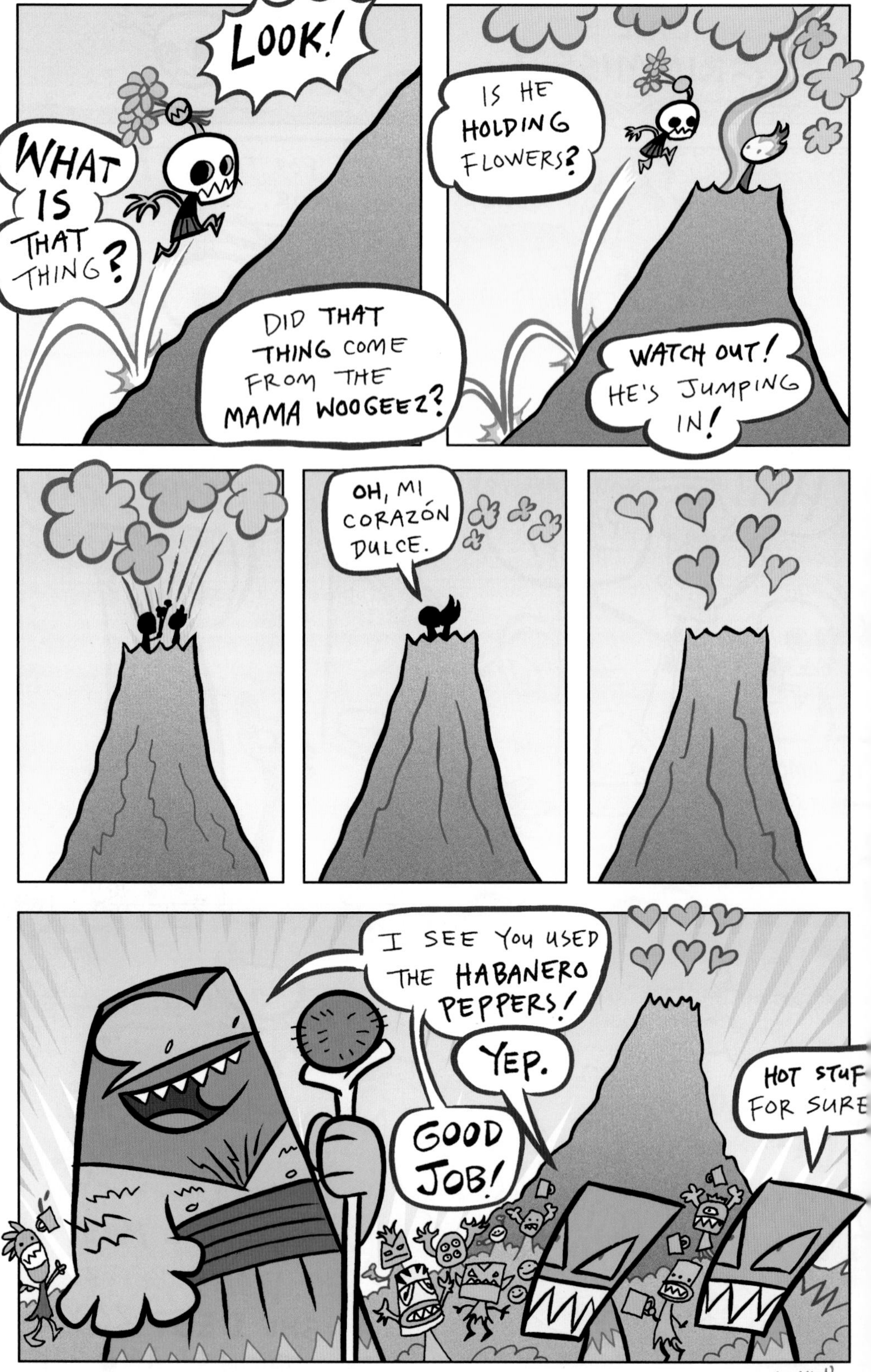
LOOK!
WHAT IS THAT THING?
DID THAT THING COME FROM THE MAMA WOOGEEZ?
IS HE HOLDING FLOWERS?
WATCH OUT! HE'S JUMPING IN!
OH, MI CORAZÓN DULCE.
I SEE YOU USED THE HABANERO PEPPERS!
YEP.
GOOD JOB!
HOT STUF
FOR SURE
-LOVIN'.

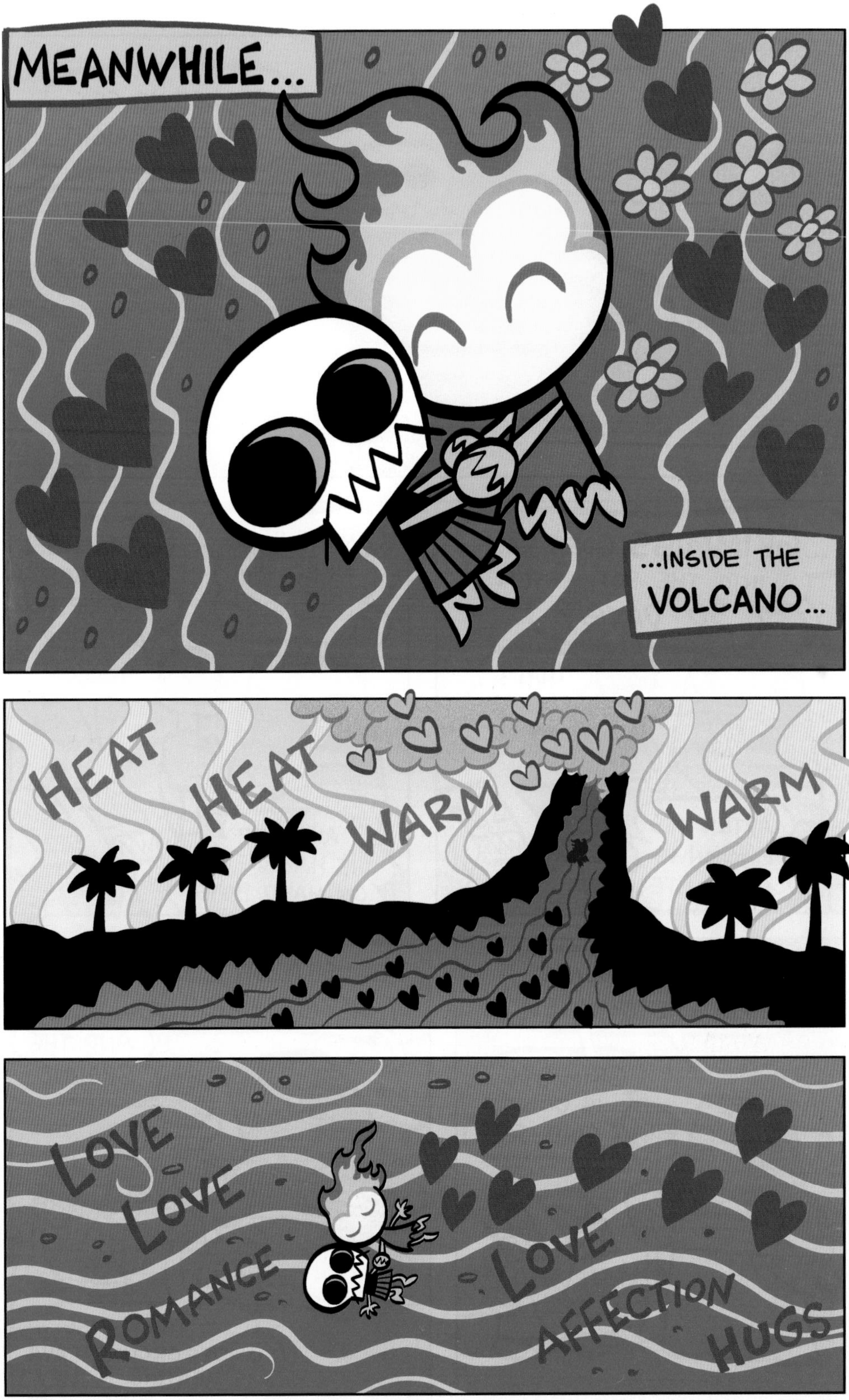
MEANWHILE...
...INSIDE THE VOLCANO...
HEAT
HEAT
WARM
WARM
LOVE
LOVE
ROMANCE
LOVE
AFFECTION
HUGS

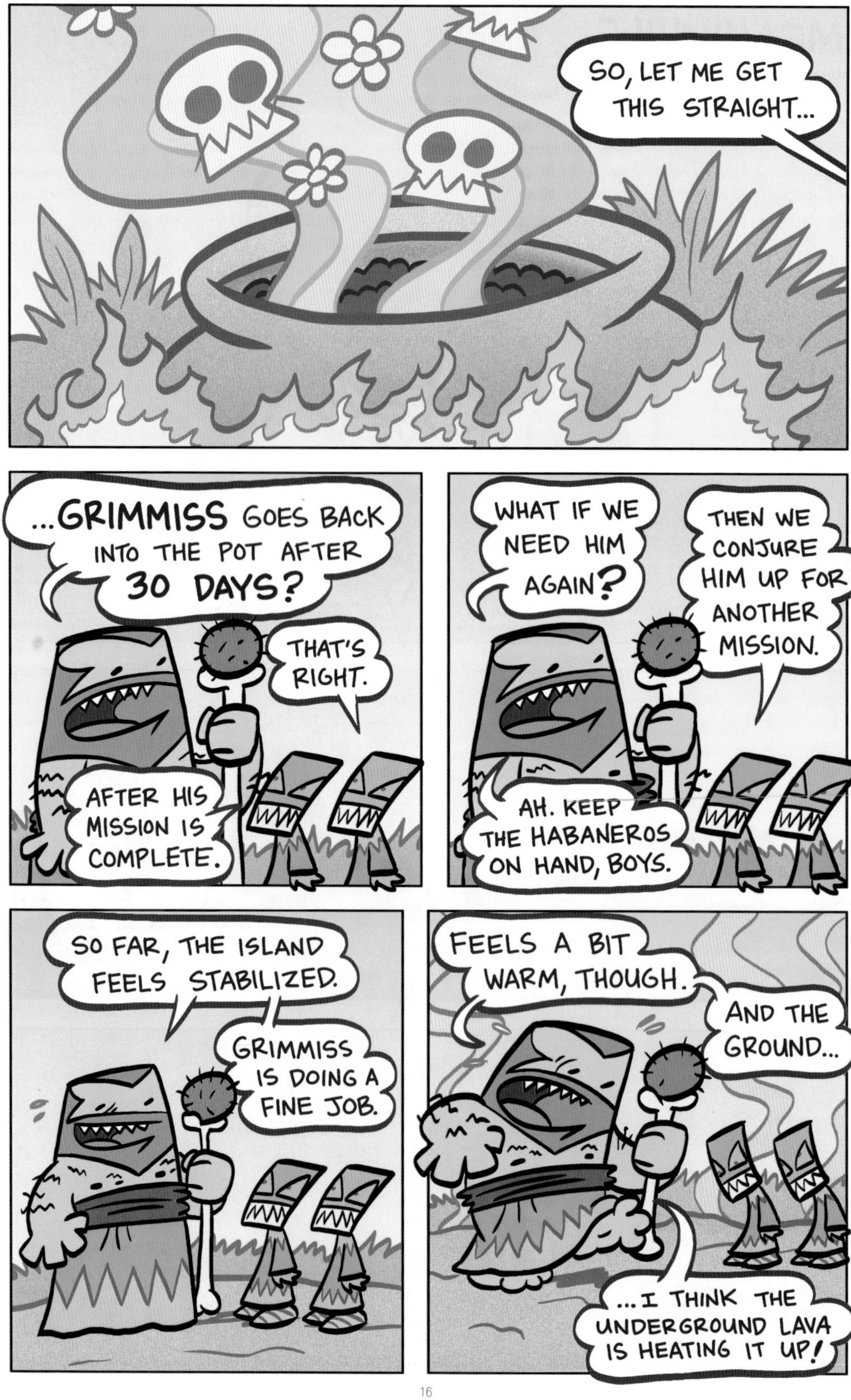
SO, LET ME GET THIS STRAIGHT...
...GRIMMISS GOES BACK INTO THE POT AFTER 30 DAYS?
THAT'S RIGHT.
AFTER HIS MISSION IS COMPLETE.
WHAT IF WE NEED HIM AGAIN?
THEN WE CONJURE HIM UP FOR ANOTHER MISSION.
AH. KEEP THE HABANEROS ON HAND, BOYS.
SO FAR, THE ISLAND FEELS STABILIZED.
GRIMMISS IS DOING A FINE JOB.
FEELS A BIT WARM, THOUGH.
AND THE GROUND...
...I THINK THE UNDERGROUND LAVA IS HEATING IT UP!

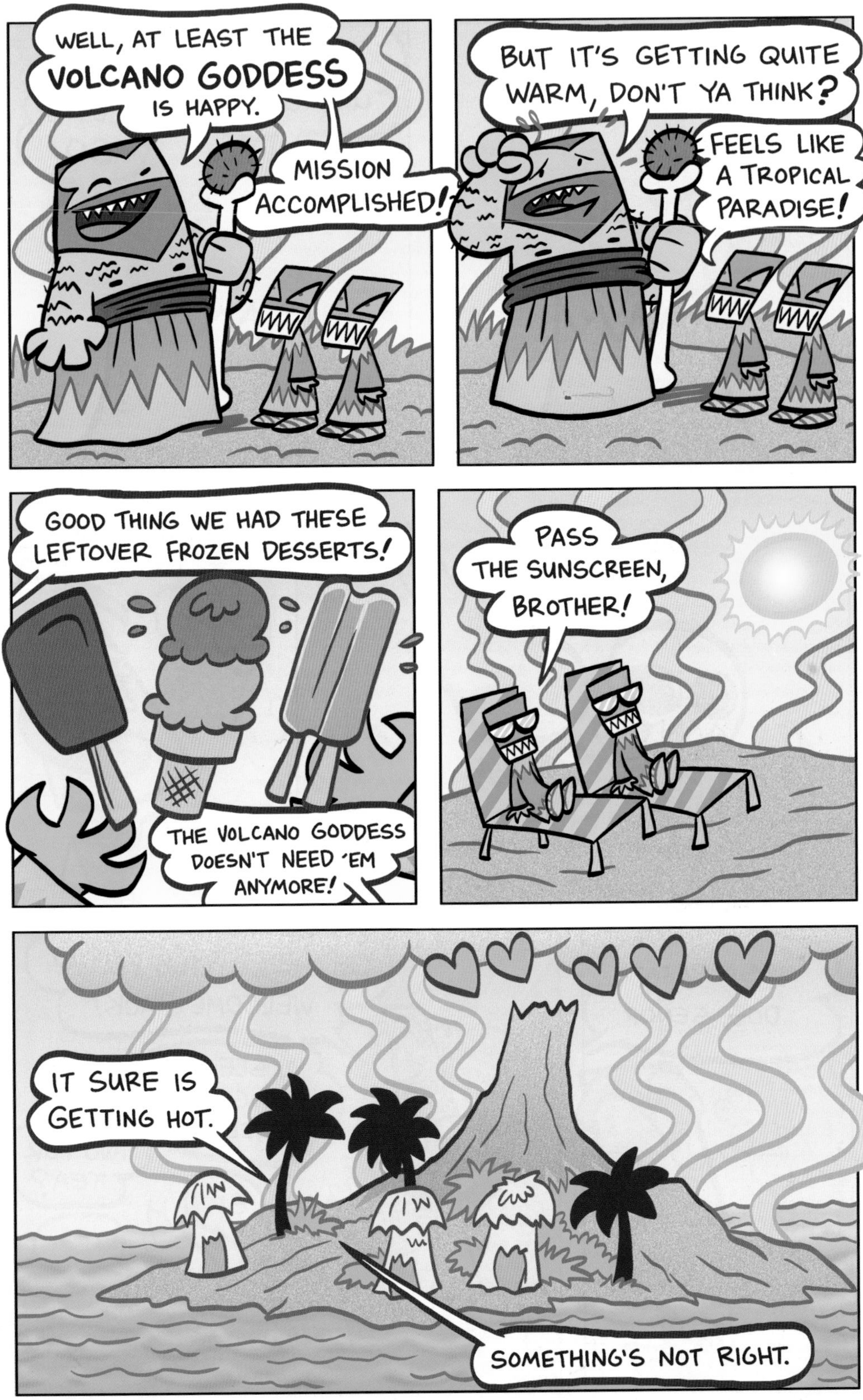
WELL, AT LEAST THE VOLCANO GODDESS IS HAPPY.
MISSION ACCOMPLISHED!
BUT IT'S GETTING QUITE WARM, DON'T YA THINK?
FEELS LIKE A TROPICAL PARADISE!
GOOD THING WE HAD THESE LEFTOVER FROZEN DESSERTS!
THE VOLCANO GODDESS DOESN'T NEED 'EM ANYMORE!
PASS THE SUNSCREEN, BROTHER!
IT SURE IS GETTING HOT.
SOMETHING'S NOT RIGHT.

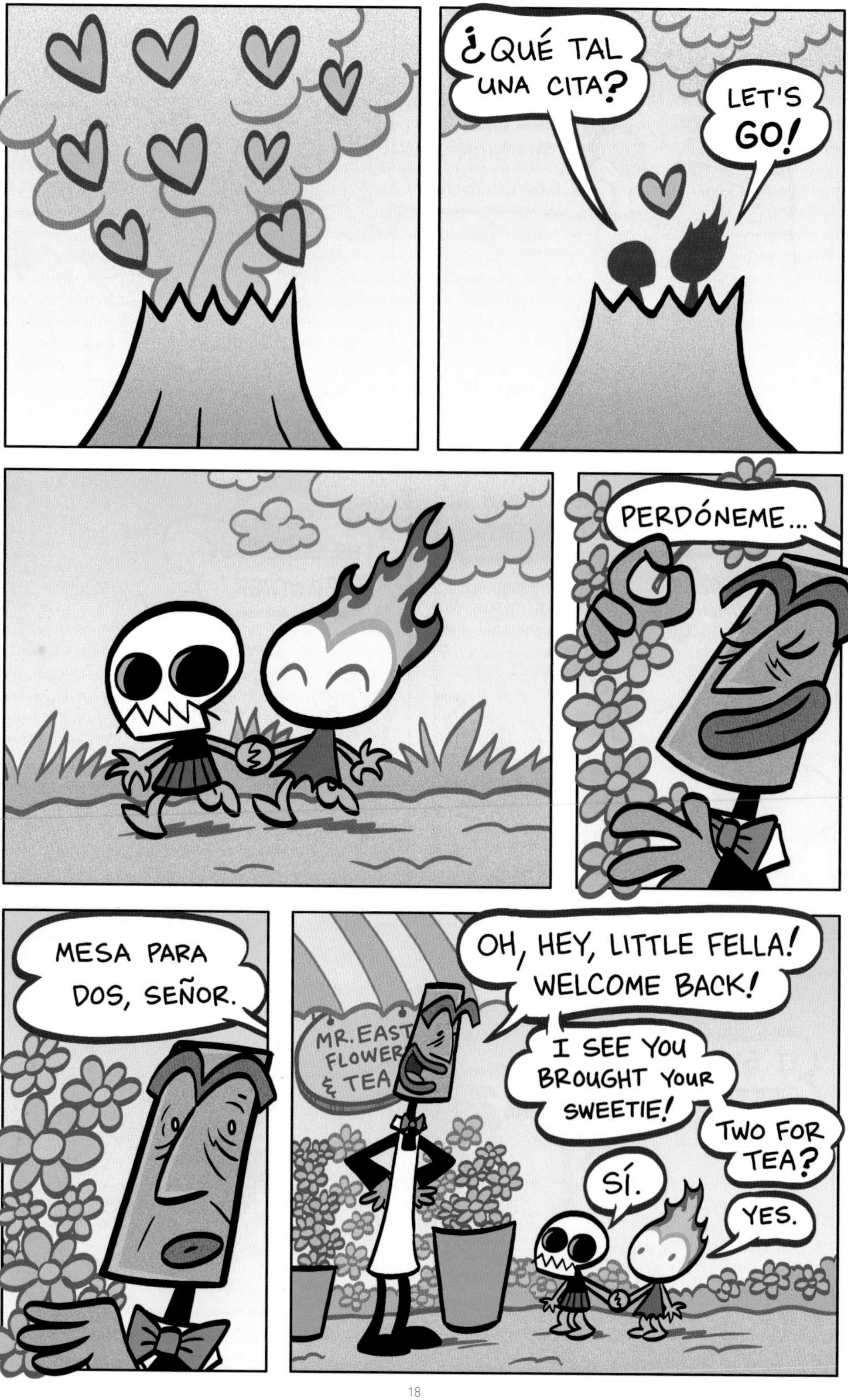
¿QUÉ TAL UNA CITA?
LET'S GO!
PERDÓNEME...
MESA PARA DOS, SEÑOR.
OH, HEY, LITTLE FELLA! WELCOME BACK!
MR. EAST FLOWER & TEA
I SEE YOU BROUGHT YOUR SWEETIE!
TWO FOR TEA?
SÍ.
YES.

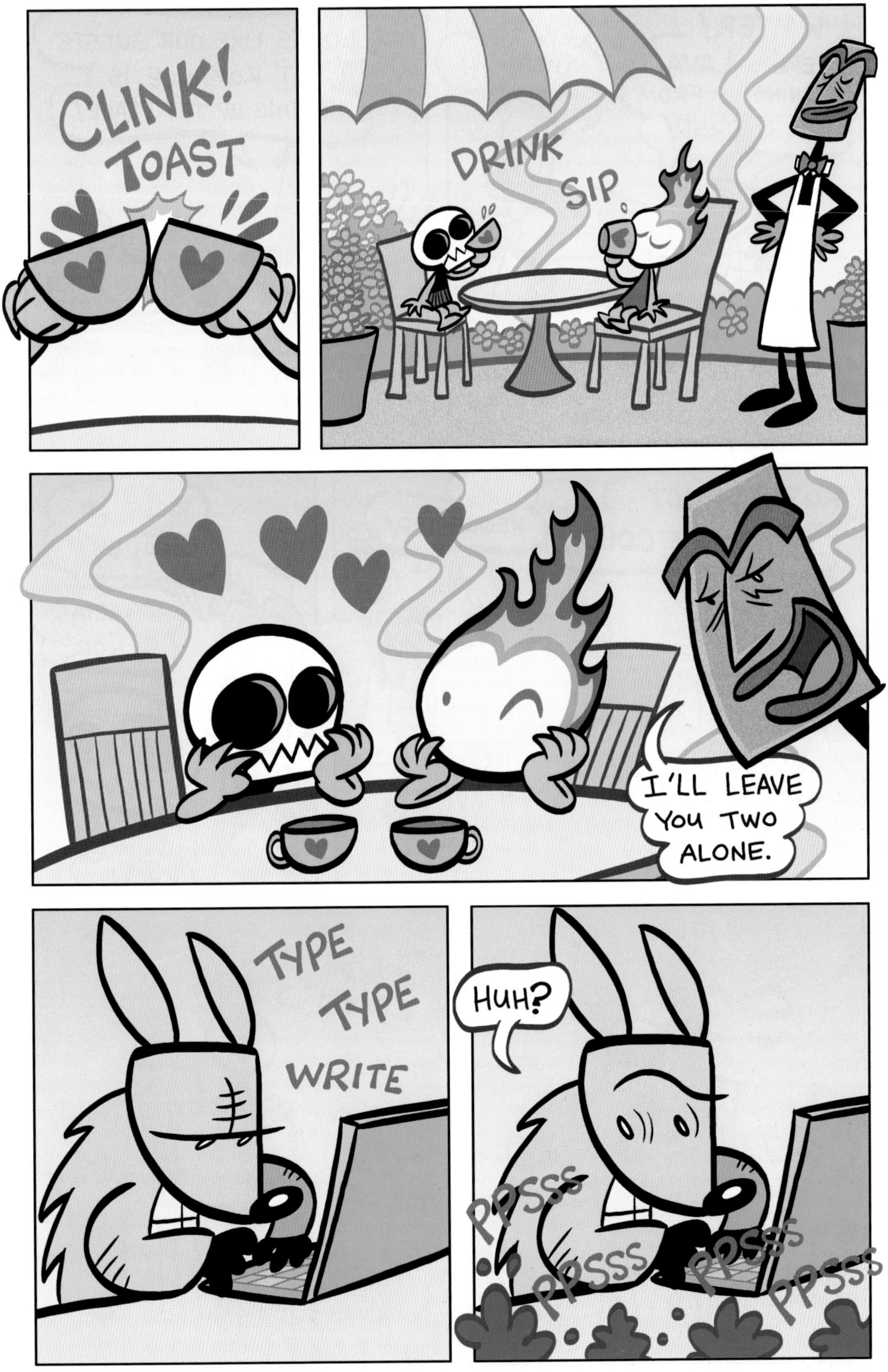
CLINK!
TOAST
DRINK
SIP
I'LL LEAVE YOU TWO ALONE.
TYPE
TYPE
WRITE
HUH?
PPSSS
PPSSS
PPSSS
PPSSS

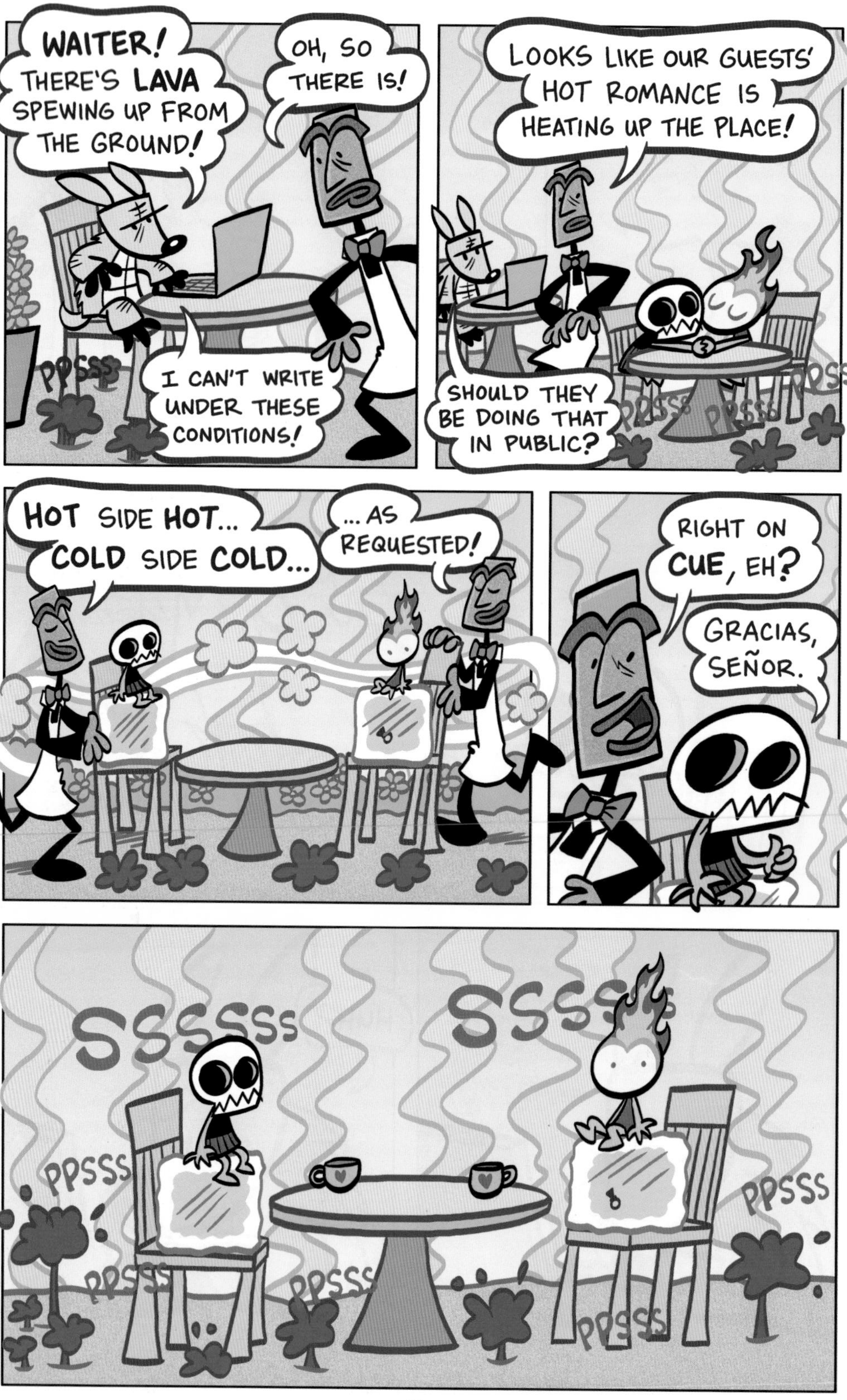
WAITER! THERE'S LAVA SPEWING UP FROM THE GROUND!
OH, SO THERE IS!
I CAN'T WRITE UNDER THESE CONDITIONS!
PPSSS
LOOKS LIKE OUR GUESTS' HOT ROMANCE IS HEATING UP THE PLACE!
SHOULD THEY BE DOING THAT IN PUBLIC?
PPSSS
PPSSS
PPSSS
HOT SIDE HOT... COLD SIDE COLD...
...AS REQUESTED!
RIGHT ON CUE, EH?
GRACIAS, SEÑOR.
SSSSSS
SSSSS
PPSSS
PPSSS
PPSSS
PPSSS
PPSSS

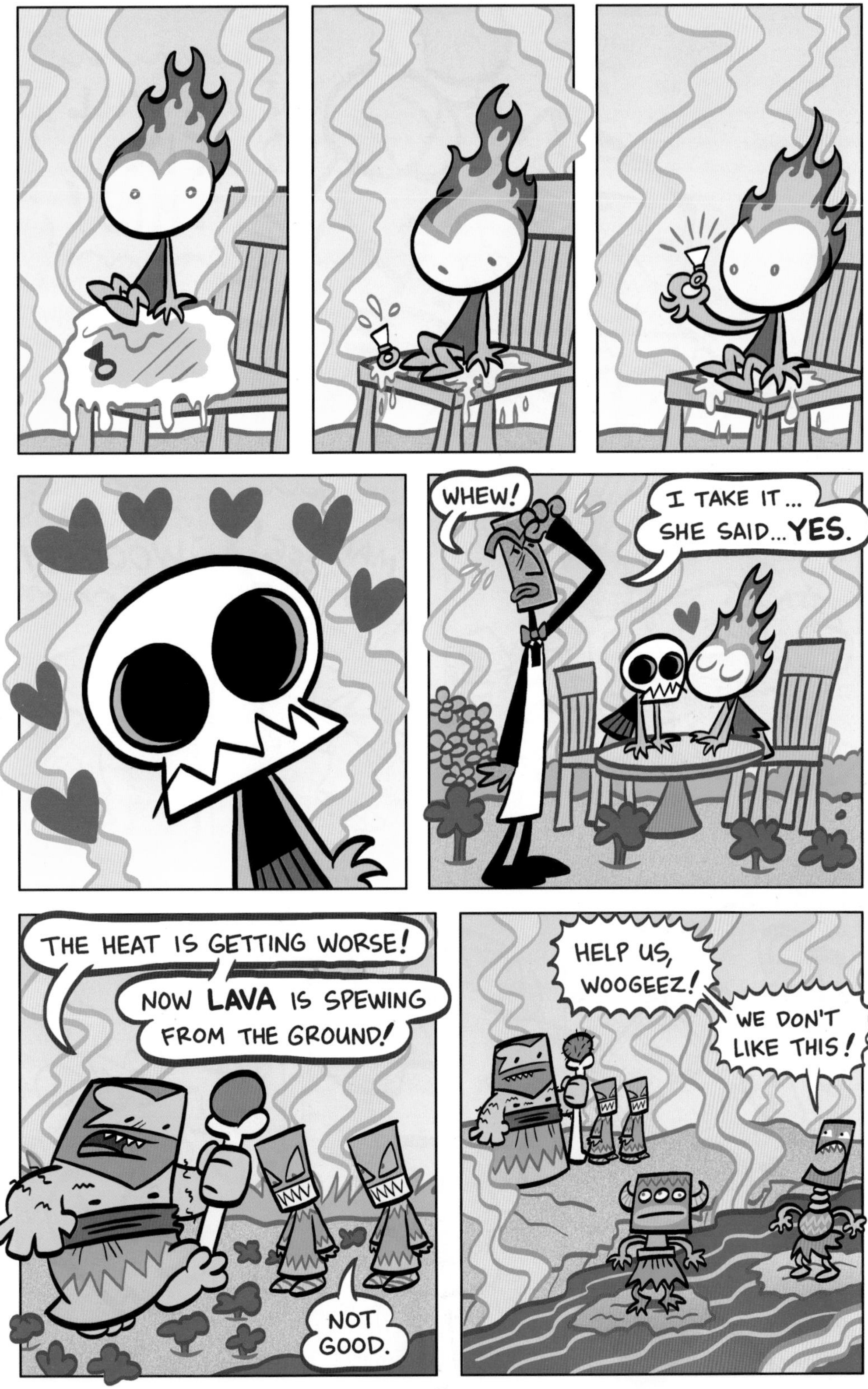
WHEW!
I TAKE IT... SHE SAID... YES.
THE HEAT IS GETTING WORSE!
NOW LAVA IS SPEWING FROM THE GROUND!
NOT GOOD.
HELP US, WOOGEEZ!
WE DON'T LIKE THIS!

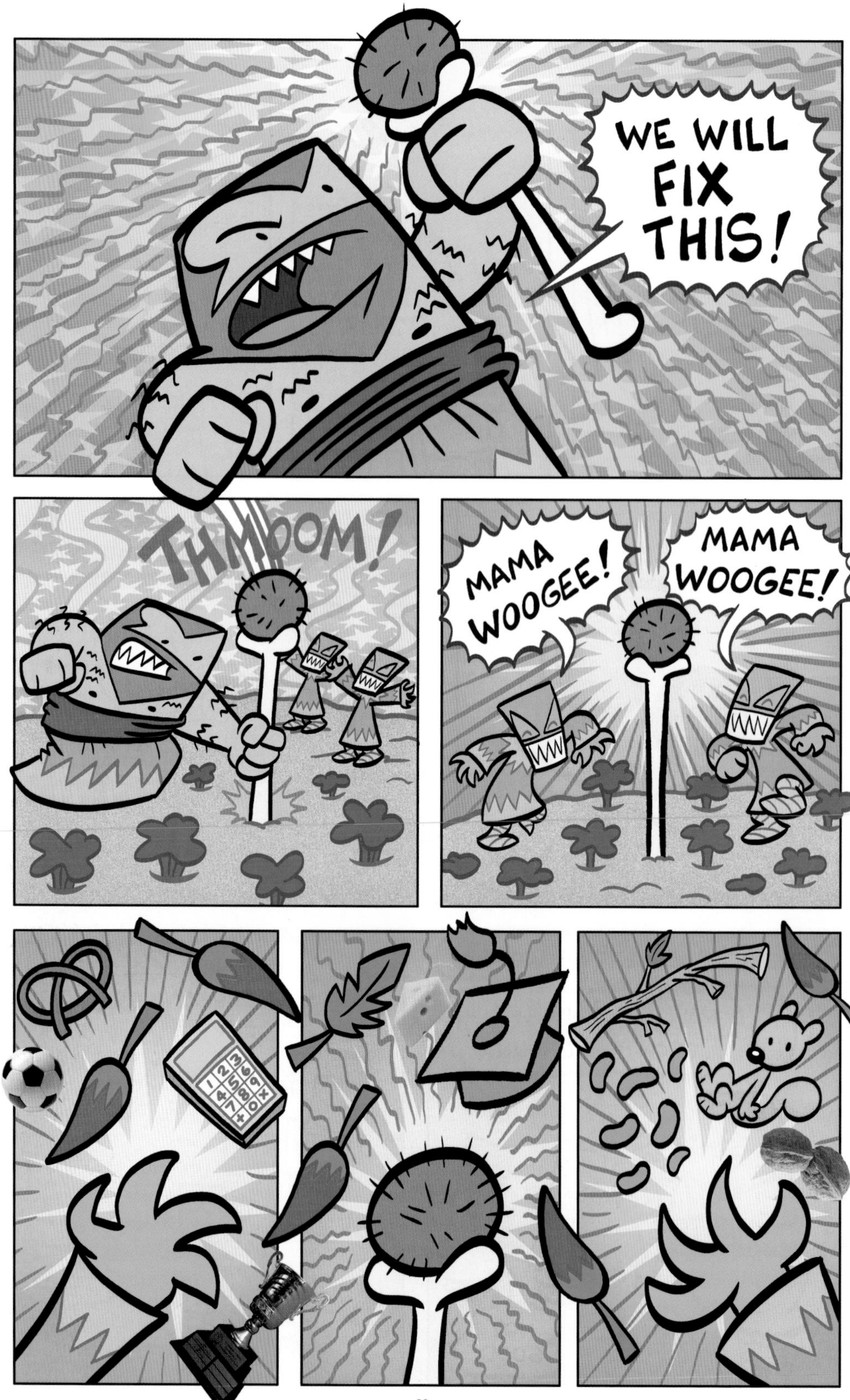
WE WILL FIX THIS!
THMOOM!
MAMA WOOGEE!
MAMA WOOGEE!

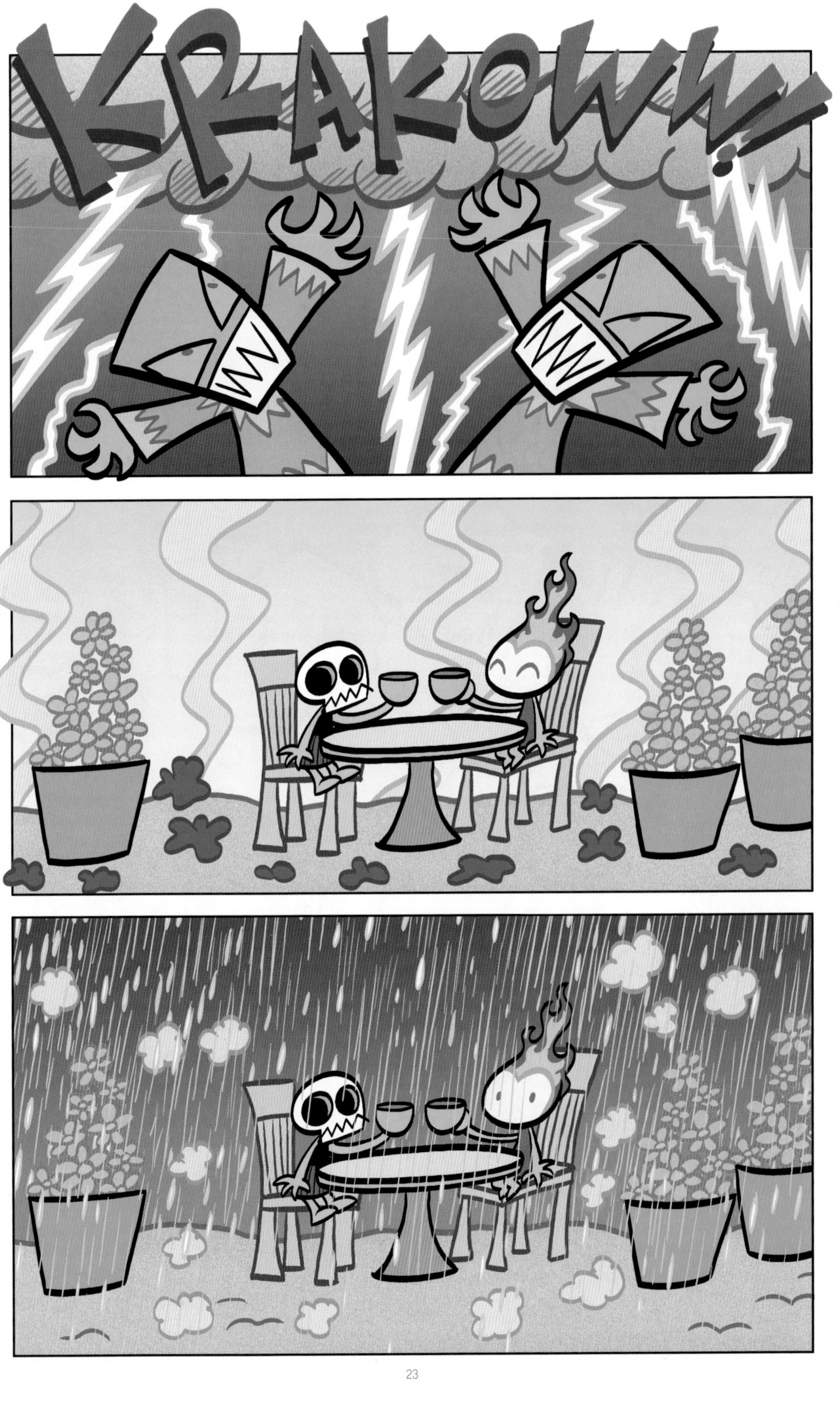
KRAKOW!!

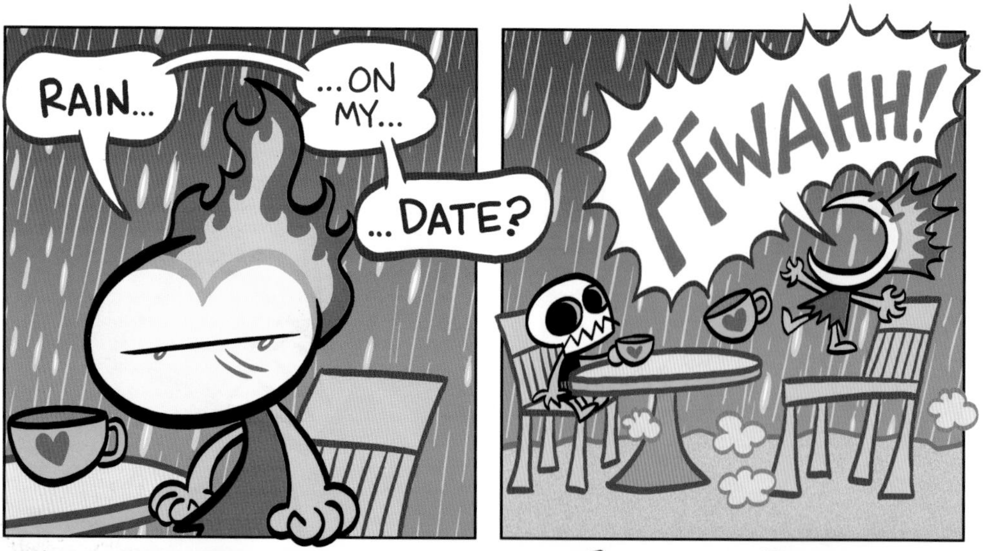
RAIN...
...ON MY...
...DATE?
FFWAHH!

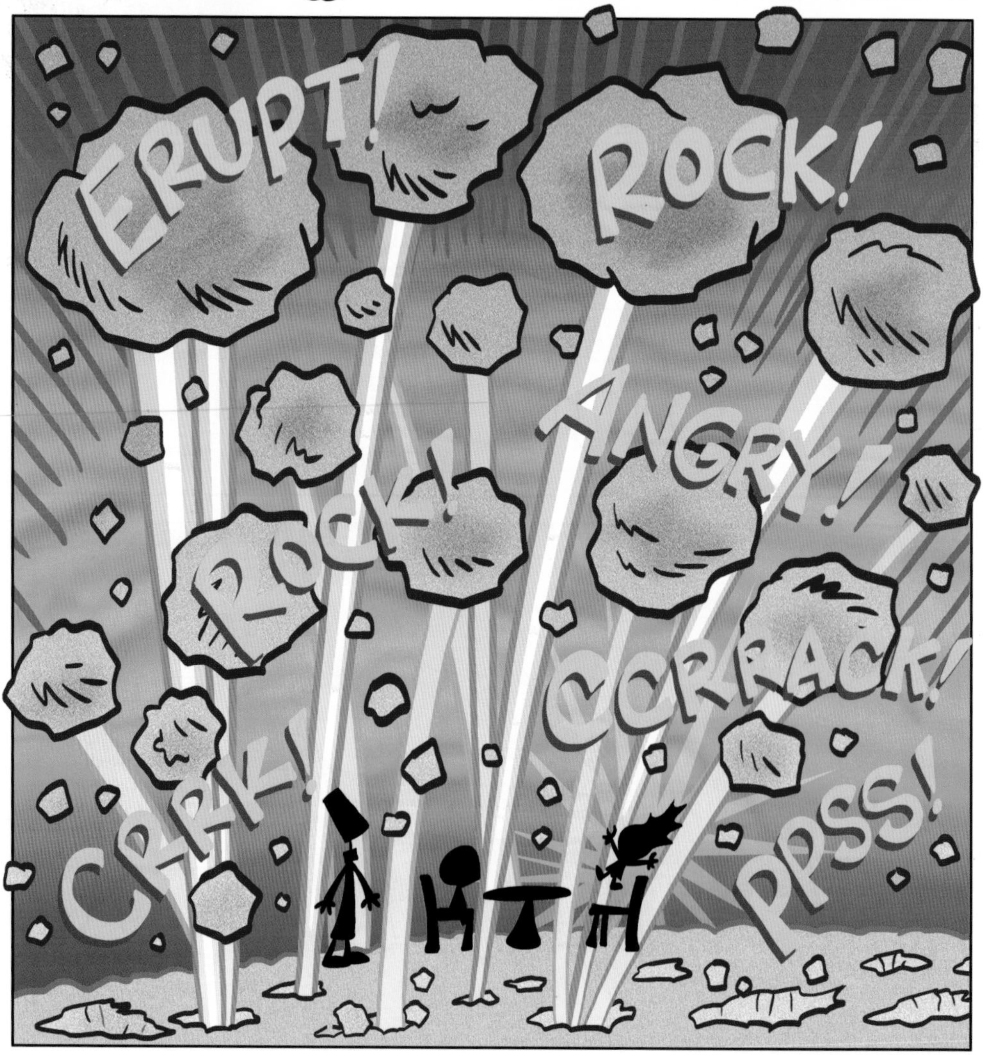
ERUPT!
ROCK!
ANGRY!
ROCK!
CORRACK!
CRRK!
PPSSS!

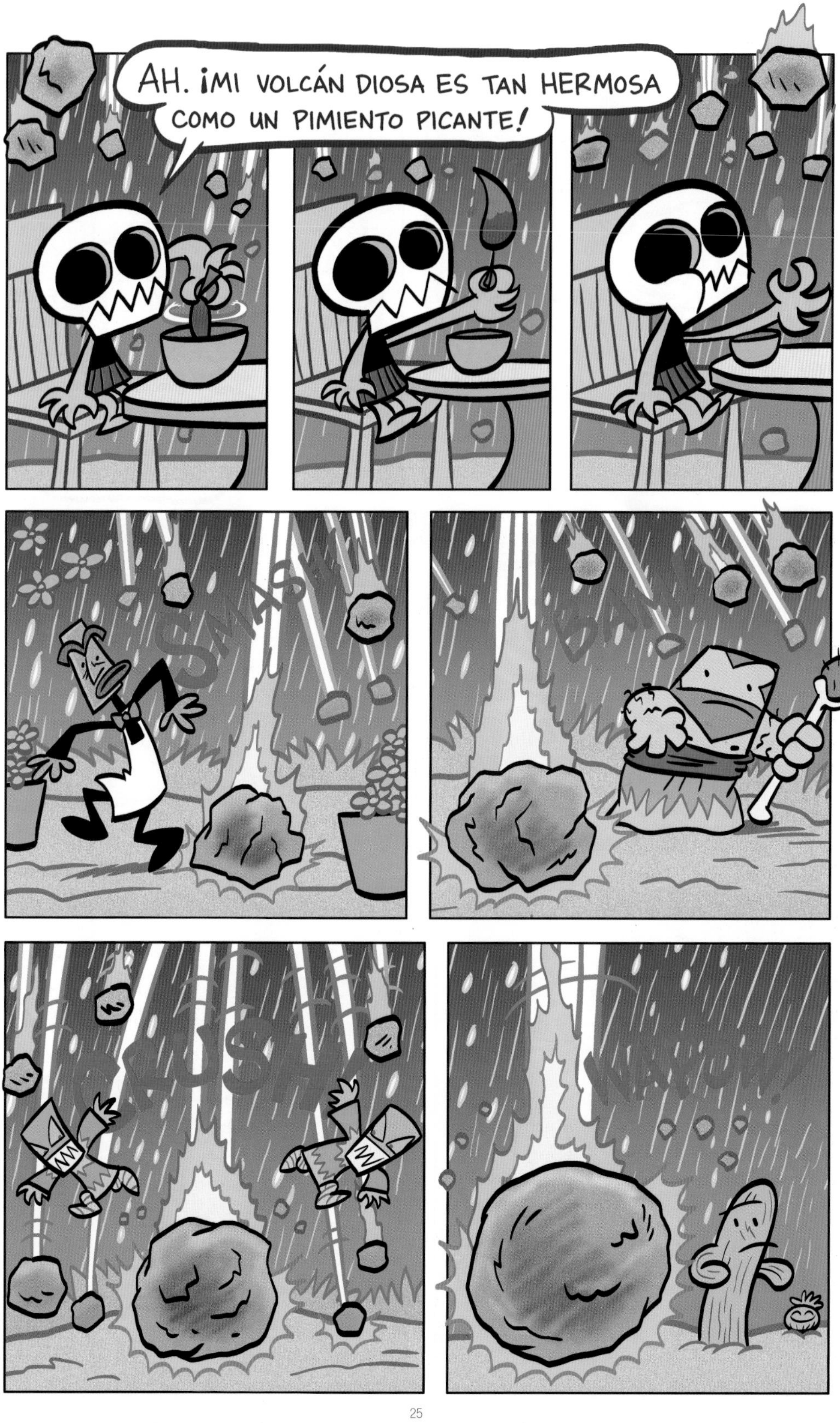
AH. ¡MI VOLCÁN DIOSA ES TAN HERMOSA COMO UN PIMIENTO PICANTE!
SMASH

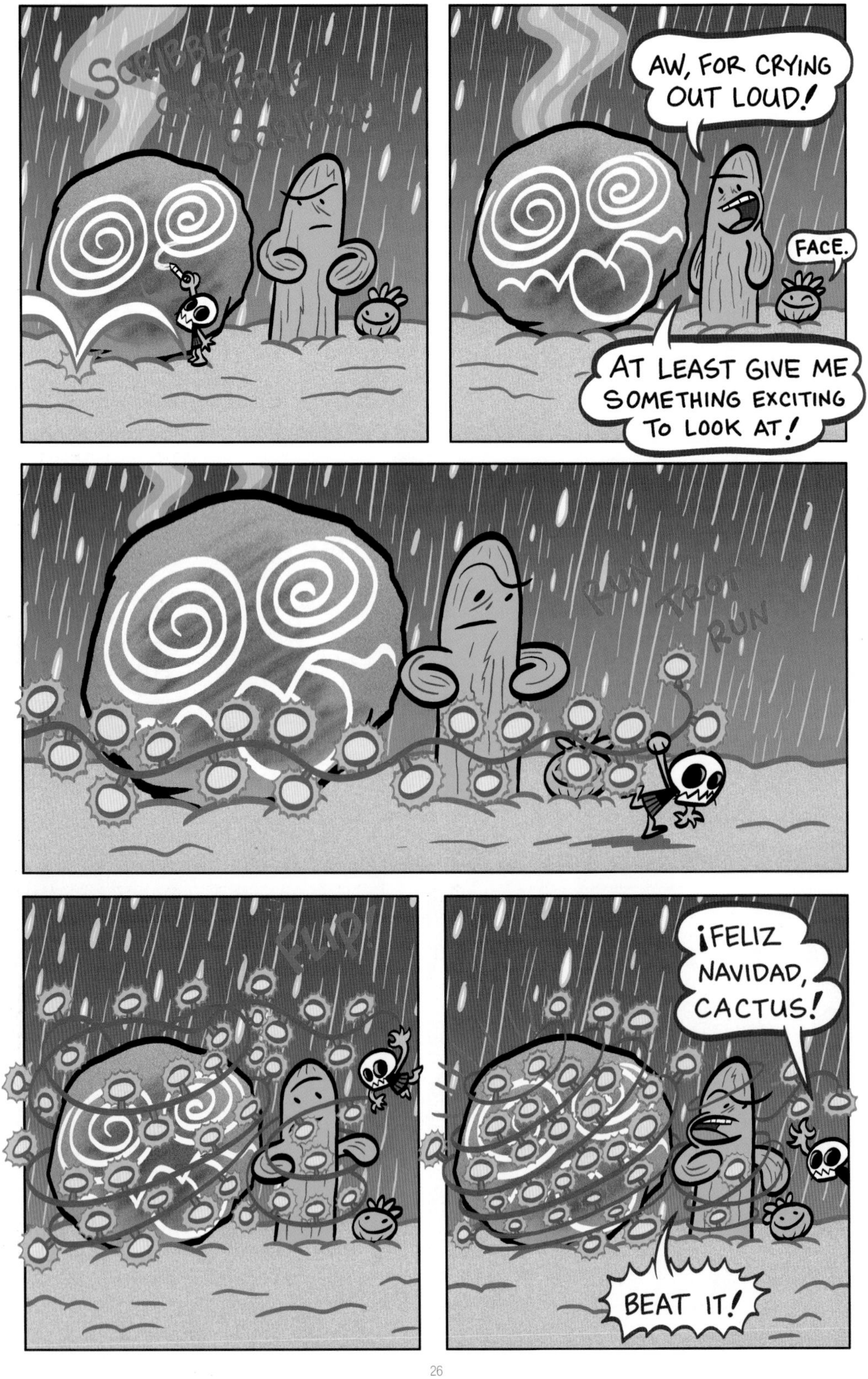
SCRIBBLE SCRIBBLE SCRIBBLE
AW, FOR CRYING OUT LOUD!
FACE.
AT LEAST GIVE ME SOMETHING EXCITING TO LOOK AT!
RUN TROT RUN
FLIP!
¡FELIZ NAVIDAD, CACTUS!
BEAT IT!

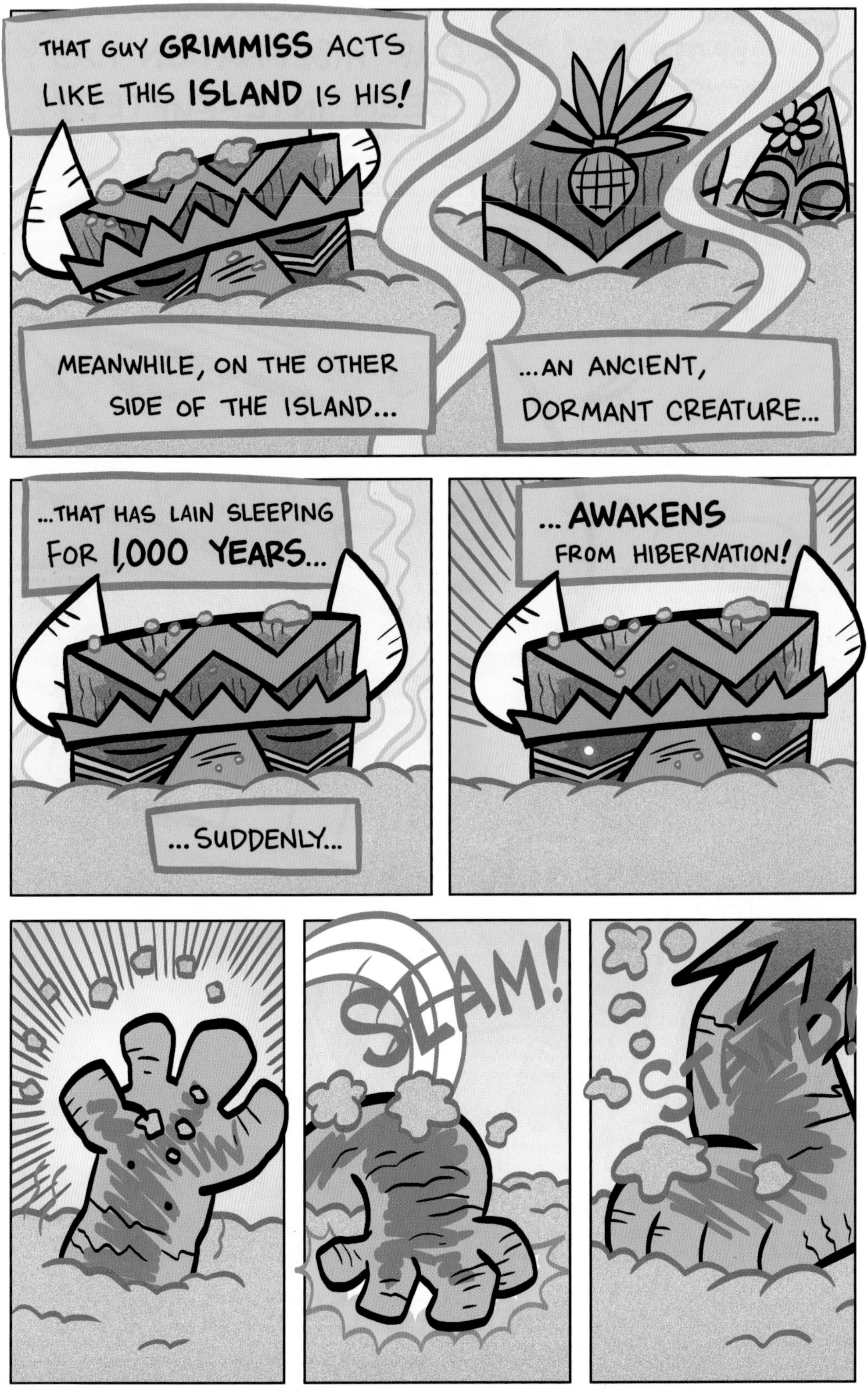

THAT GUY GRIMMISS ACTS LIKE THIS ISLAND IS HIS!
MEANWHILE, ON THE OTHER SIDE OF THE ISLAND...
...AN ANCIENT, DORMANT CREATURE...
...THAT HAS LAIN SLEEPING FOR 1,000 YEARS...
...SUDDENLY...
...AWAKENS FROM HIBERNATION!
SLAM!
STAND!

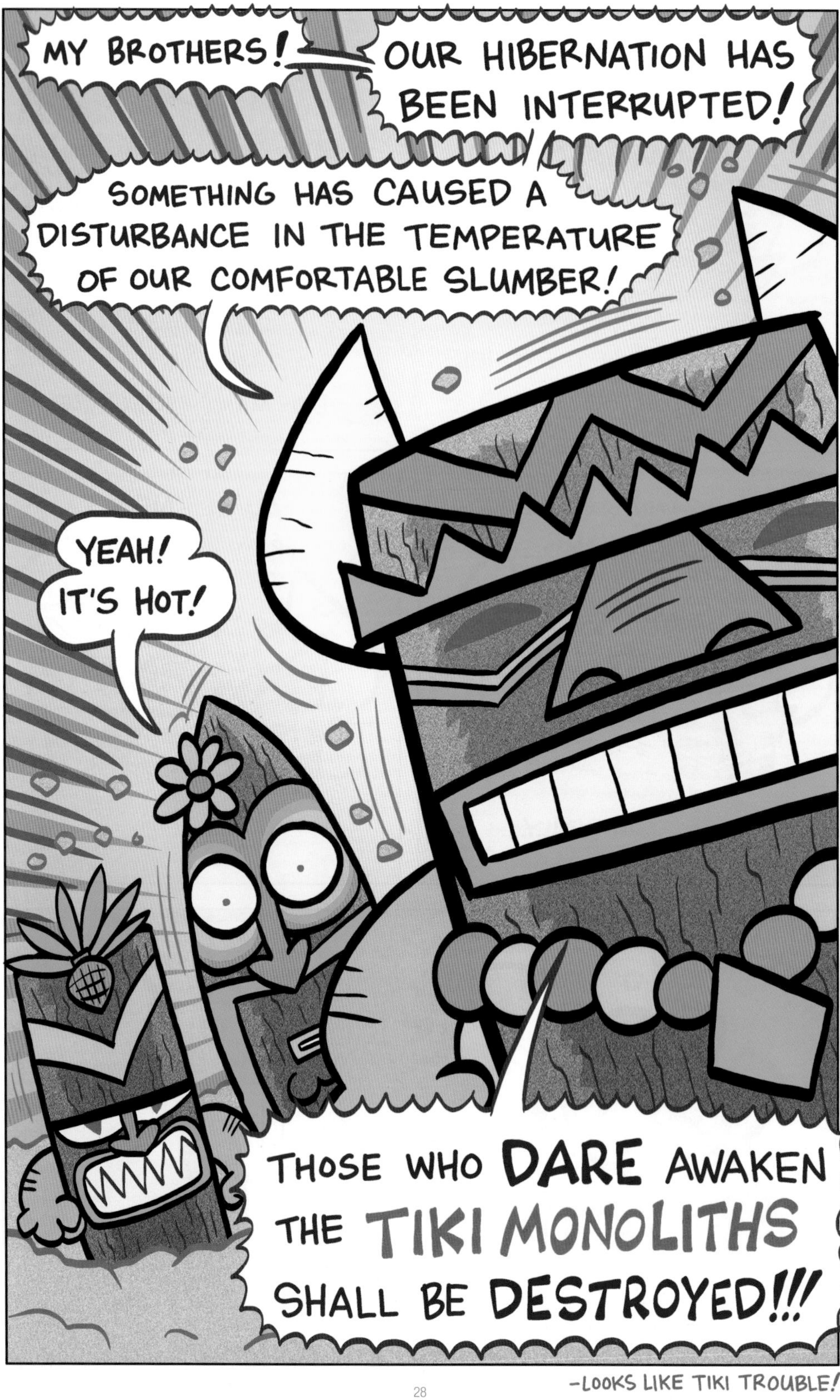
MY BROTHERS!
OUR HIBERNATION HAS BEEN INTERRUPTED!
SOMETHING HAS CAUSED A DISTURBANCE IN THE TEMPERATURE OF OUR COMFORTABLE SLUMBER!
YEAH! IT'S HOT!
THOSE WHO DARE AWAKEN THE TIKI MONOLITHS SHALL BE DESTROYED!!!

-LOOKS LIKE TIKI TROUBLE!

CHAPTER TWO

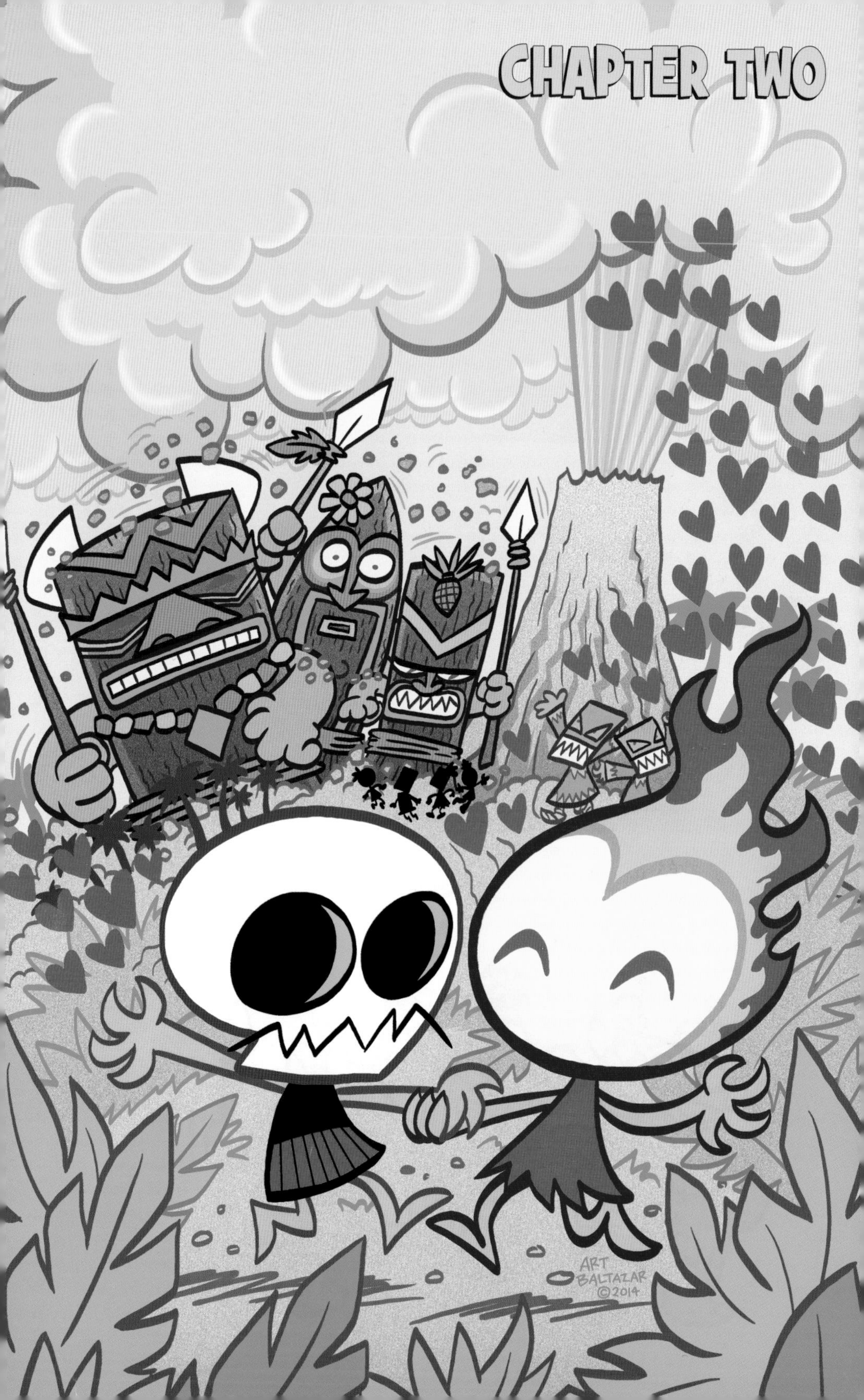
ART BALTAZAR ©2014

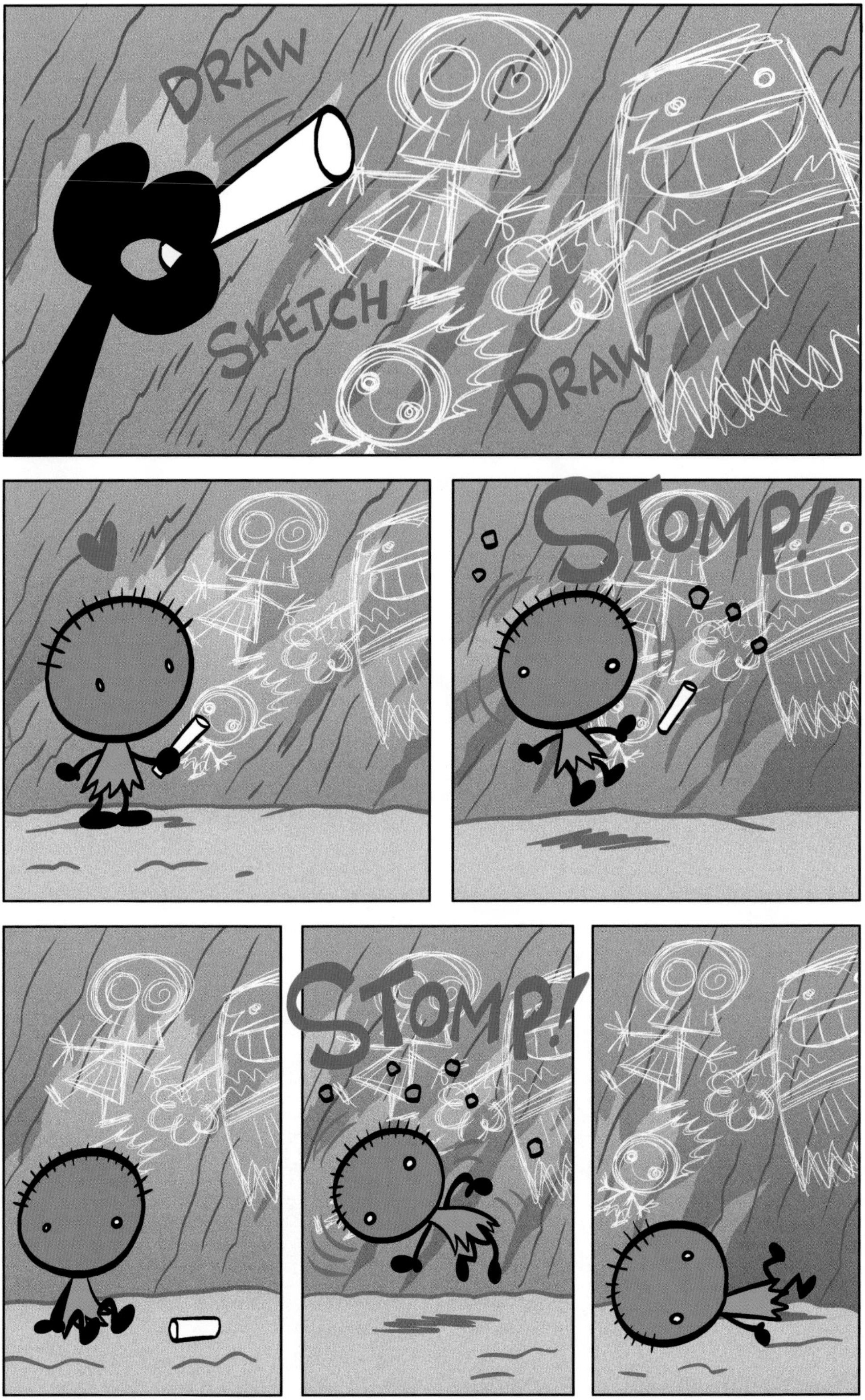
DRAW
SKETCH
DRAW
STOMP!
STOMP!

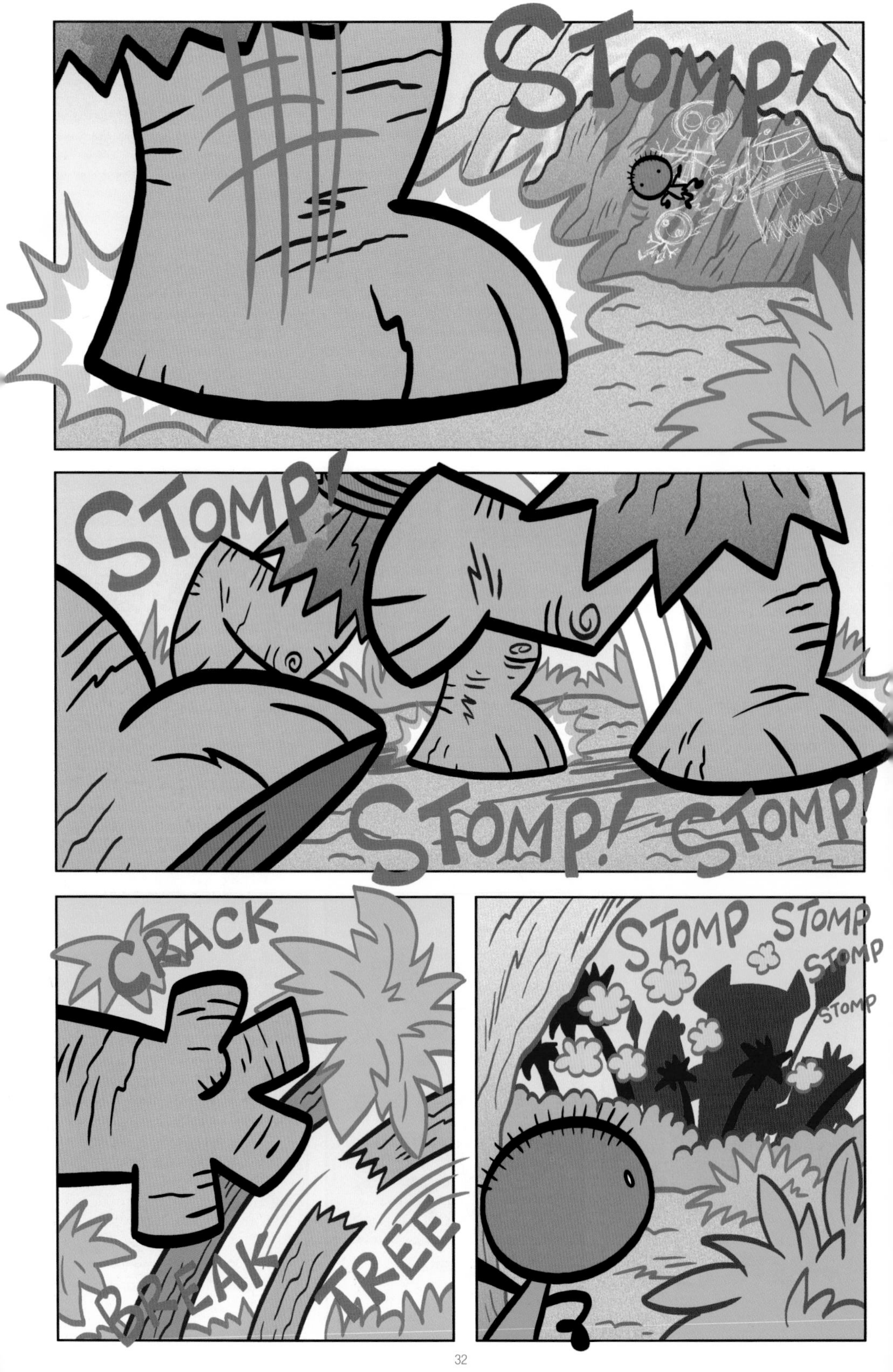
STOMP!
STOMP!
STOMP! STOMP!
CRACK
BREAK
TREE
STOMP STOMP
STOMP
STOMP

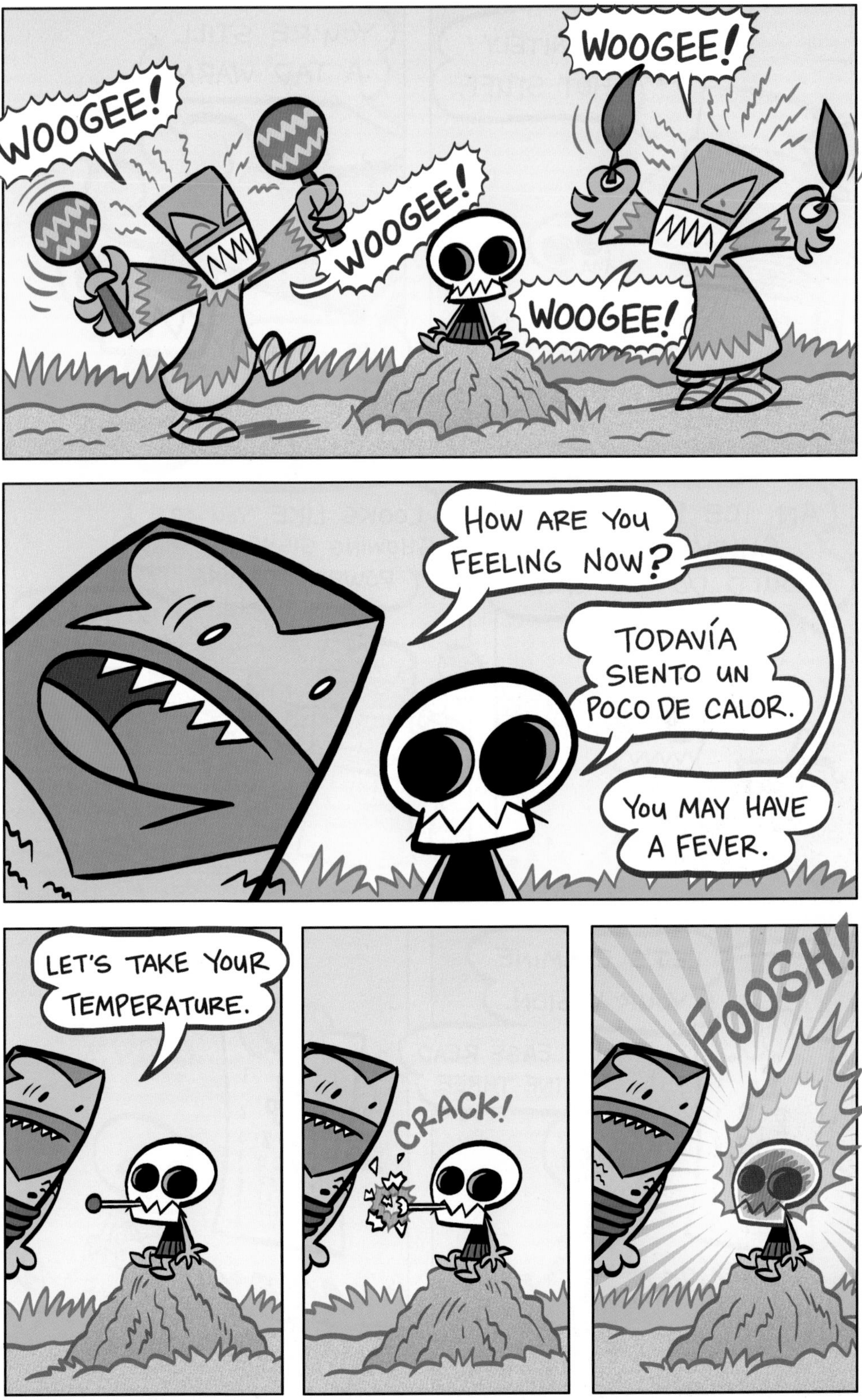
WOOGEE!
WOOGEE!
WOOGEE!
WOOGEE!
HOW ARE YOU FEELING NOW?
TODAVÍA SIENTO UN POCO DE CALOR.
YOU MAY HAVE A FEVER.
LET'S TAKE YOUR TEMPERATURE.
CRACK!
FOOSH!

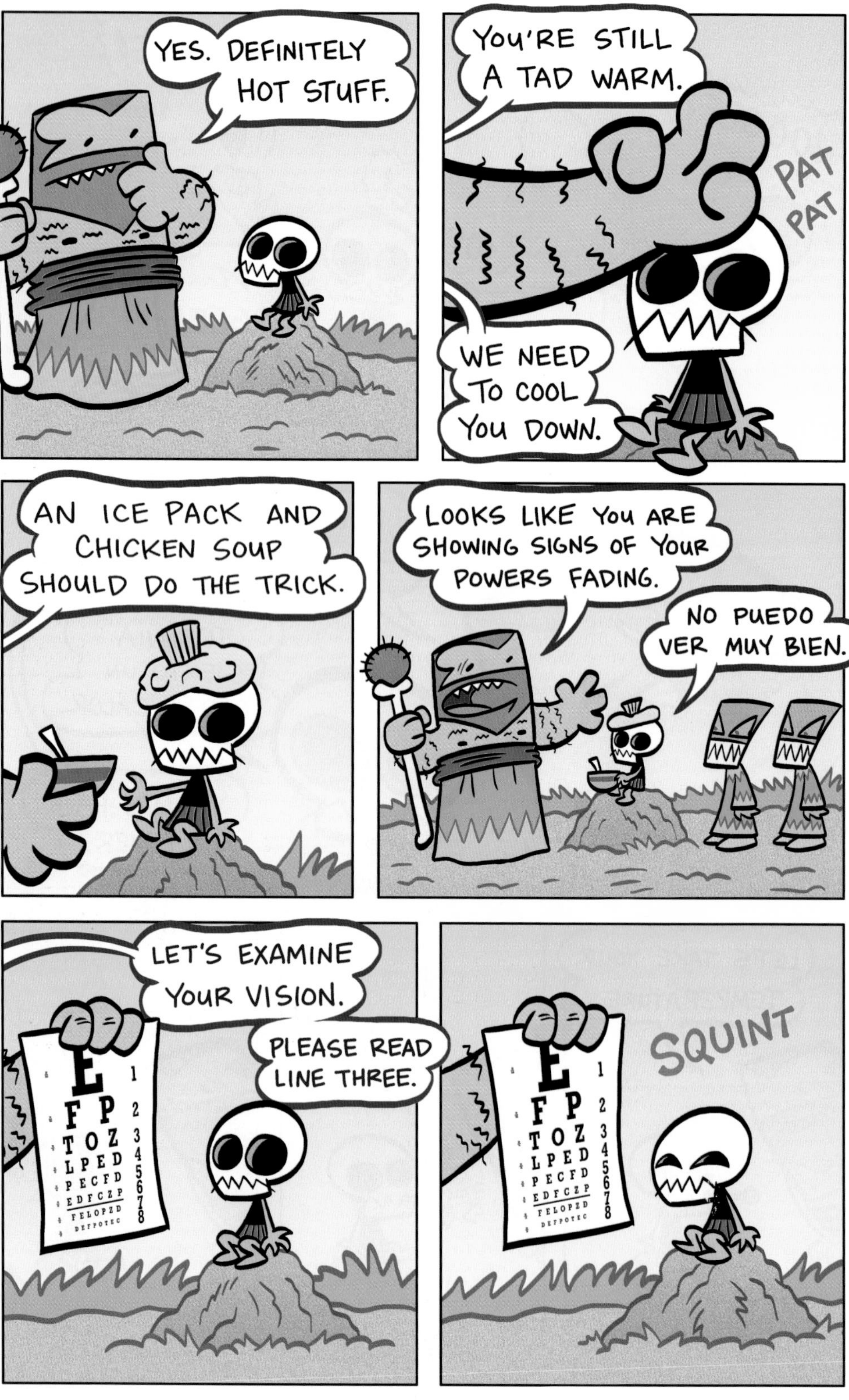
YES. DEFINITELY HOT STUFF.
YOU'RE STILL A TAD WARM.
PAT PAT
WE NEED TO COOL YOU DOWN.
AN ICE PACK AND CHICKEN SOUP SHOULD DO THE TRICK.
LOOKS LIKE YOU ARE SHOWING SIGNS OF YOUR POWERS FADING.
NO PUEDO VER MUY BIEN.
LET'S EXAMINE YOUR VISION.
PLEASE READ LINE THREE.
SQUINT

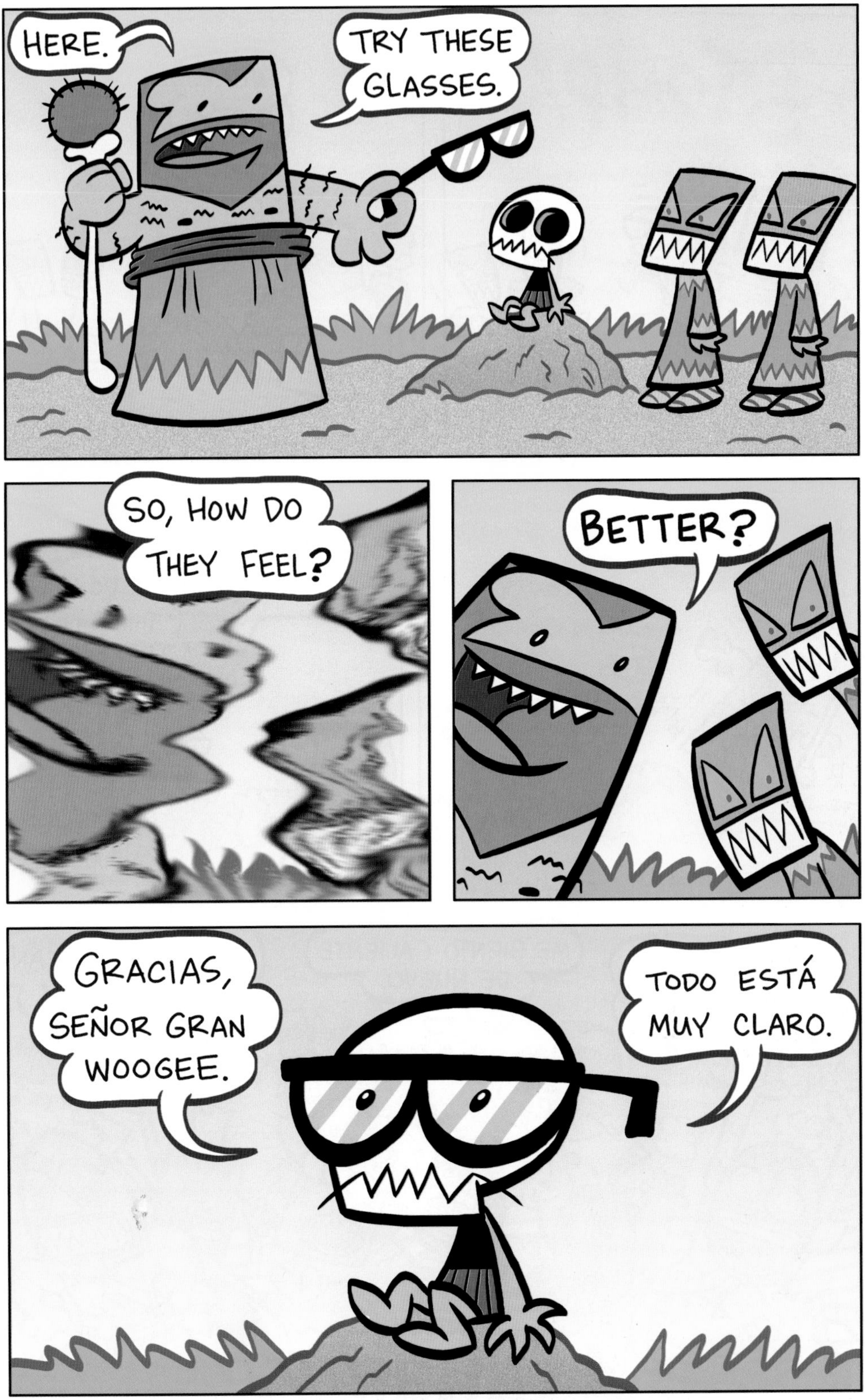
HERE.
TRY THESE GLASSES.
SO, HOW DO THEY FEEL?
BETTER?
GRACIAS, SEÑOR GRAN WOOGEE.
TODO ESTÁ MUY CLARO.

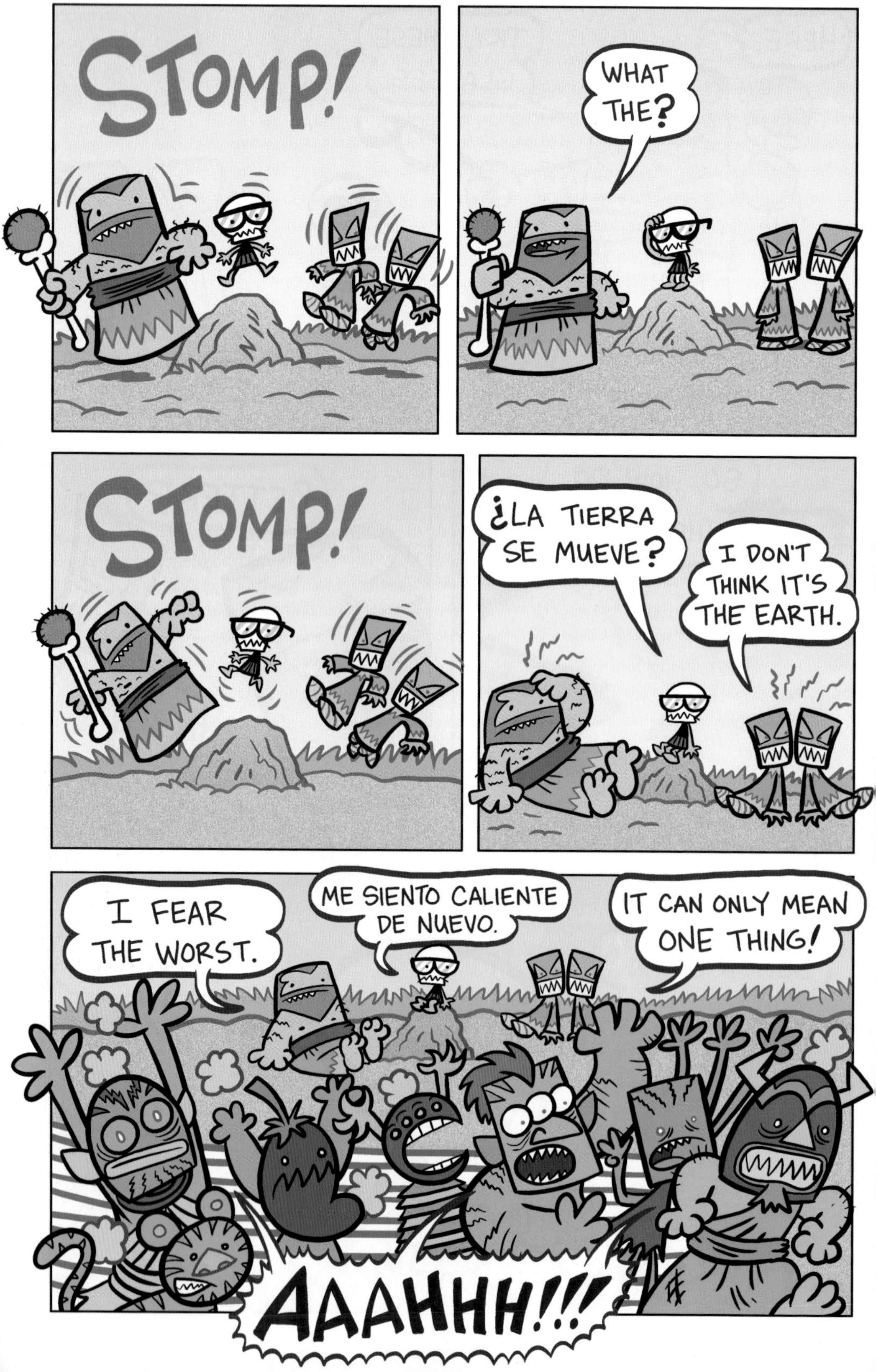
STOMP!
WHAT THE?
STOMP!
¿LA TIERRA SE MUEVE?
I DON'T THINK IT'S THE EARTH.
I FEAR THE WORST.
ME SIENTO CALIENTE DE NUEVO.
IT CAN ONLY MEAN ONE THING!
AAAHHH!!!

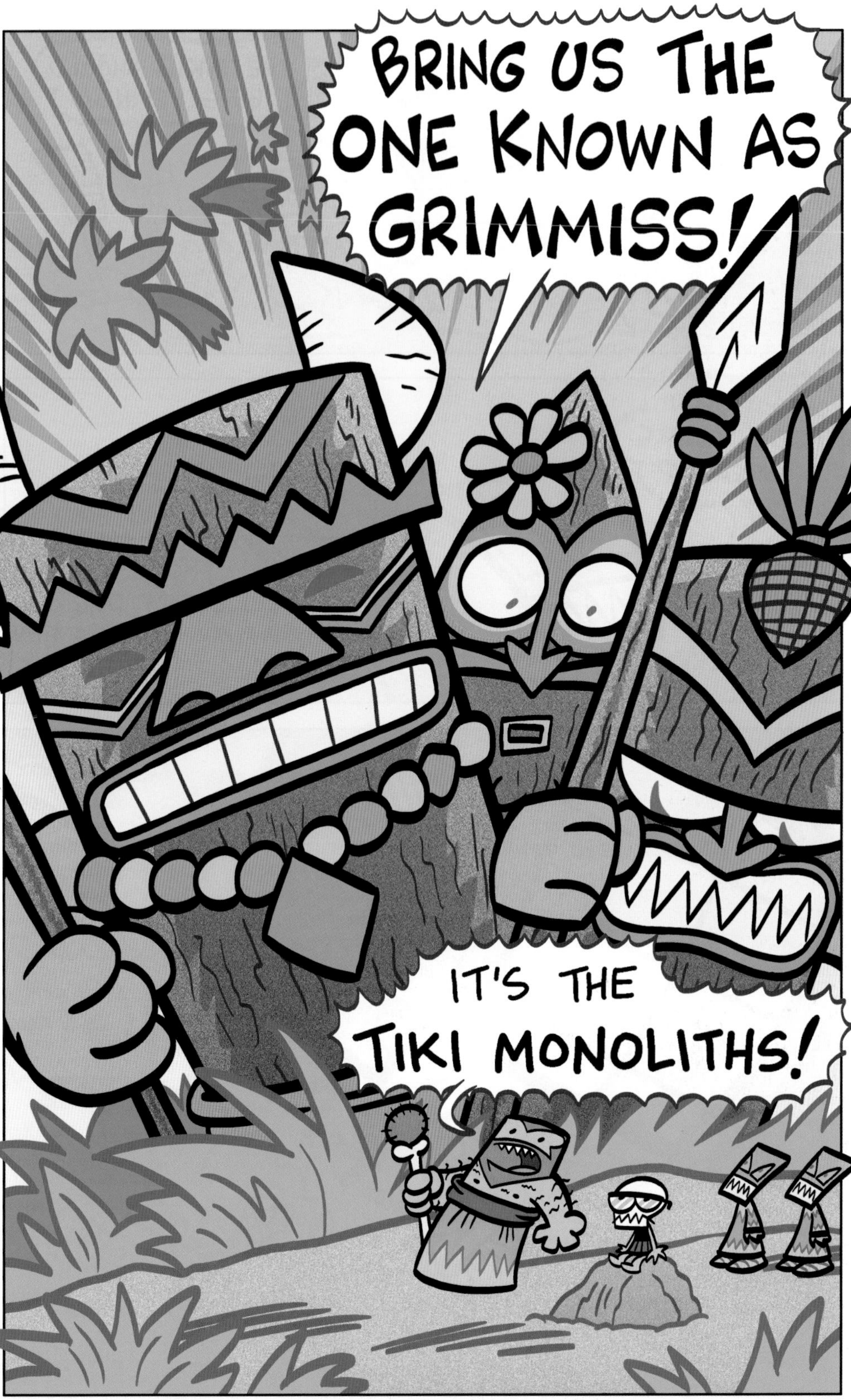
BRING US THE ONE KNOWN AS GRIMMISS!
IT'S THE TIKI MONOLITHS!

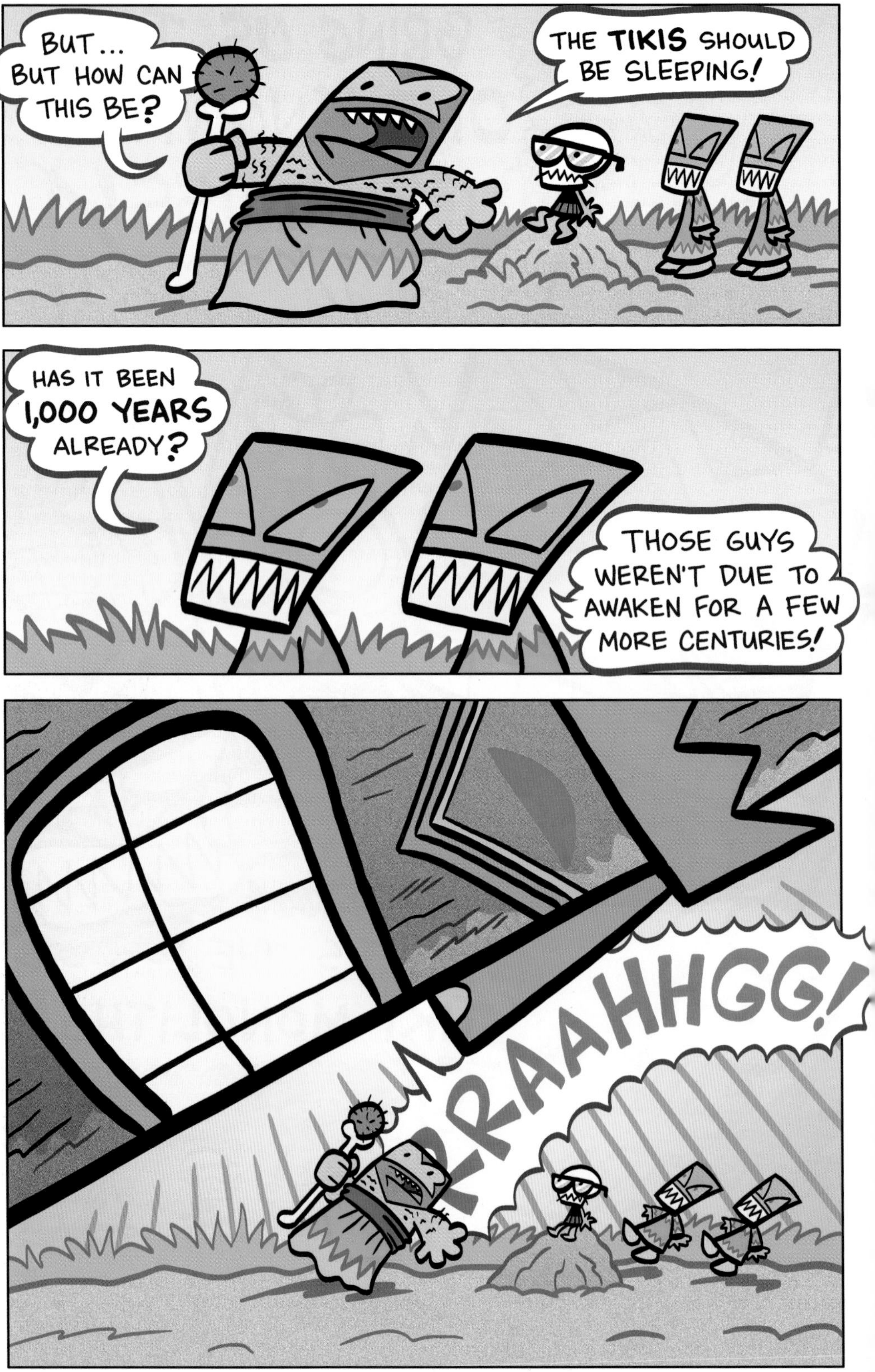
BUT... BUT HOW CAN THIS BE?
THE **TIKIS** SHOULD BE SLEEPING!
HAS IT BEEN **1,000 YEARS** ALREADY?
THOSE GUYS WEREN'T DUE TO AWAKEN FOR A FEW MORE CENTURIES!
RRAAHHGG!

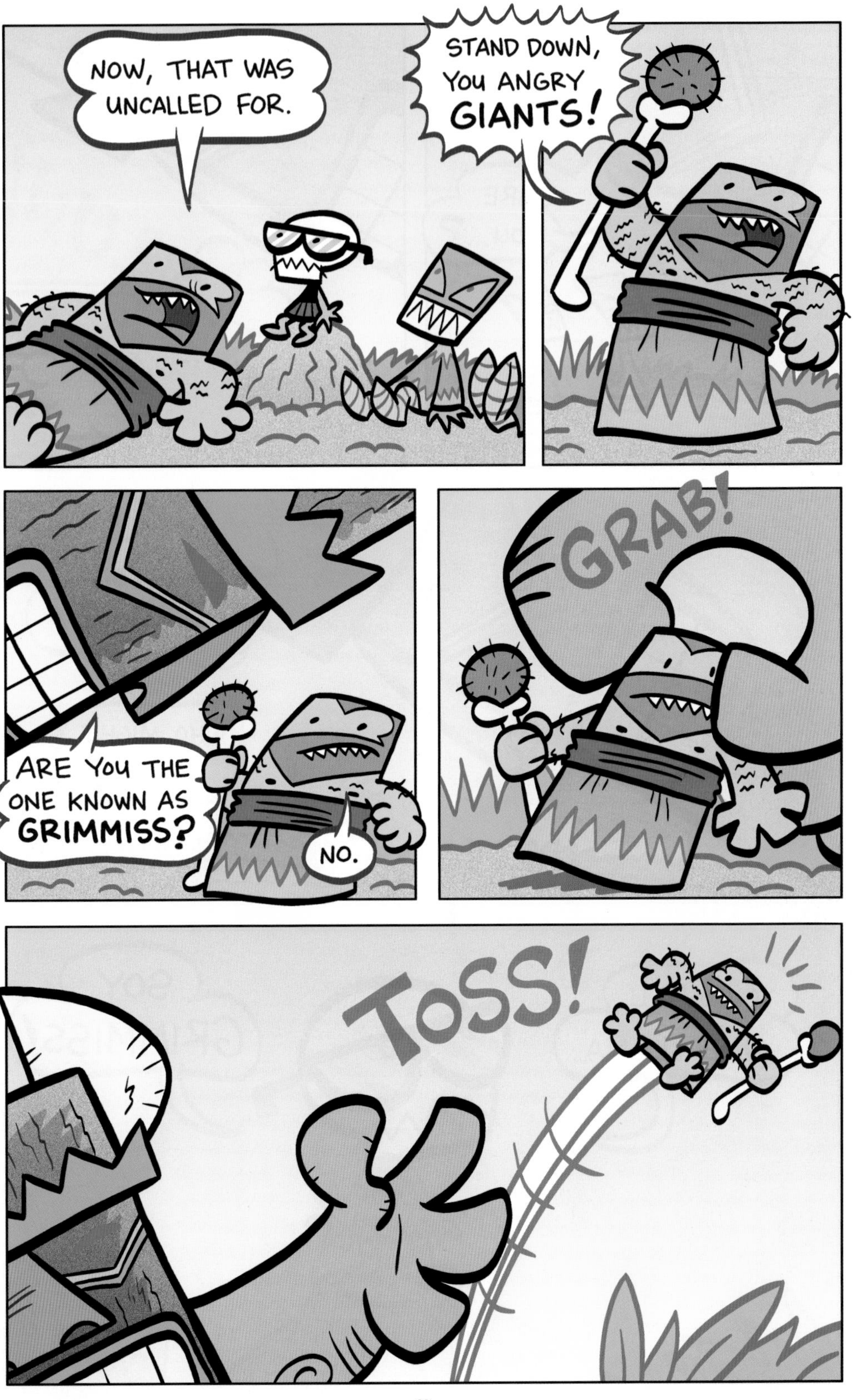
NOW, THAT WAS UNCALLED FOR.
STAND DOWN, YOU ANGRY GIANTS!
ARE YOU THE ONE KNOWN AS GRIMMISS?
NO.
GRAB!
TOSS!

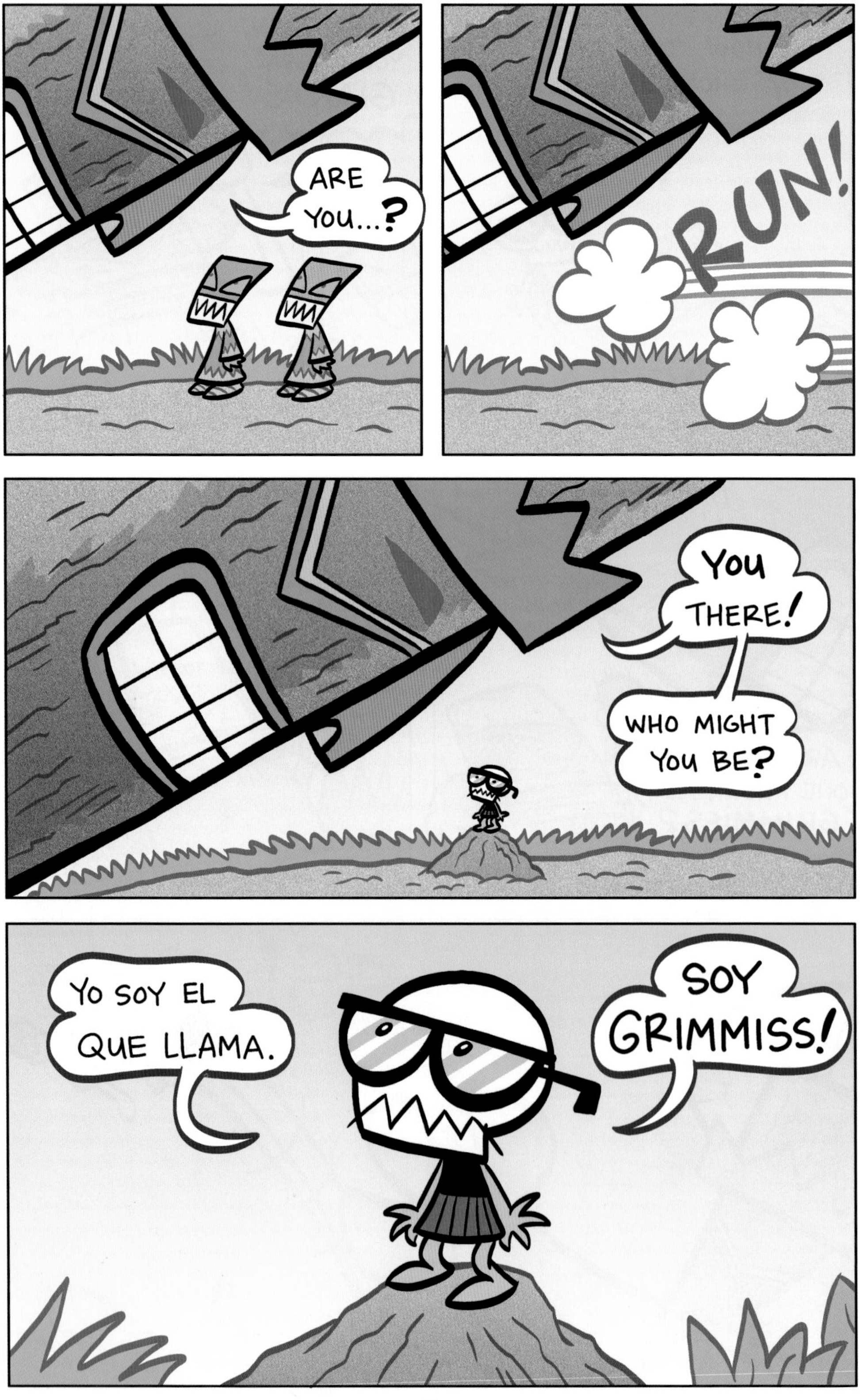
ARE YOU...?
RUN!
YOU THERE!
WHO MIGHT YOU BE?
YO SOY EL QUE LLAMA.
SOY GRIMMISS!

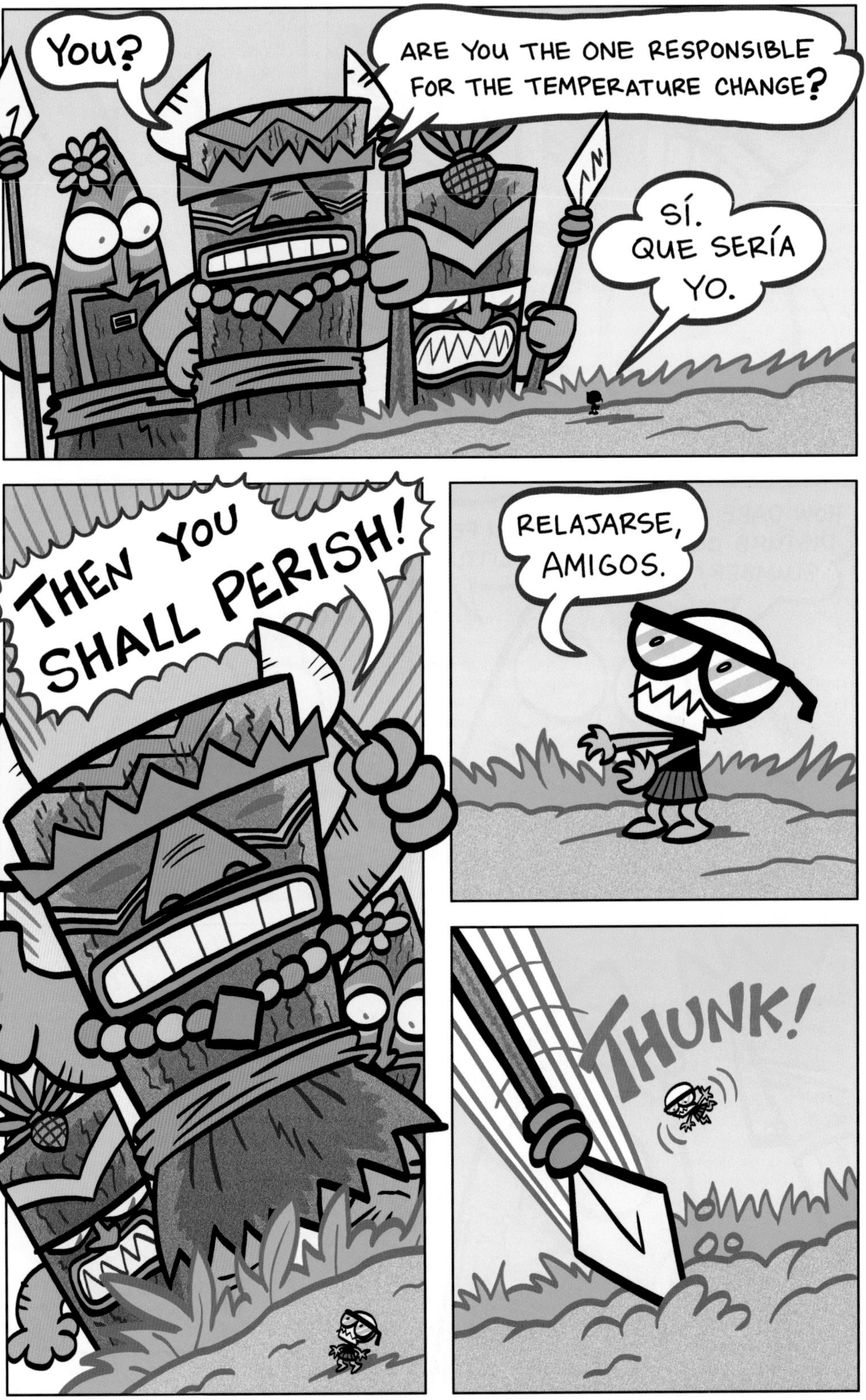

YOU?
ARE YOU THE ONE RESPONSIBLE FOR THE TEMPERATURE CHANGE?
SÍ. QUE SERÍA YO.
THEN YOU SHALL PERISH!
RELAJARSE, AMIGOS.
THUNK!

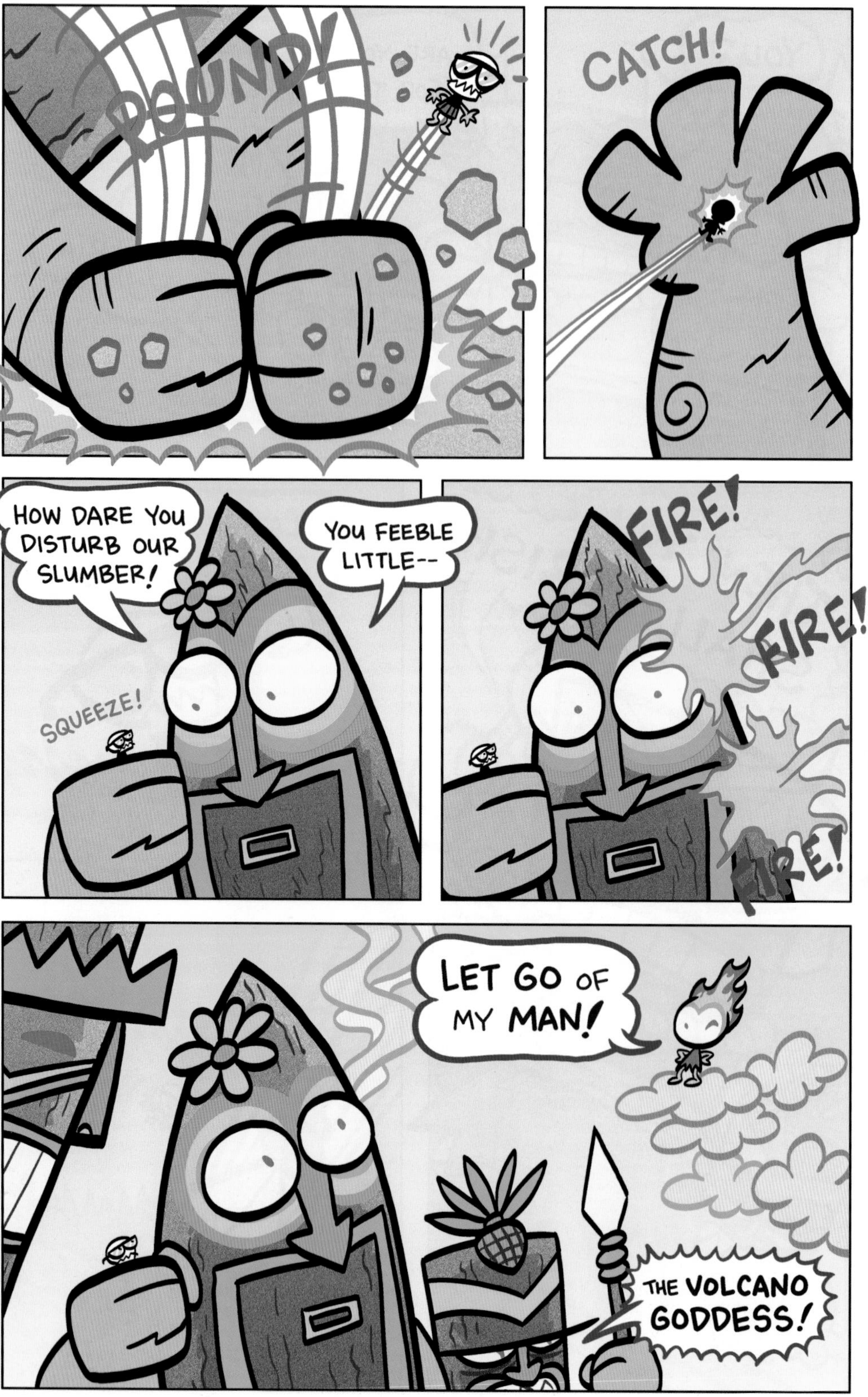
POUND!
CATCH!
HOW DARE YOU DISTURB OUR SLUMBER!
YOU FEEBLE LITTLE--
SQUEEZE!
FIRE!
FIRE!
FIRE!
LET GO OF MY MAN!
THE VOLCANO GODDESS!

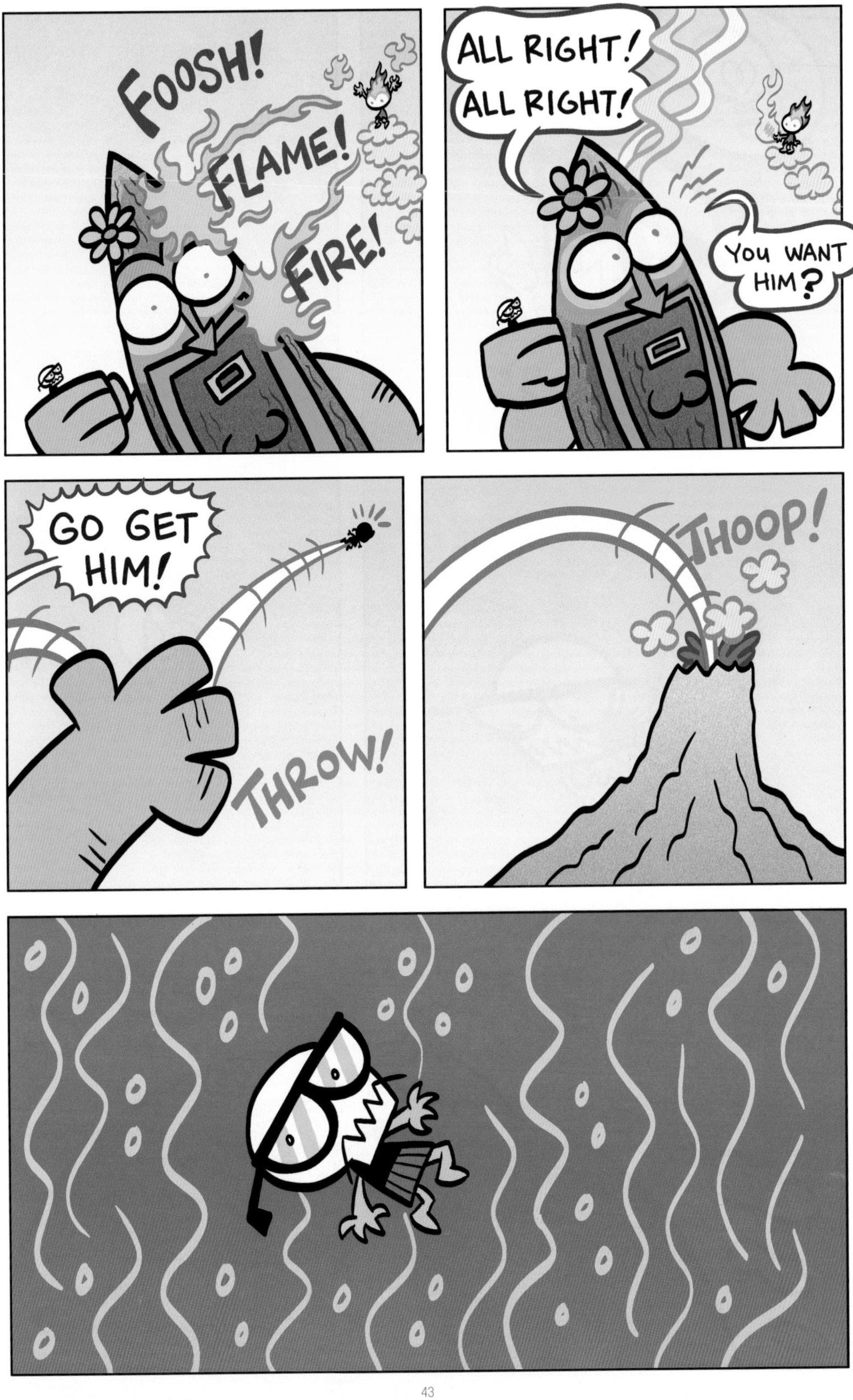
FOOSH!
FLAME!
FIRE!
ALL RIGHT! ALL RIGHT!
YOU WANT HIM?
GO GET HIM!
THROW!
THOOP!

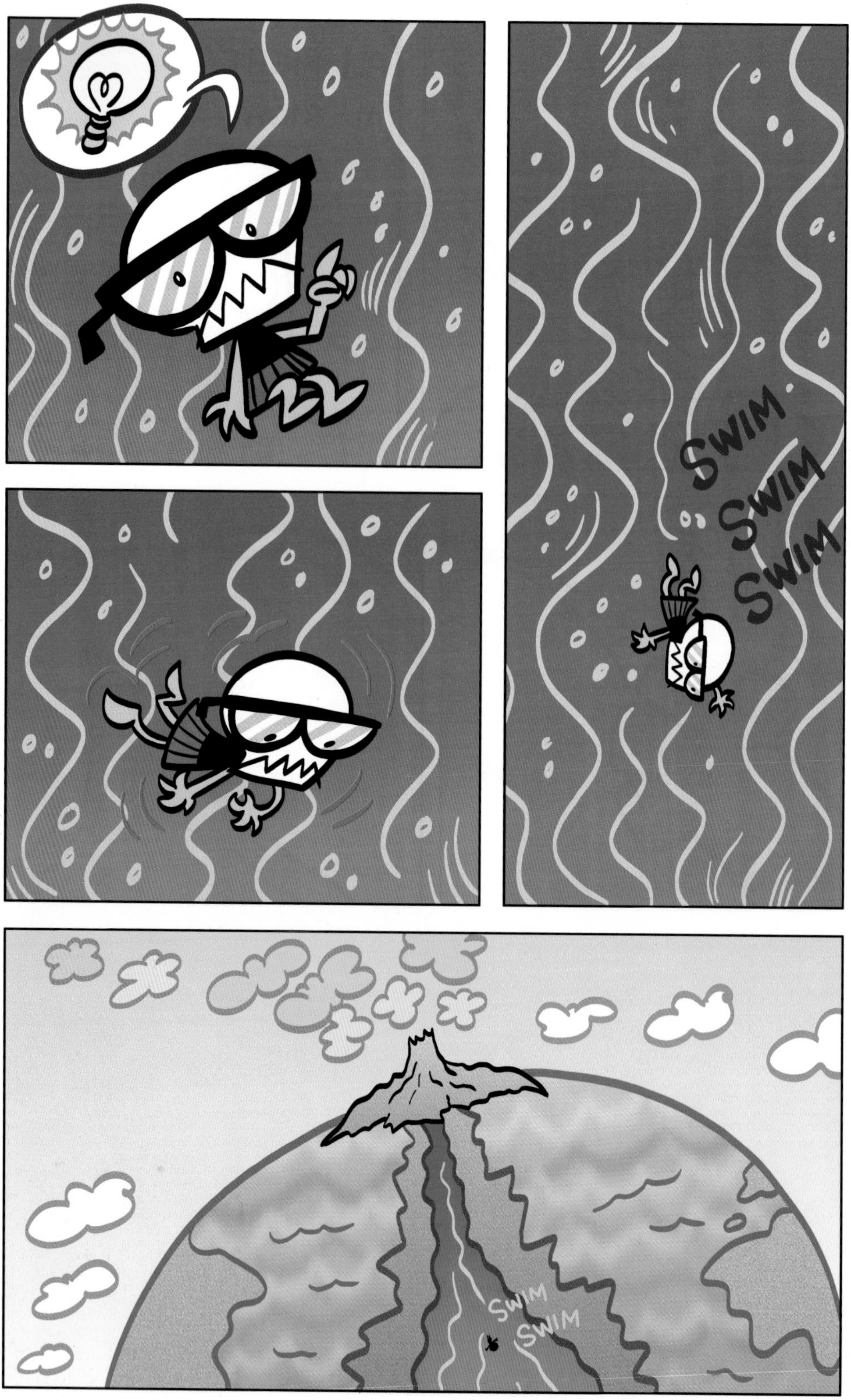
SWIM
SWIM
SWIM
SWIM
SWIM

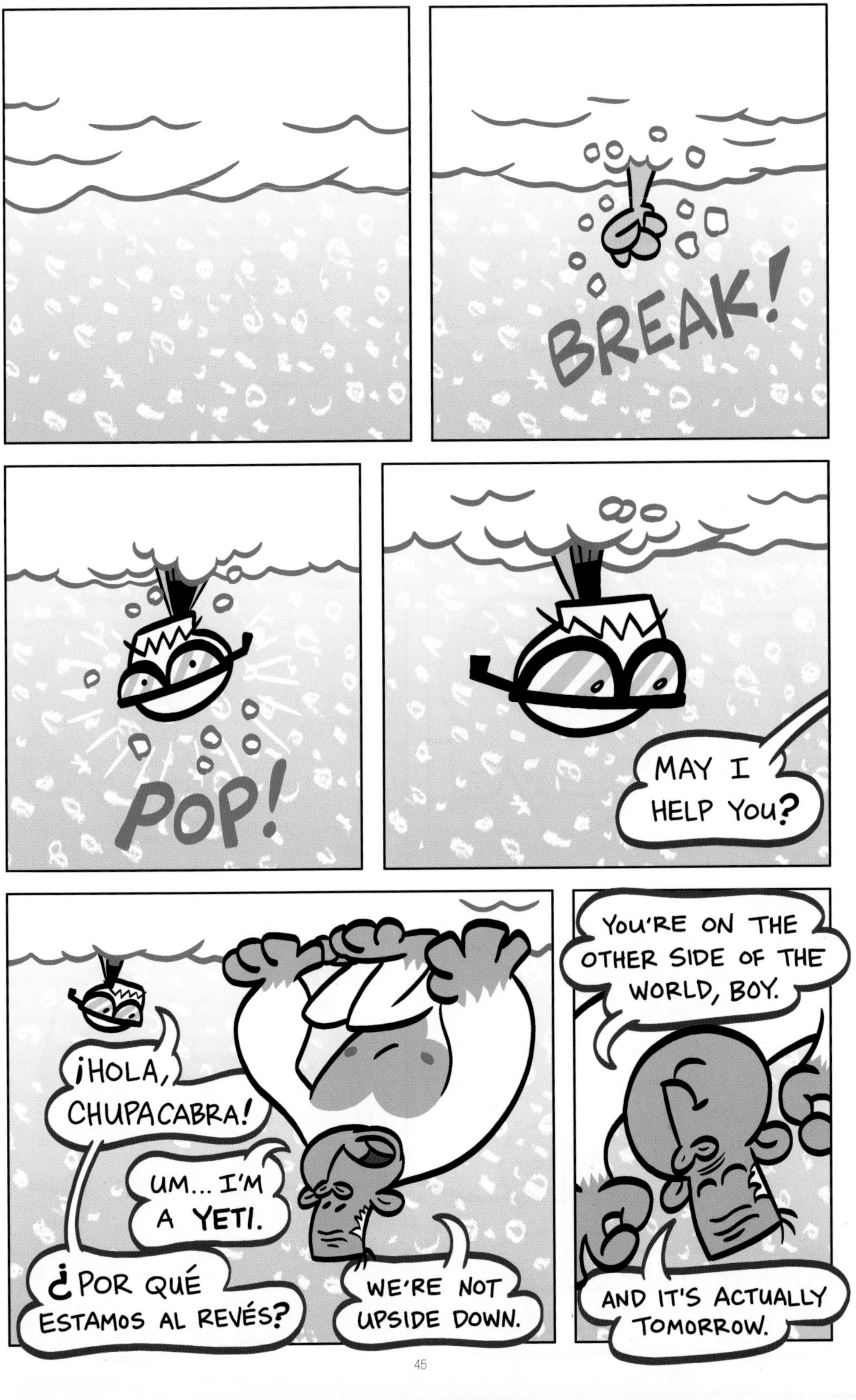
BREAK!
POP!
MAY I HELP YOU?
¡HOLA, CHUPACABRA!
UM... I'M A YETI.
¿POR QUÉ ESTAMOS AL REVÉS?
WE'RE NOT UPSIDE DOWN.
YOU'RE ON THE OTHER SIDE OF THE WORLD, BOY.
AND IT'S ACTUALLY TOMORROW.

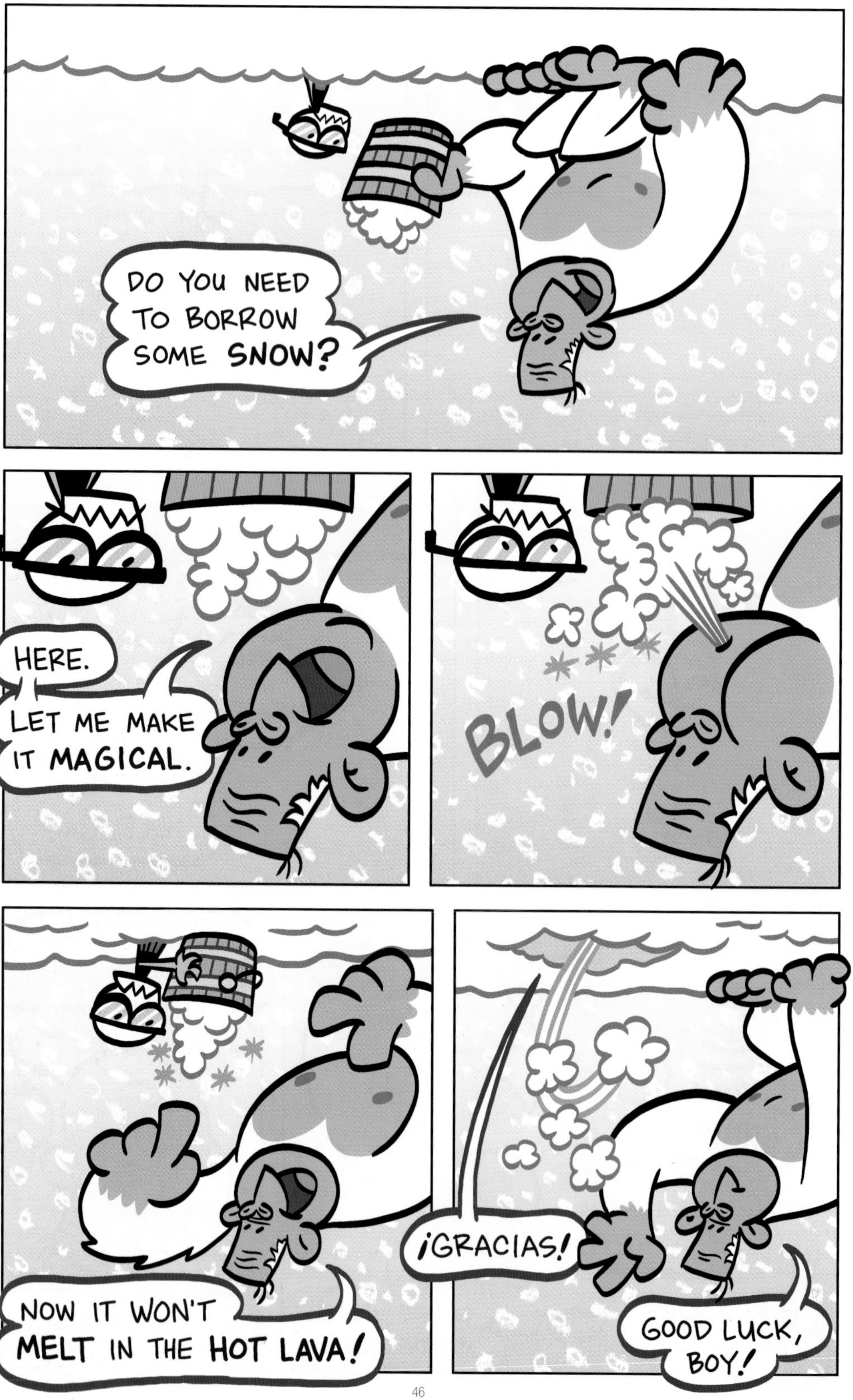
DO YOU NEED TO BORROW SOME SNOW?
HERE.
LET ME MAKE IT MAGICAL.
BLOW!
NOW IT WON'T MELT IN THE HOT LAVA!
¡GRACIAS!
GOOD LUCK, BOY!

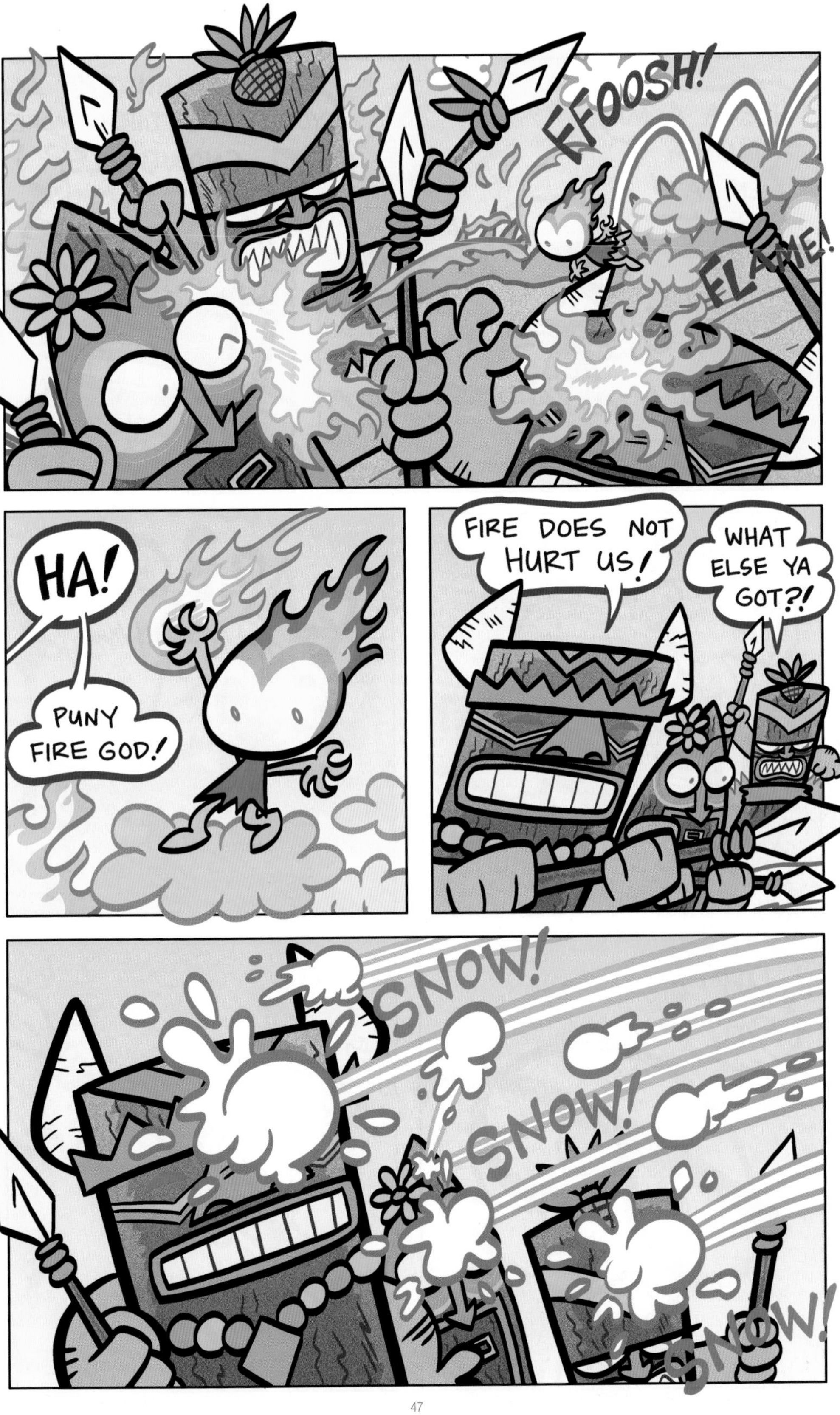
FFOOSH!
FLAME!
HA!
PUNY FIRE GOD!
FIRE DOES NOT HURT US!
WHAT ELSE YA GOT?!
SNOW!
SNOW!
SNOW!

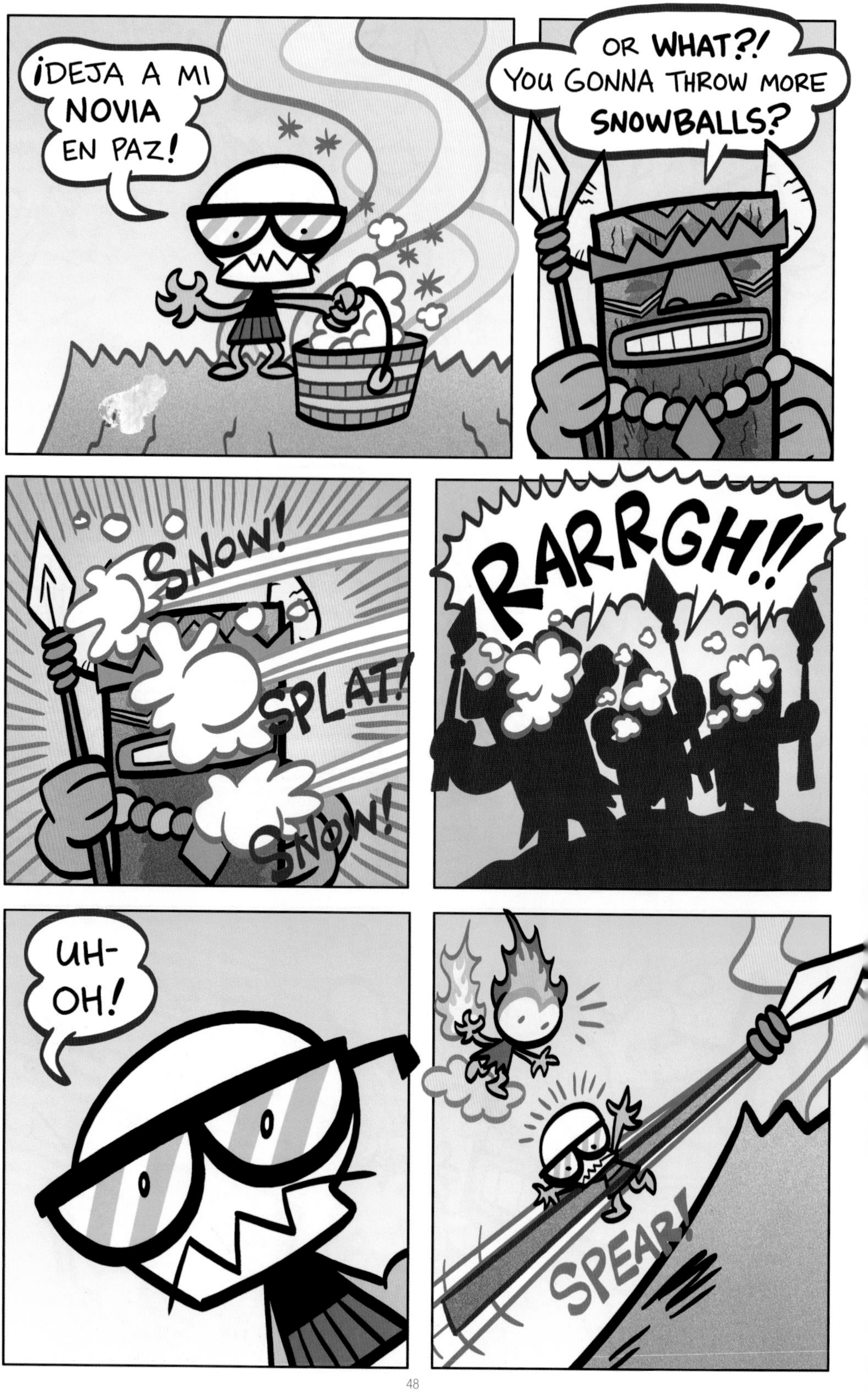
¡DEJA A MI NOVIA EN PAZ!
OR WHAT?! YOU GONNA THROW MORE SNOWBALLS?
SNOW!
SPLAT!
SNOW!
RARRGH!!
UH-OH!
SPEAR!

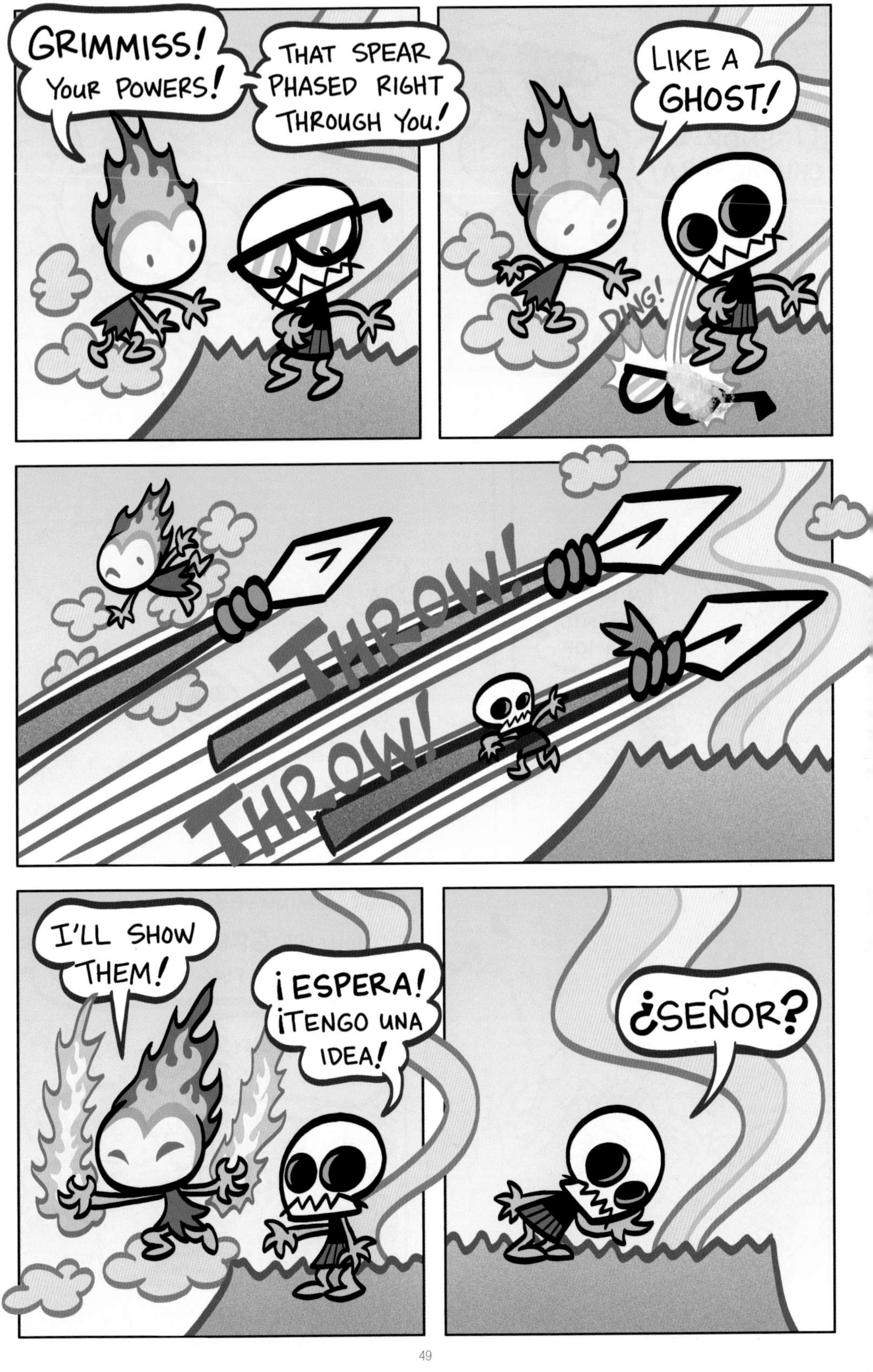
GRIMMISS! YOUR POWERS!
THAT SPEAR PHASED RIGHT THROUGH YOU!
LIKE A GHOST!
DING!
THROW!
THROW!
I'LL SHOW THEM!
¡ESPERA! ¡TENGO UNA IDEA!
¿SEÑOR?

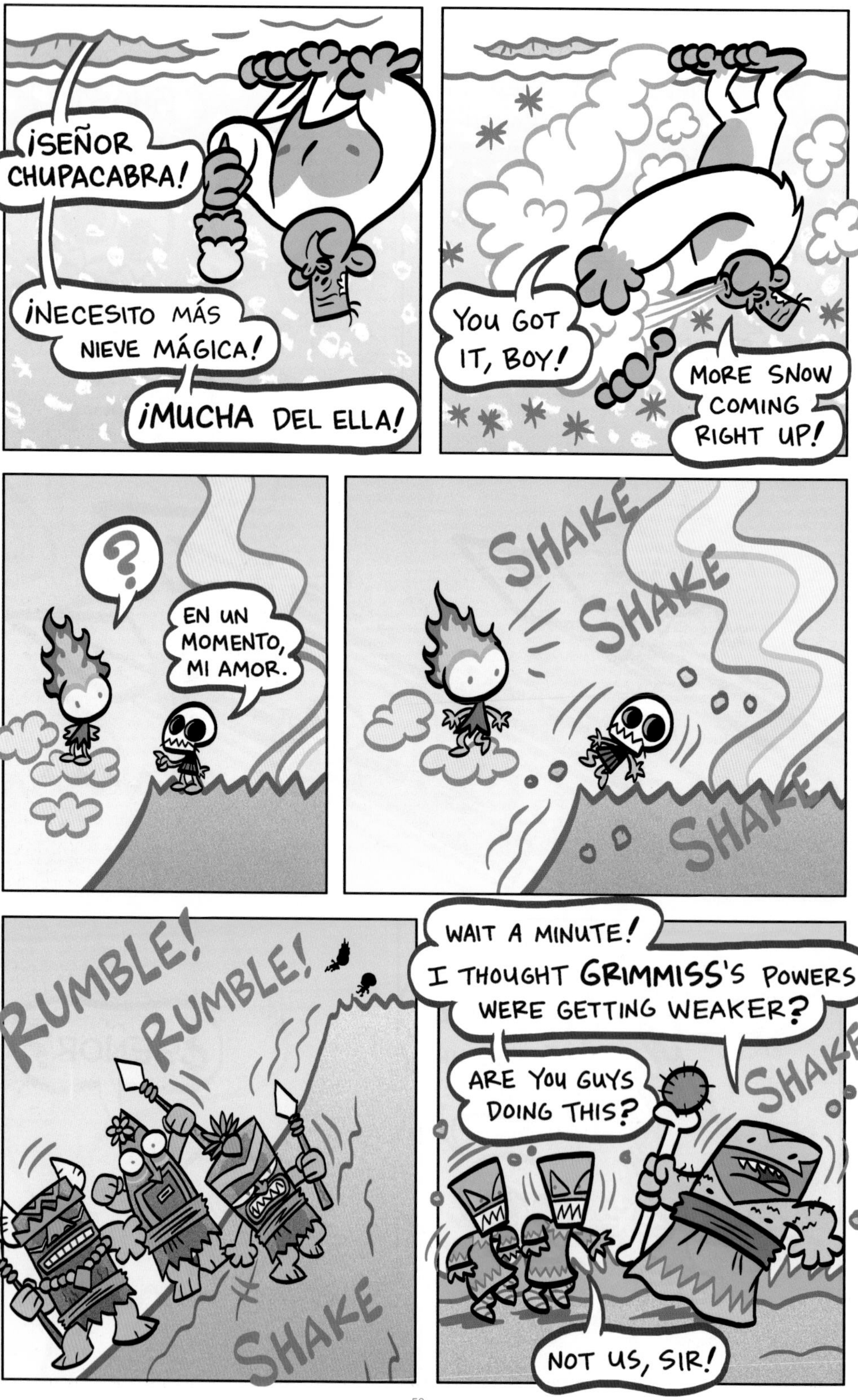

¡SEÑOR CHUPACABRA!
¡NECESITO MÁS NIEVE MÁGICA!
¡MUCHA DEL ELLA!
YOU GOT IT, BOY!
MORE SNOW COMING RIGHT UP!
?
EN UN MOMENTO, MI AMOR.
SHAKE
SHAKE
SHAKE
RUMBLE!
RUMBLE!
SHAKE
WAIT A MINUTE!
I THOUGHT GRIMMISS'S POWERS WERE GETTING WEAKER?
ARE YOU GUYS DOING THIS?
SHAKE
NOT US, SIR!

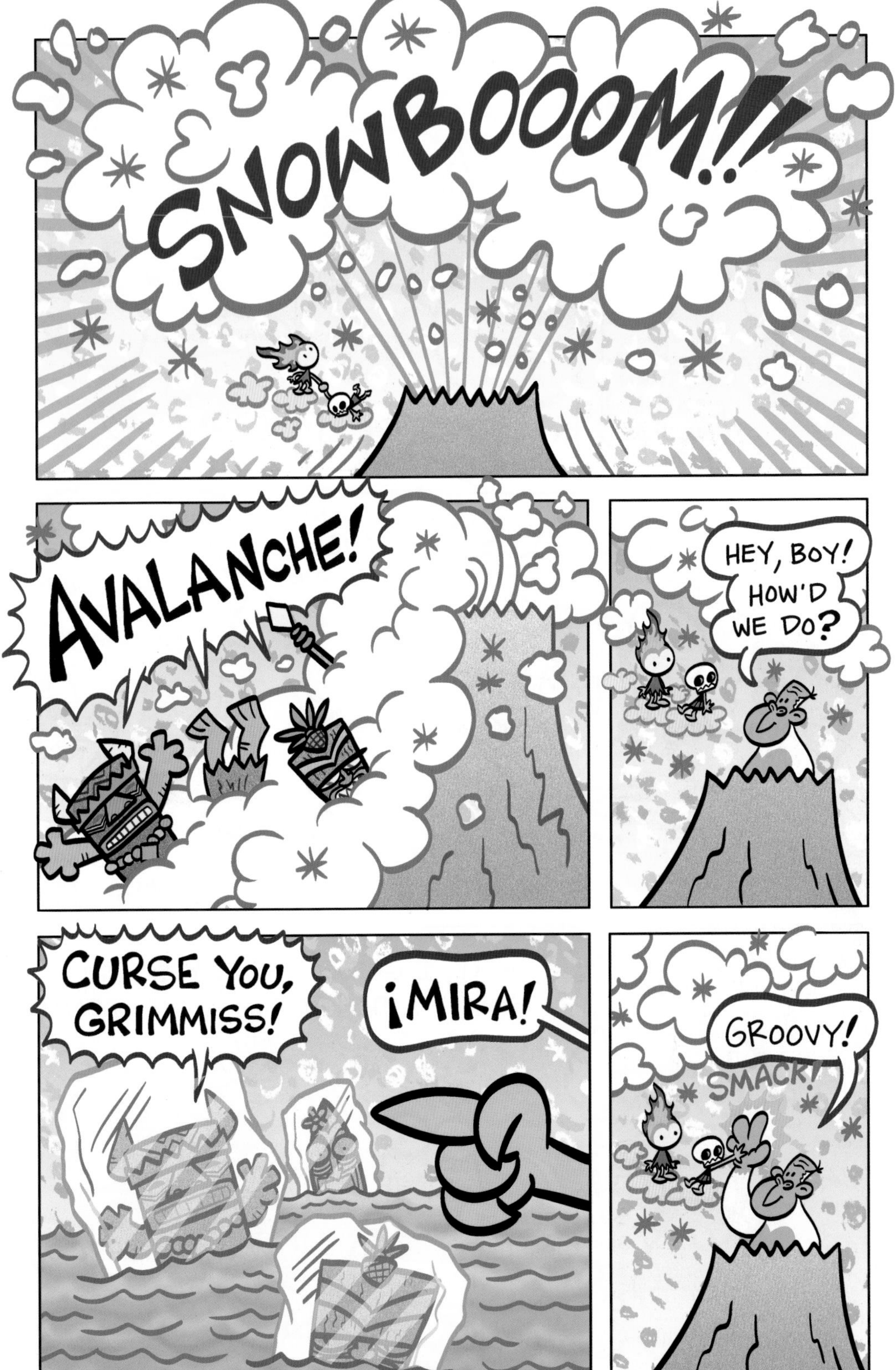
SNOWBOOOM!!
AVALANCHE!
HEY, BOY! HOW'D WE DO?
CURSE YOU, GRIMMISS!
¡MIRA!
GROOVY!
SMACK!

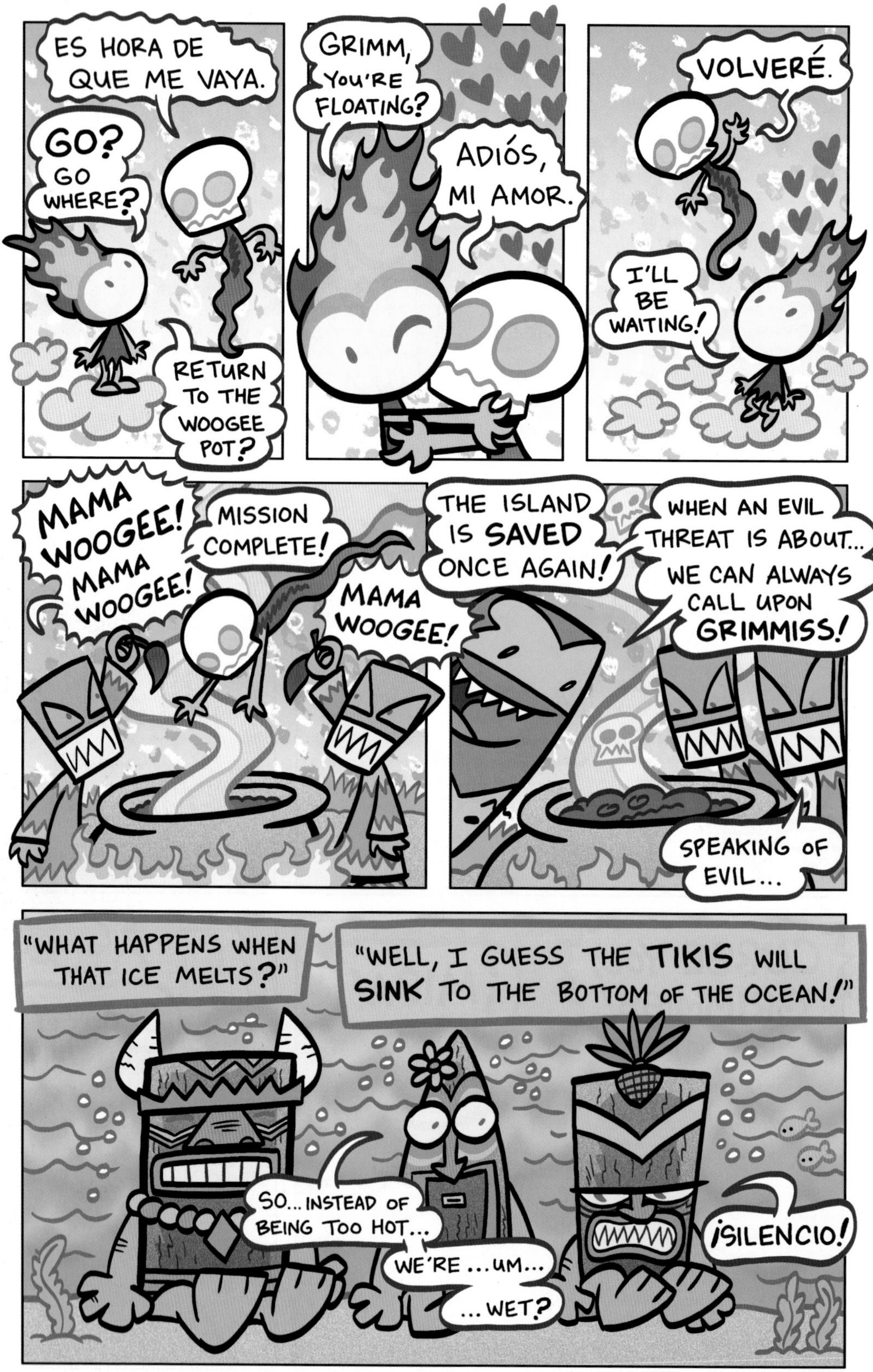
ES HORA DE QUE ME VAYA.
GO? GO WHERE?
RETURN TO THE WOOGEE POT?
GRIMM, YOU'RE FLOATING?
ADIÓS, MI AMOR.
VOLVERÉ.
I'LL BE WAITING!
MAMA WOOGEE! MAMA WOOGEE!
MISSION COMPLETE!
MAMA WOOGEE!
THE ISLAND IS SAVED ONCE AGAIN!
WHEN AN EVIL THREAT IS ABOUT... WE CAN ALWAYS CALL UPON GRIMMISS!
SPEAKING OF EVIL...
"WHAT HAPPENS WHEN THAT ICE MELTS?"
"WELL, I GUESS THE TIKIS WILL SINK TO THE BOTTOM OF THE OCEAN!"
SO... INSTEAD OF BEING TOO HOT...
WE'RE ... UM...
... WET?
¡SILENCIO!

-SUBMERGED.

CHAPTER THREE

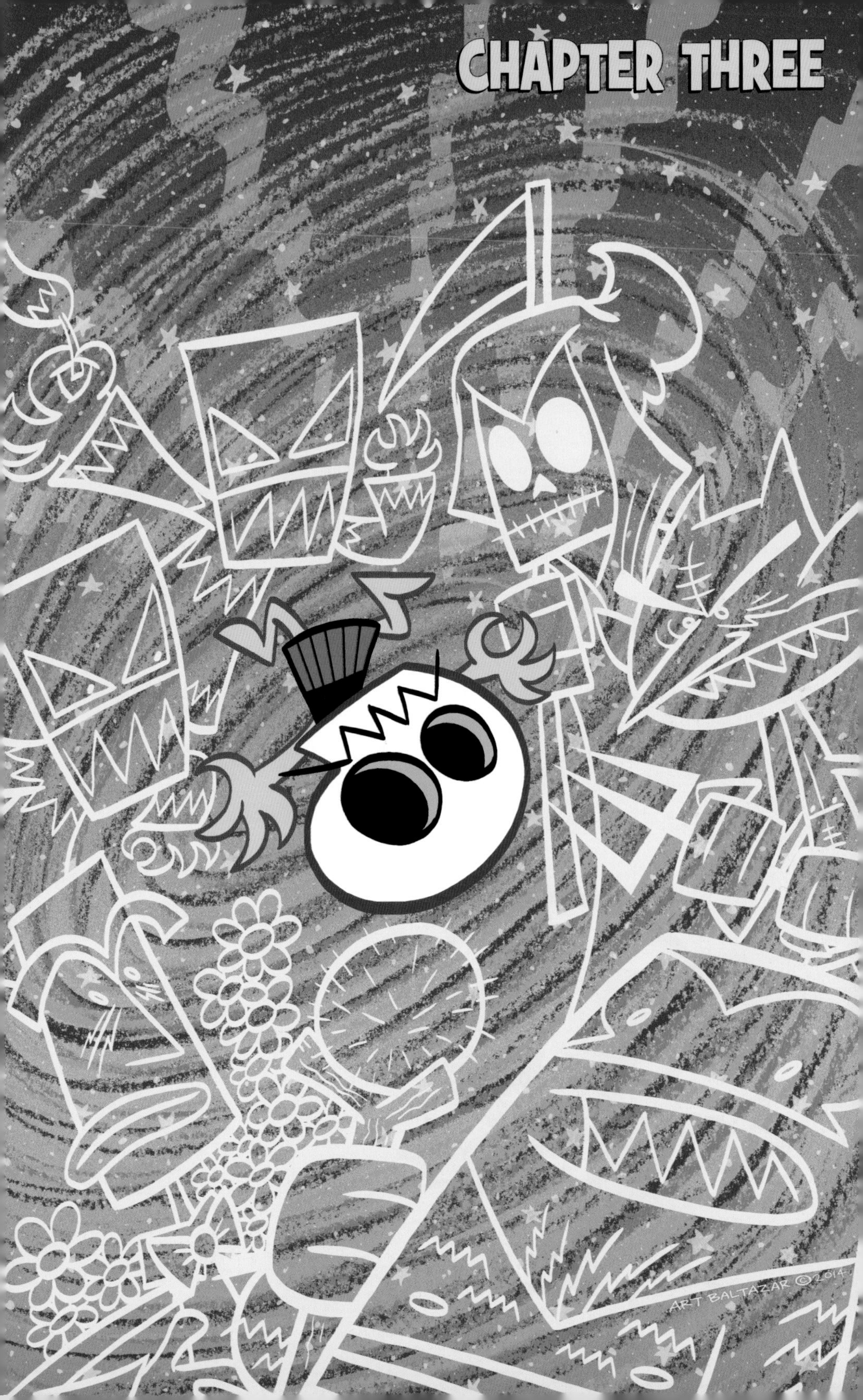
ART BALTAZAR ©2014

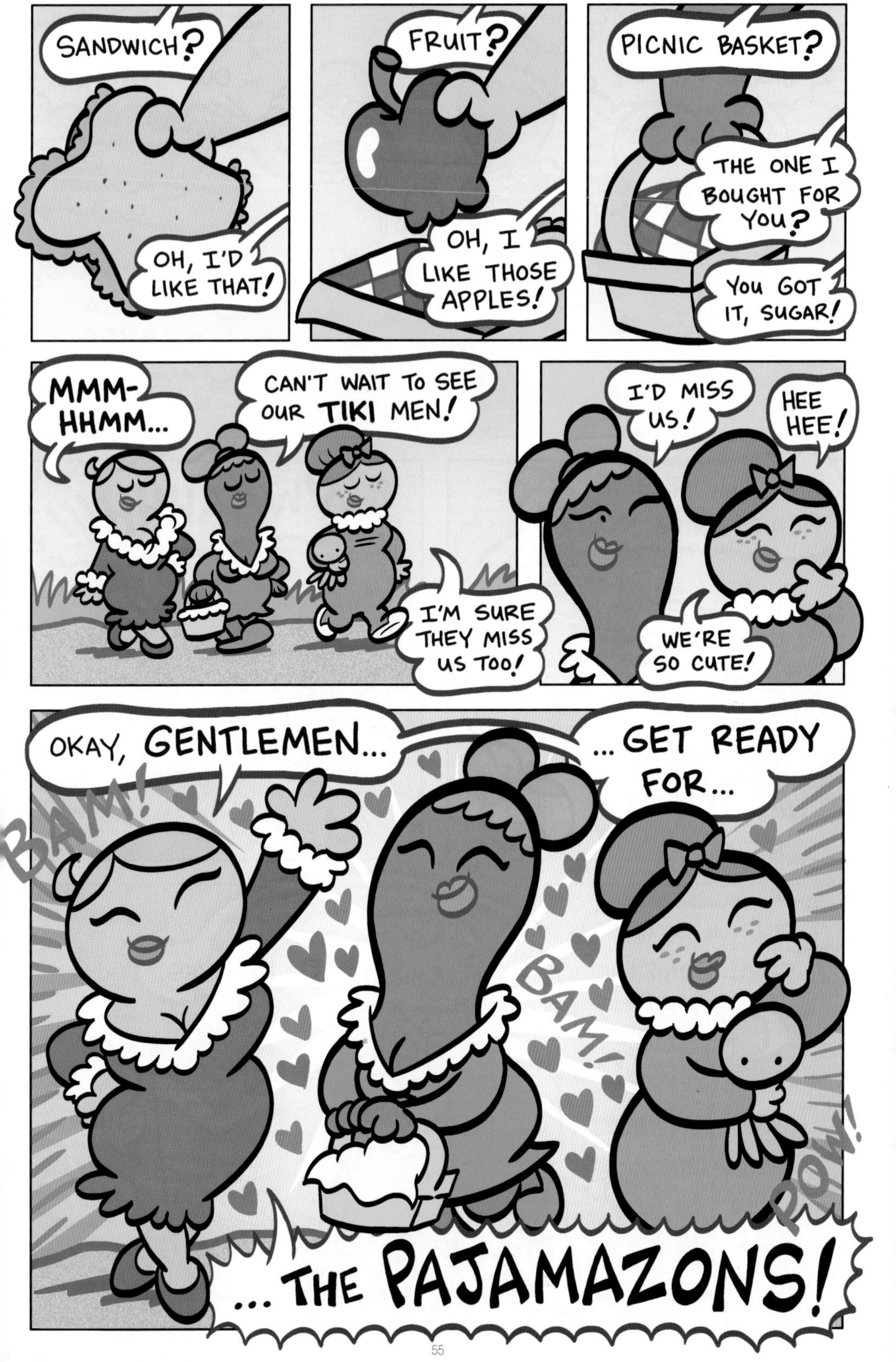
SANDWICH?
OH, I'D LIKE THAT!
FRUIT?
OH, I LIKE THOSE APPLES!
PICNIC BASKET?
THE ONE I BOUGHT FOR YOU?
YOU GOT IT, SUGAR!
MMM-HHMM...
CAN'T WAIT TO SEE OUR TIKI MEN!
I'M SURE THEY MISS US TOO!
I'D MISS US!
HEE HEE!
WE'RE SO CUTE!
OKAY, GENTLEMEN...
...GET READY FOR...
BAM!
BAM!
POW!
...THE PAJAMAZONS!

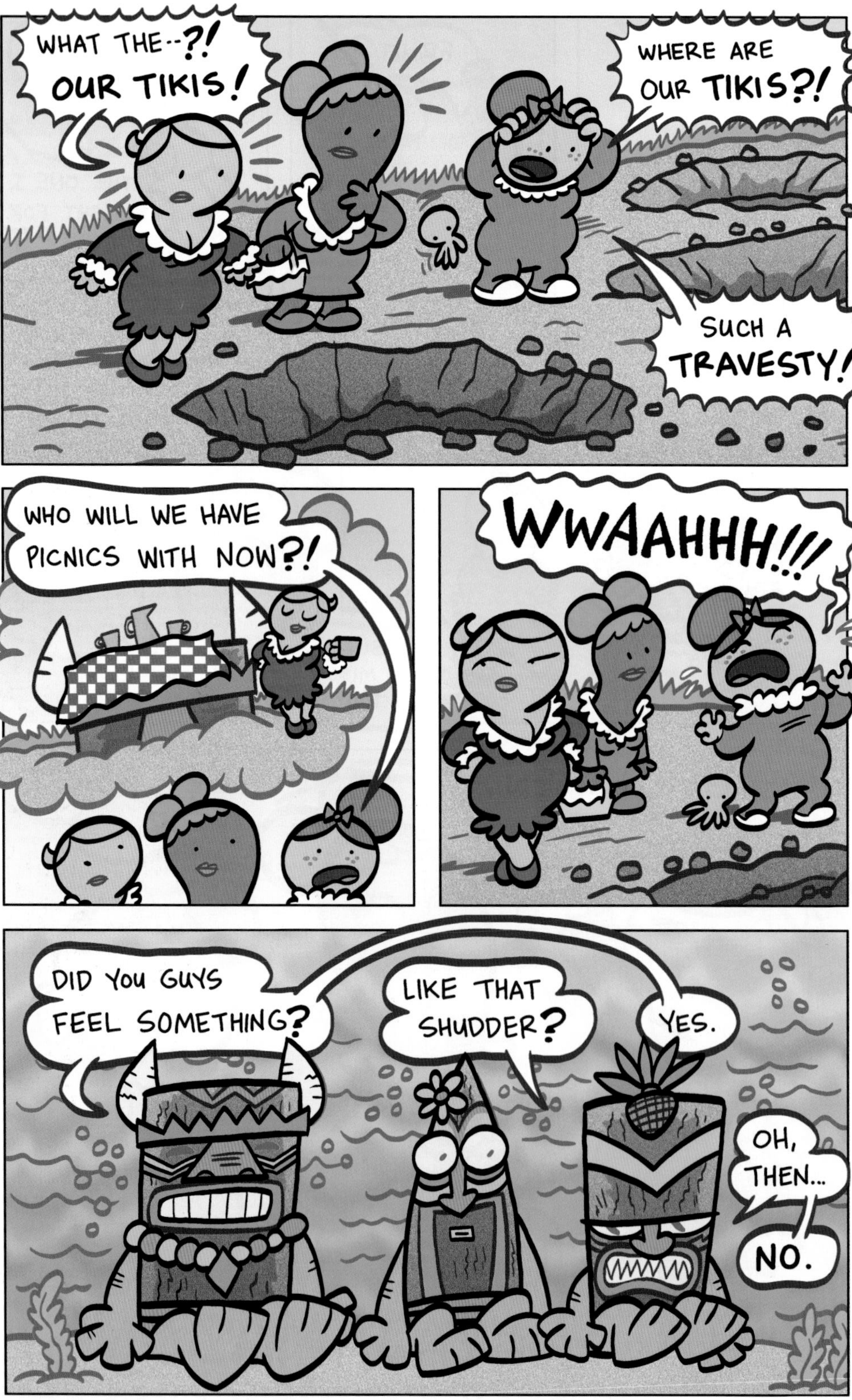
WHAT THE--?! OUR TIKIS!
WHERE ARE OUR TIKIS?!
SUCH A TRAVESTY!
WHO WILL WE HAVE PICNICS WITH NOW?!
WWAAHHH!!!
DID YOU GUYS FEEL SOMETHING?
LIKE THAT SHUDDER?
YES.
OH, THEN...
NO.

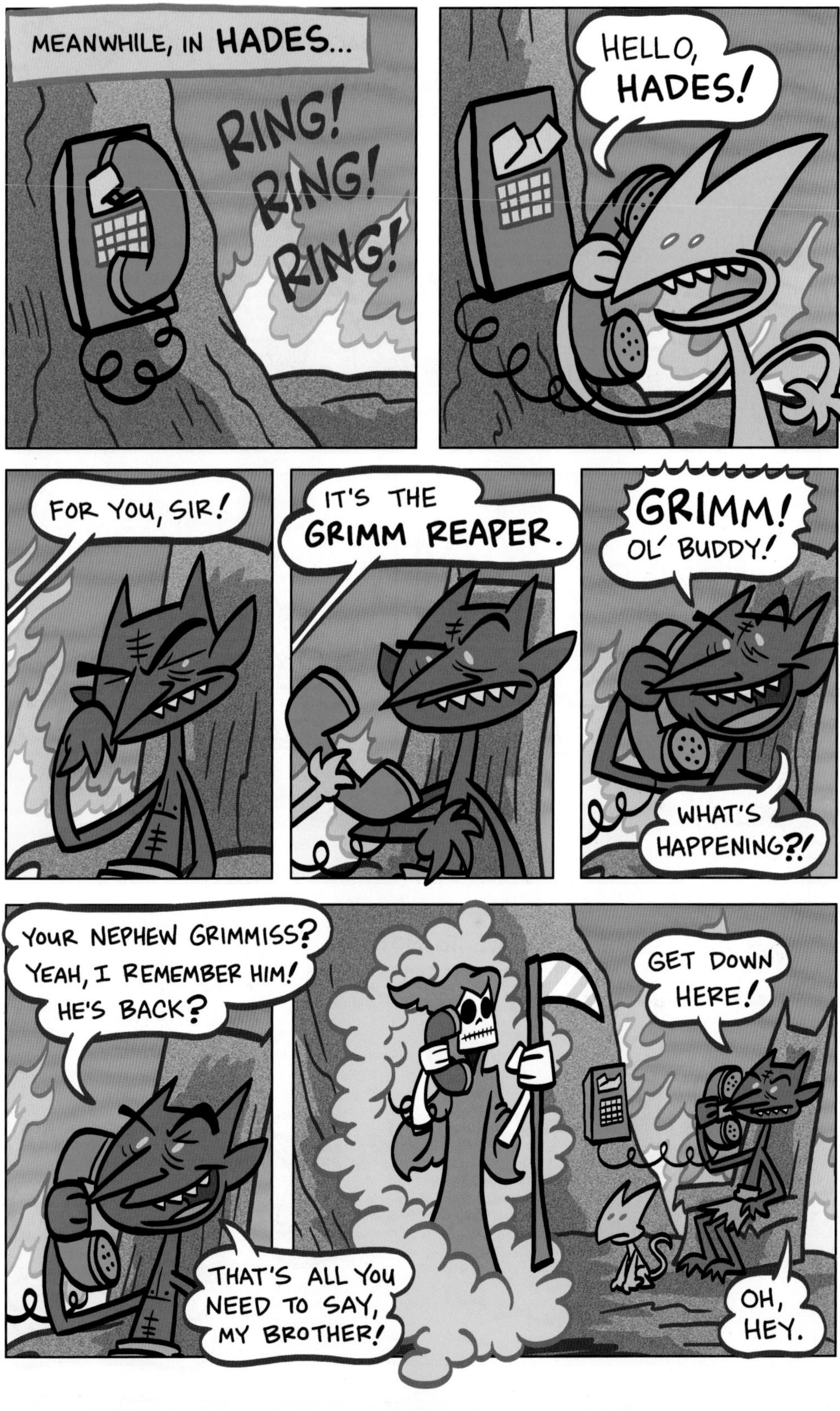
MEANWHILE, IN HADES...
RING! RING! RING!
HELLO, HADES!
FOR YOU, SIR!
IT'S THE GRIMM REAPER.
GRIMM! OL' BUDDY!
WHAT'S HAPPENING?!
YOUR NEPHEW GRIMMISS? YEAH, I REMEMBER HIM! HE'S BACK?
THAT'S ALL YOU NEED TO SAY, MY BROTHER!
GET DOWN HERE!
OH, HEY.

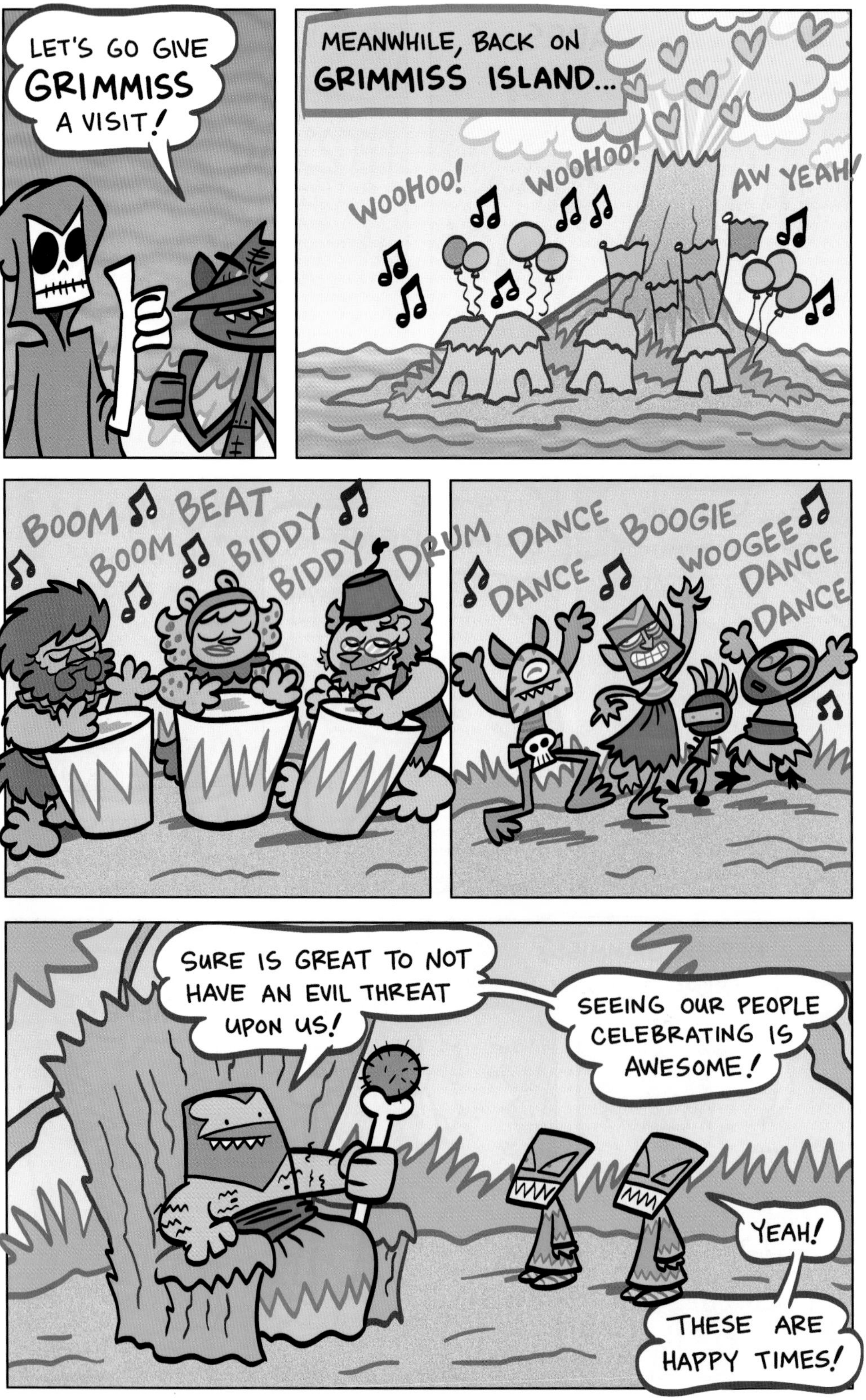
LET'S GO GIVE GRIMMISS A VISIT!
MEANWHILE, BACK ON GRIMMISS ISLAND...
WOOHOO!
WOOHOO!
AW YEAH!
BOOM BOOM
BEAT BIDDY BIDDY
DRUM
DANCE DANCE
BOOGIE WOOGEE
DANCE DANCE
SURE IS GREAT TO NOT HAVE AN EVIL THREAT UPON US!
SEEING OUR PEOPLE CELEBRATING IS AWESOME!
YEAH!
THESE ARE HAPPY TIMES!

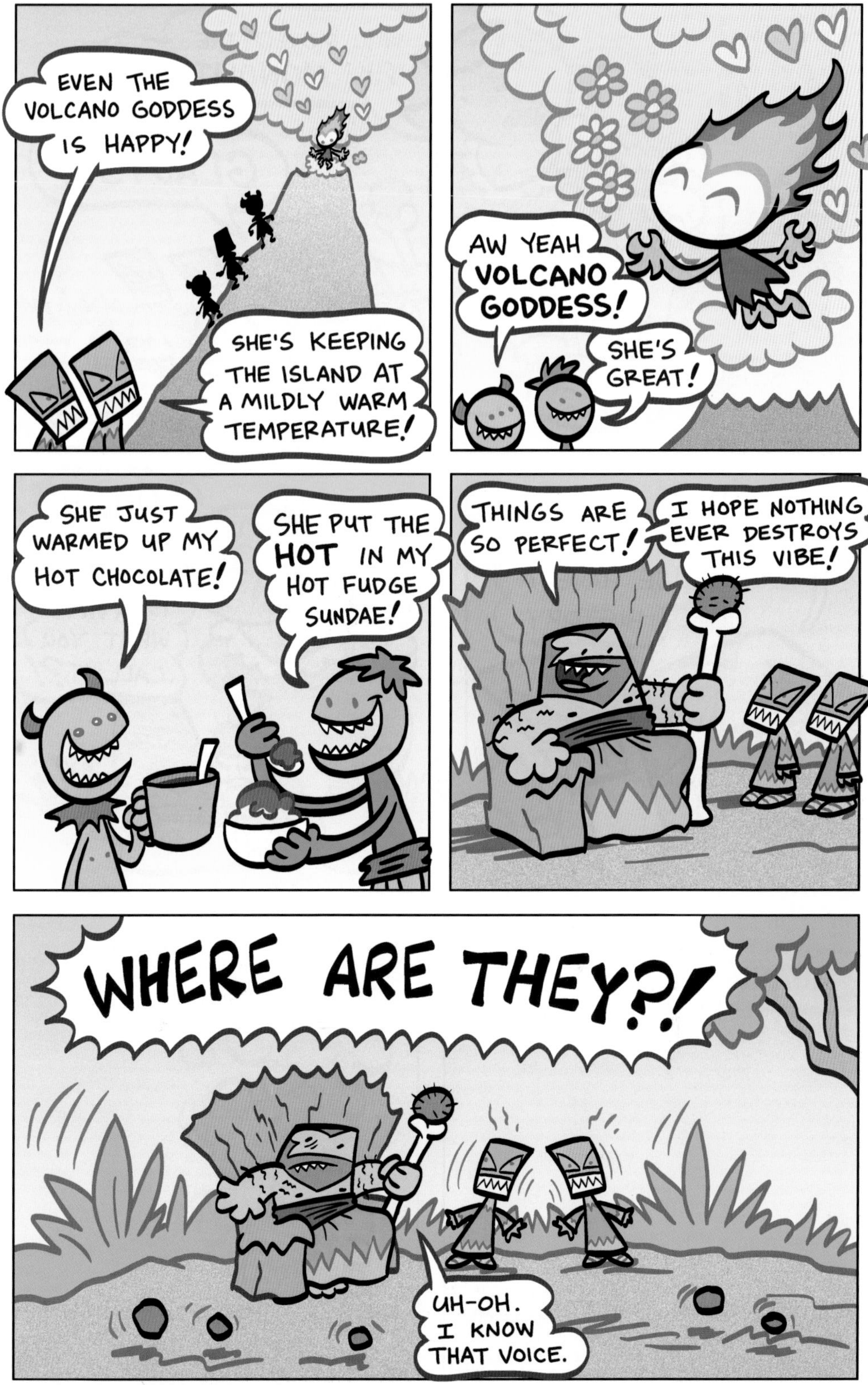
EVEN THE VOLCANO GODDESS IS HAPPY!
SHE'S KEEPING THE ISLAND AT A MILDLY WARM TEMPERATURE!
AW YEAH VOLCANO GODDESS!
SHE'S GREAT!
SHE JUST WARMED UP MY HOT CHOCOLATE!
SHE PUT THE HOT IN MY HOT FUDGE SUNDAE!
THINGS ARE SO PERFECT!
I HOPE NOTHING EVER DESTROYS THIS VIBE!
WHERE ARE THEY?!
UH-OH. I KNOW THAT VOICE.

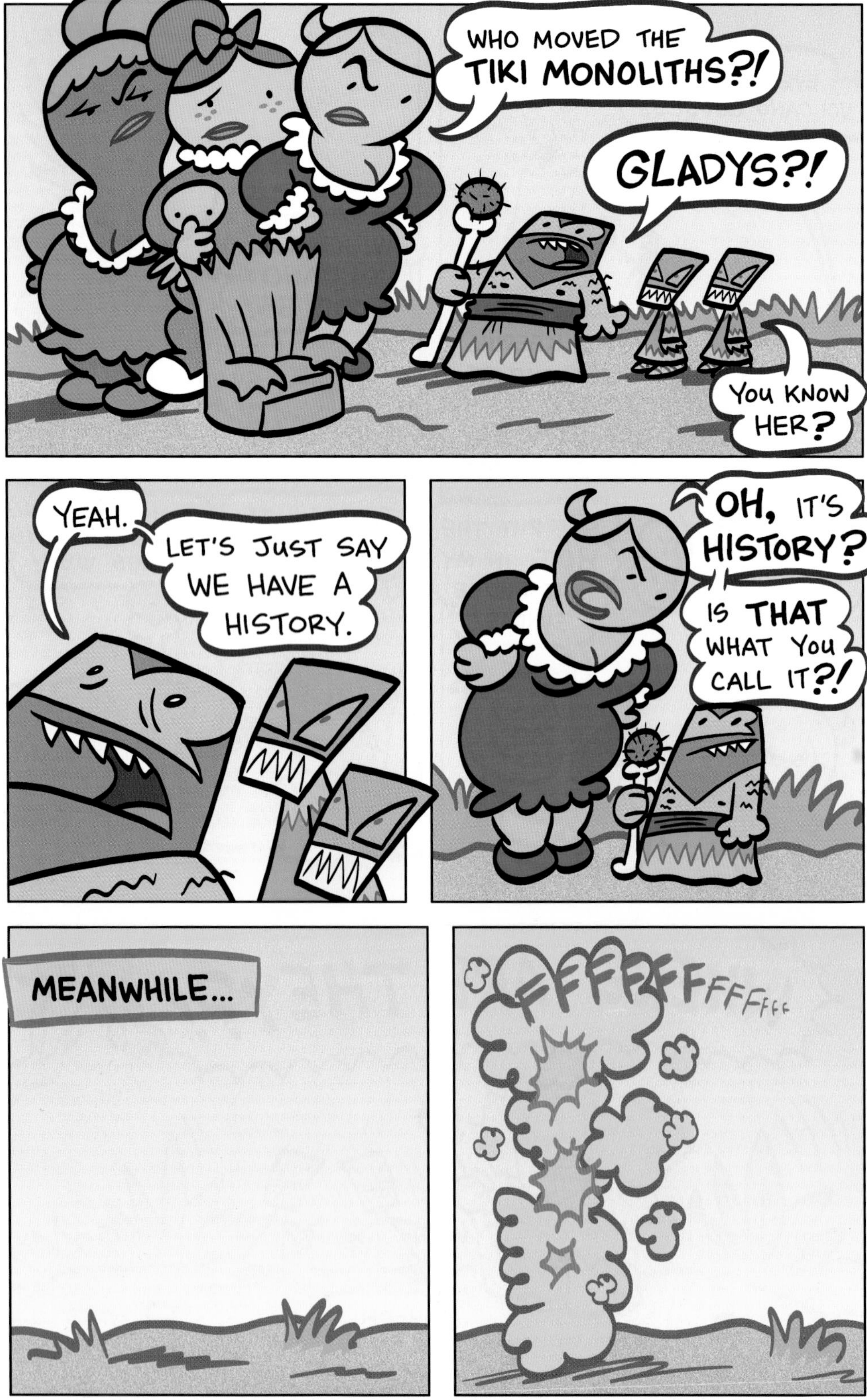
WHO MOVED THE TIKI MONOLITHS?!
GLADYS?!
YOU KNOW HER?
YEAH.
LET'S JUST SAY WE HAVE A HISTORY.
OH, IT'S HISTORY?
IS THAT WHAT YOU CALL IT?!
MEANWHILE...
FFFFFFFFFfff

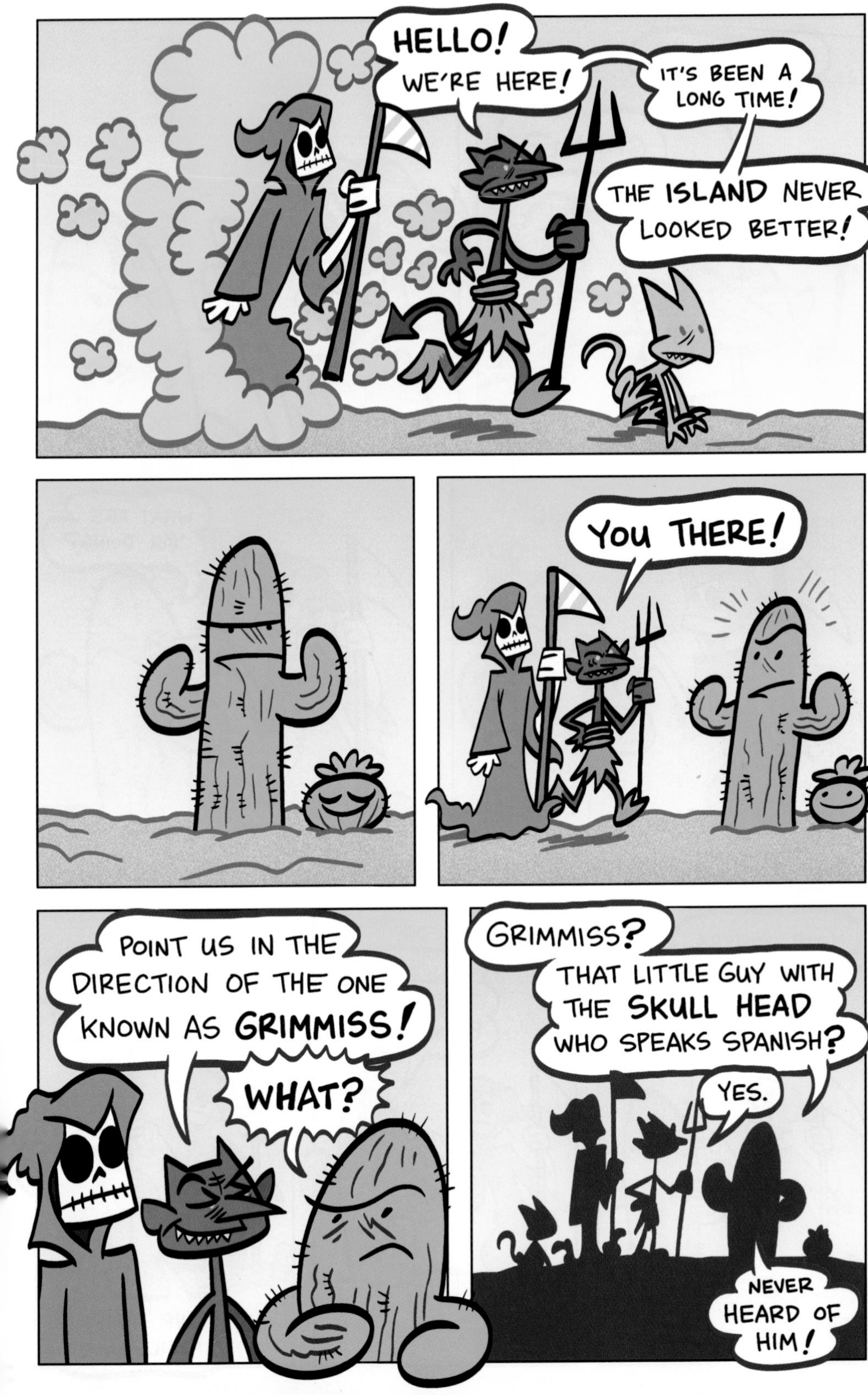
HELLO!
WE'RE HERE!
IT'S BEEN A LONG TIME!
THE **ISLAND** NEVER LOOKED BETTER!
YOU THERE!
POINT US IN THE DIRECTION OF THE ONE KNOWN AS **GRIMMISS**!
WHAT?
GRIMMISS?
THAT LITTLE GUY WITH THE **SKULL HEAD** WHO SPEAKS SPANISH?
YES.
NEVER HEARD OF HIM!

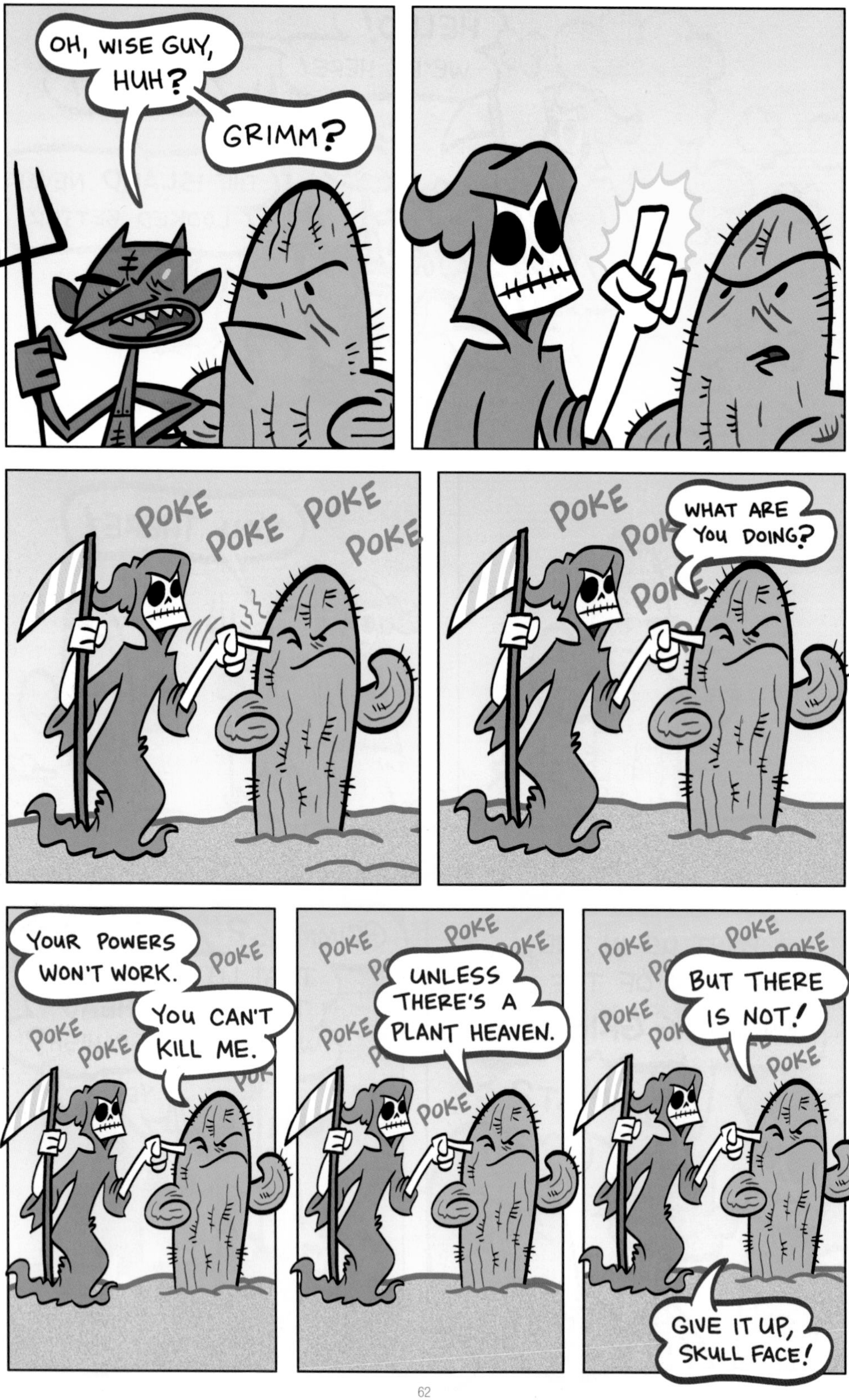
OH, WISE GUY, HUH?
GRIMM?
POKE
POKE
POKE
POKE
POKE
WHAT ARE YOU DOING?
YOUR POWERS WON'T WORK.
POKE
POKE
POKE
YOU CAN'T KILL ME.
POKE
POKE
UNLESS THERE'S A PLANT HEAVEN.
POKE
POKE
POKE
BUT THERE IS NOT!
POKE
POKE
GIVE IT UP, SKULL FACE!

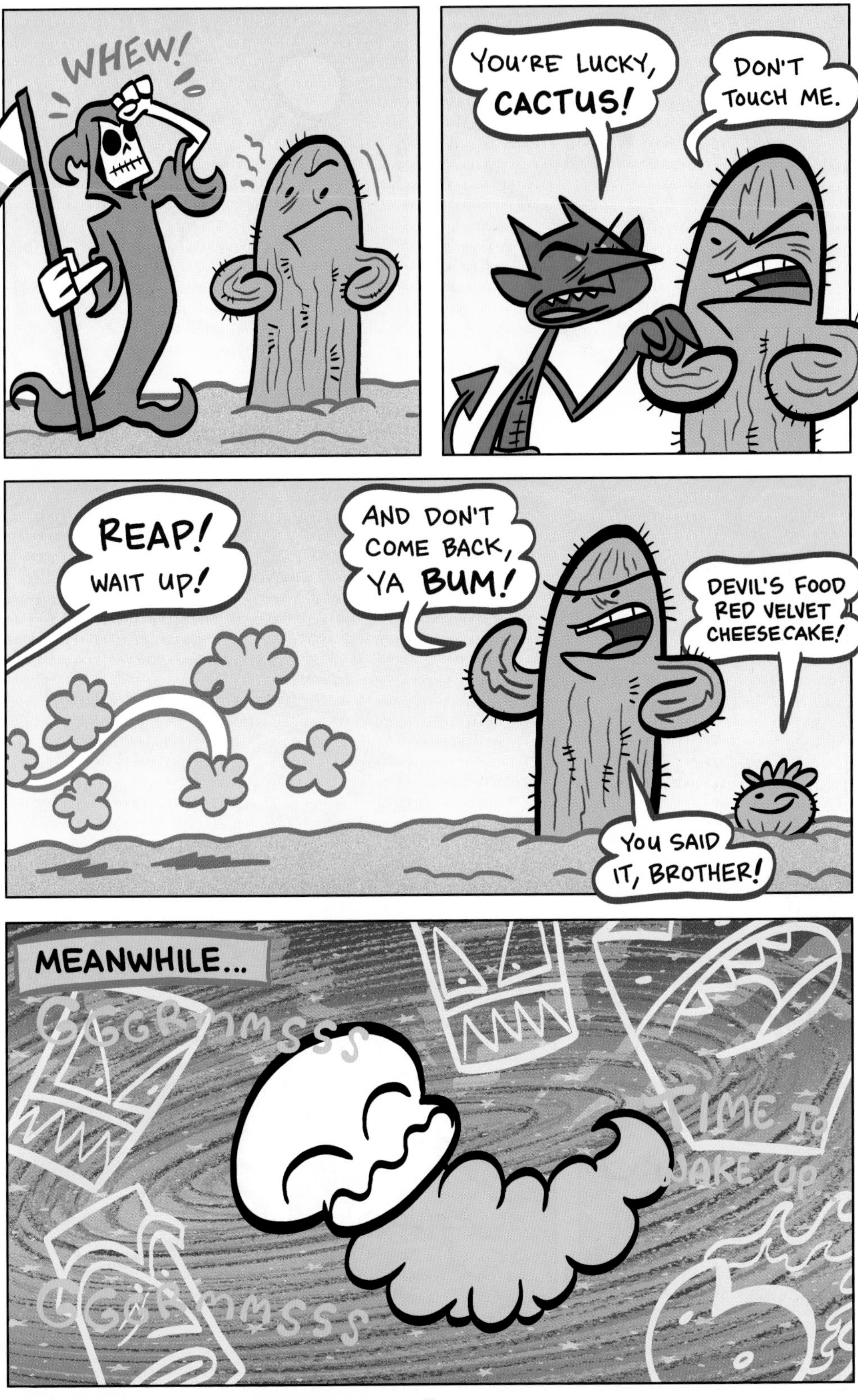
WHEW!
YOU'RE LUCKY, CACTUS!
DON'T TOUCH ME.
REAP! WAIT UP!
AND DON'T COME BACK, YA BUM!
DEVIL'S FOOD RED VELVET CHEESECAKE!
YOU SAID IT, BROTHER!
MEANWHILE...
GGRmmSSS
TIME TO WAKE UP.
GGRmmSSS

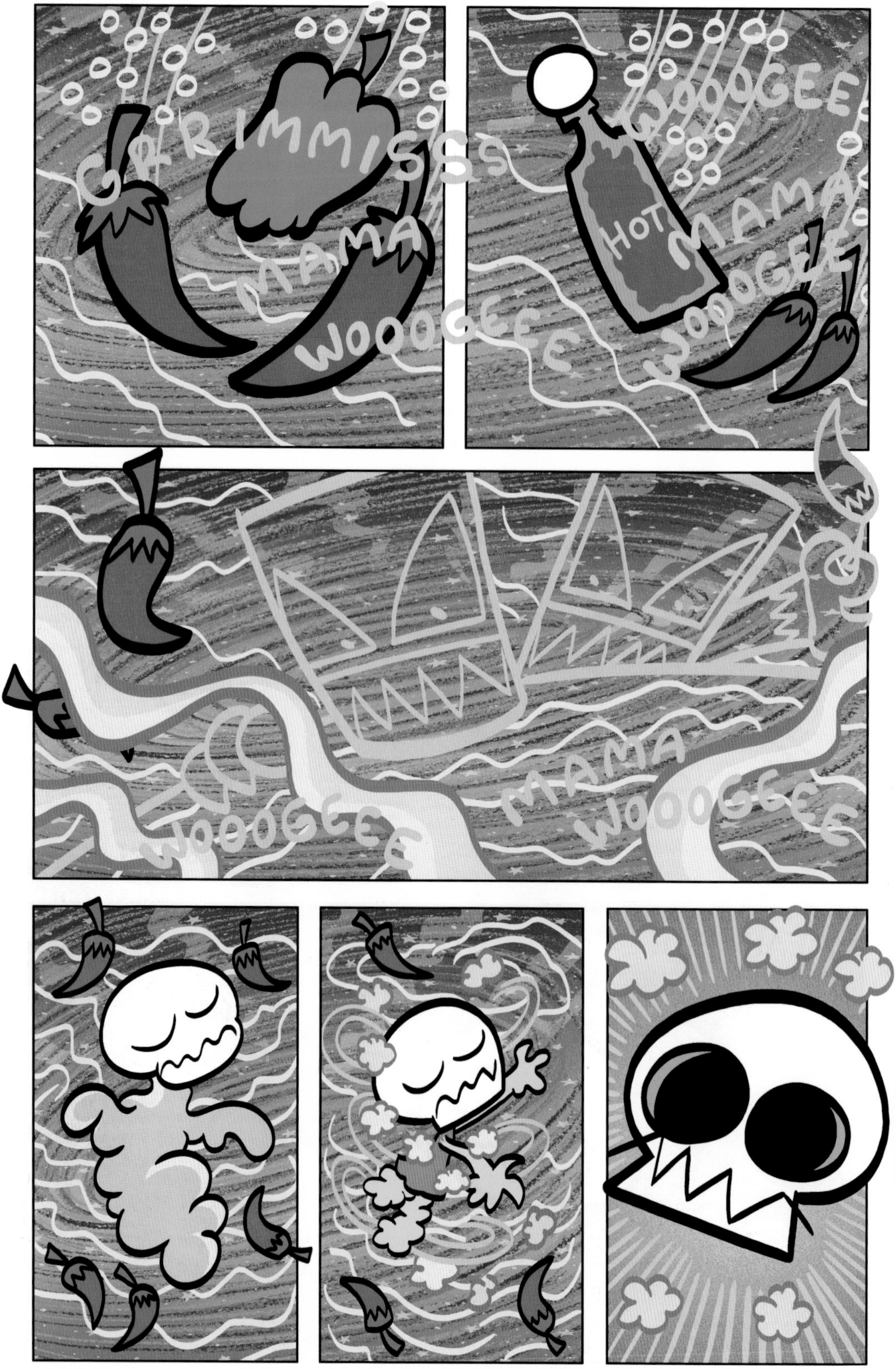
GRRIMMISSS
MAMA
WOOOGEE
WOOOGEE
HOT
MAMA
WOOOGEE
MAMA
WOOOGEE
WOOOGEE

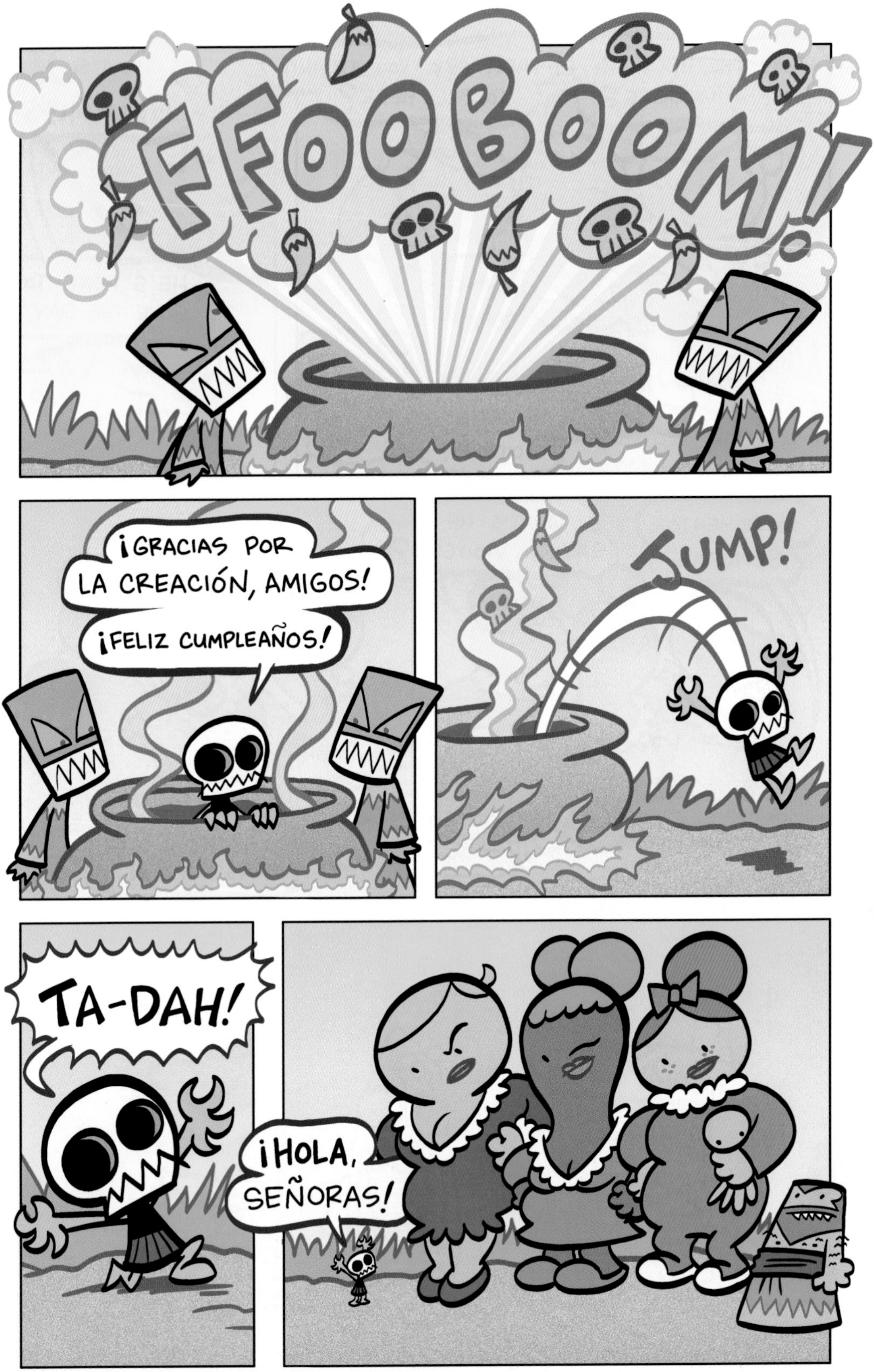
¡FFOOBOOM!
¡GRACIAS POR LA CREACIÓN, AMIGOS!
¡FELIZ CUMPLEAÑOS!
JUMP!
TA-DAH!
¡HOLA, SEÑORAS!

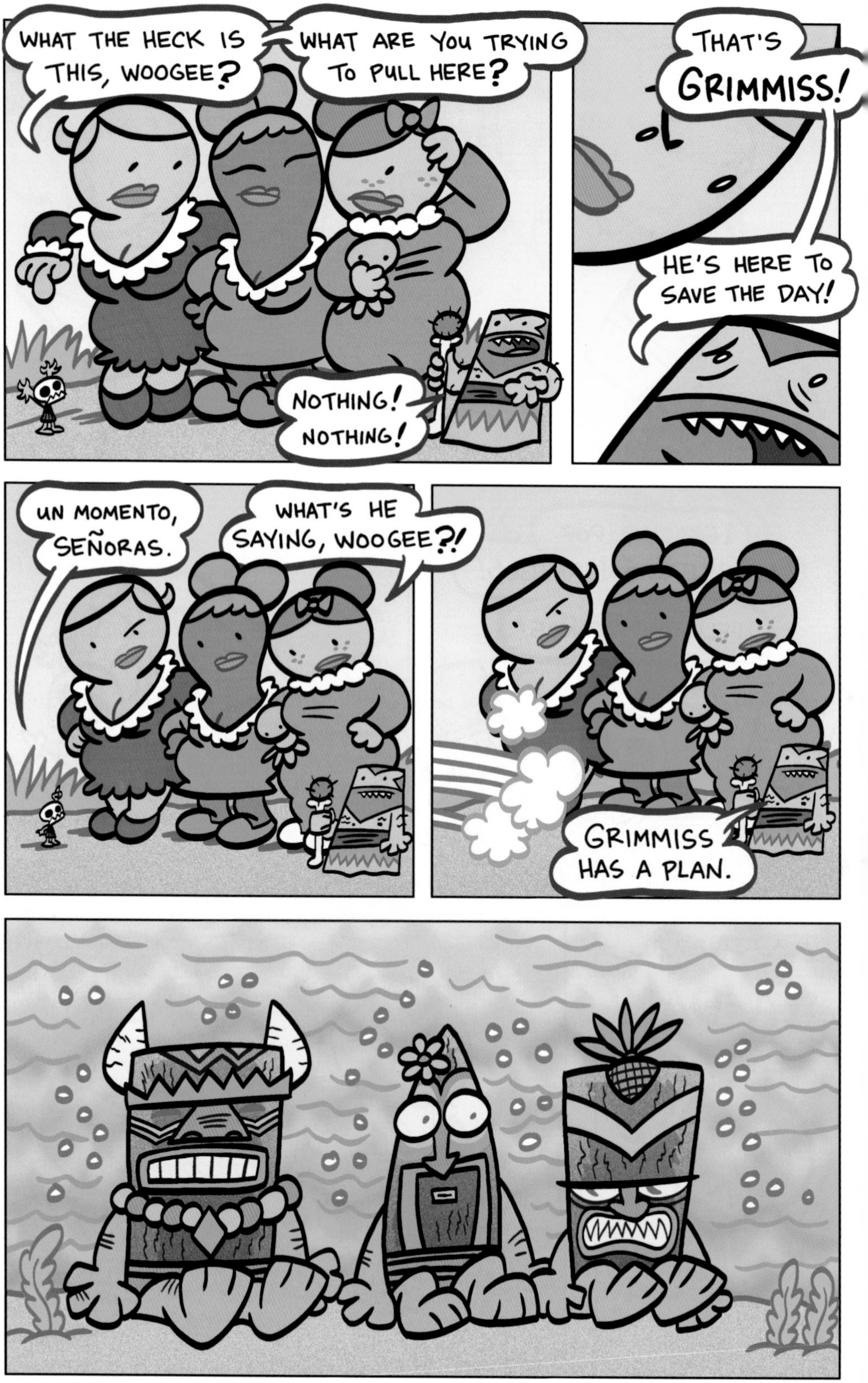
WHAT THE HECK IS THIS, WOOGEE?
WHAT ARE YOU TRYING TO PULL HERE?
NOTHING! NOTHING!
THAT'S GRIMMISS!
HE'S HERE TO SAVE THE DAY!
UN MOMENTO, SEÑORAS.
WHAT'S HE SAYING, WOOGEE?!
GRIMMISS HAS A PLAN.

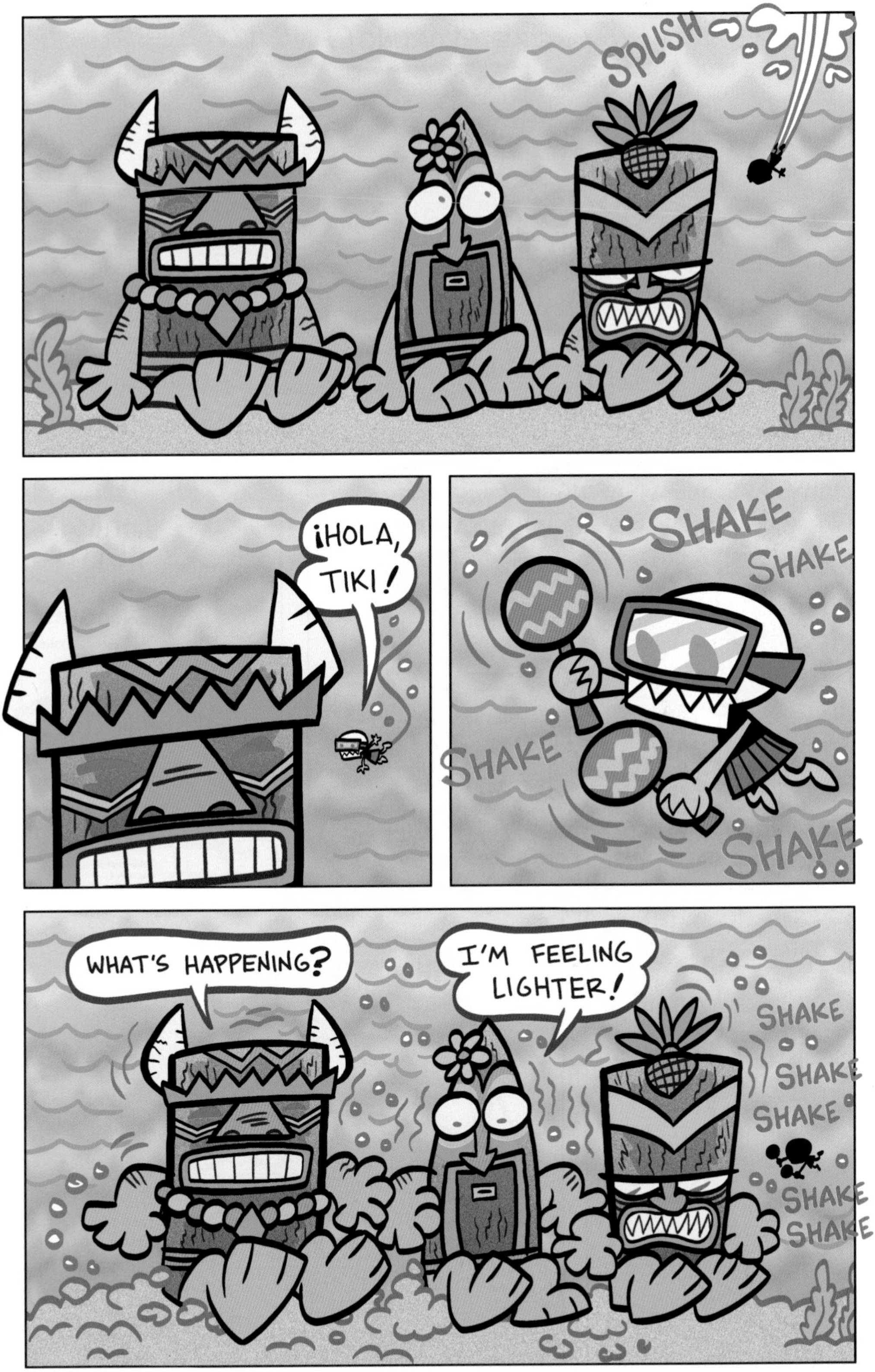
SPLISH
¡HOLA, TIKI!
SHAKE
SHAKE
SHAKE
SHAKE
WHAT'S HAPPENING?
I'M FEELING LIGHTER!
SHAKE
SHAKE
SHAKE
SHAKE
SHAKE

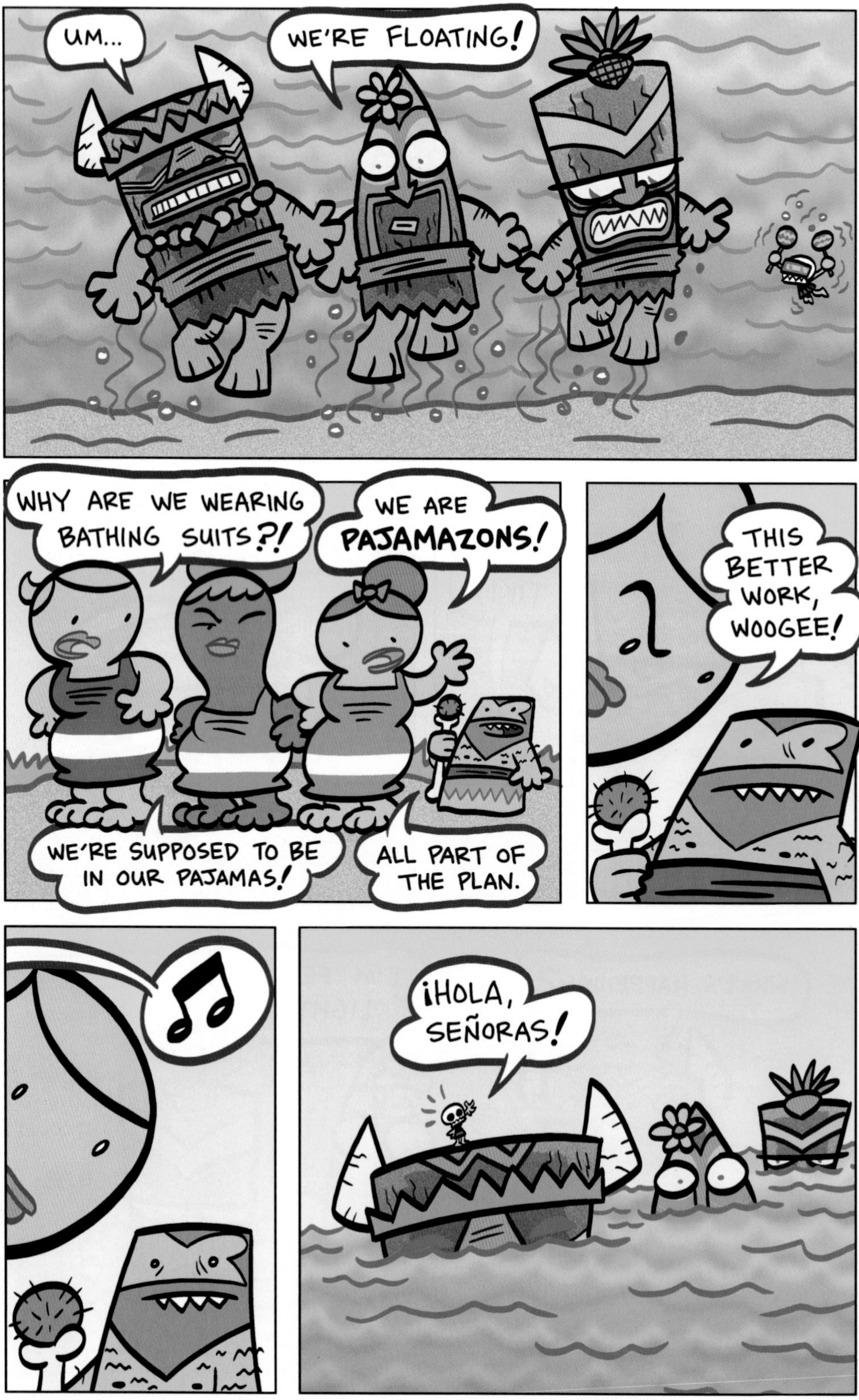
UM...
WE'RE FLOATING!
WHY ARE WE WEARING BATHING SUITS?!
WE ARE PAJAMAZONS!
WE'RE SUPPOSED TO BE IN OUR PAJAMAS!
ALL PART OF THE PLAN.
THIS BETTER WORK, WOOGEE!
♫
¡HOLA, SEÑORAS!

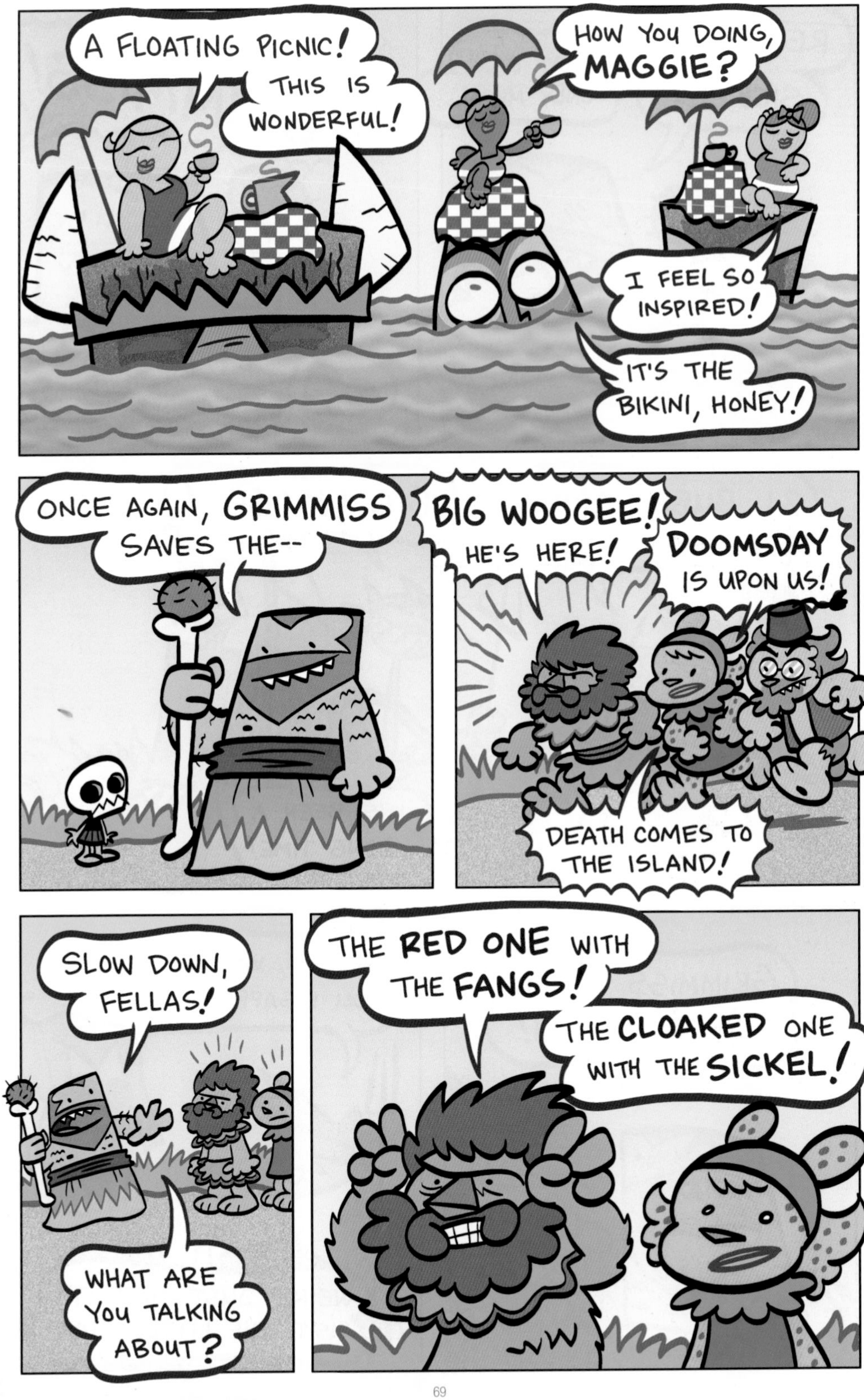
A FLOATING PICNIC!
THIS IS WONDERFUL!
HOW YOU DOING, MAGGIE?
I FEEL SO INSPIRED!
IT'S THE BIKINI, HONEY!
ONCE AGAIN, GRIMMISS SAVES THE--
BIG WOOGEE!
HE'S HERE!
DOOMSDAY IS UPON US!
DEATH COMES TO THE ISLAND!
SLOW DOWN, FELLAS!
WHAT ARE YOU TALKING ABOUT?
THE RED ONE WITH THE FANGS!
THE CLOAKED ONE WITH THE SICKEL!

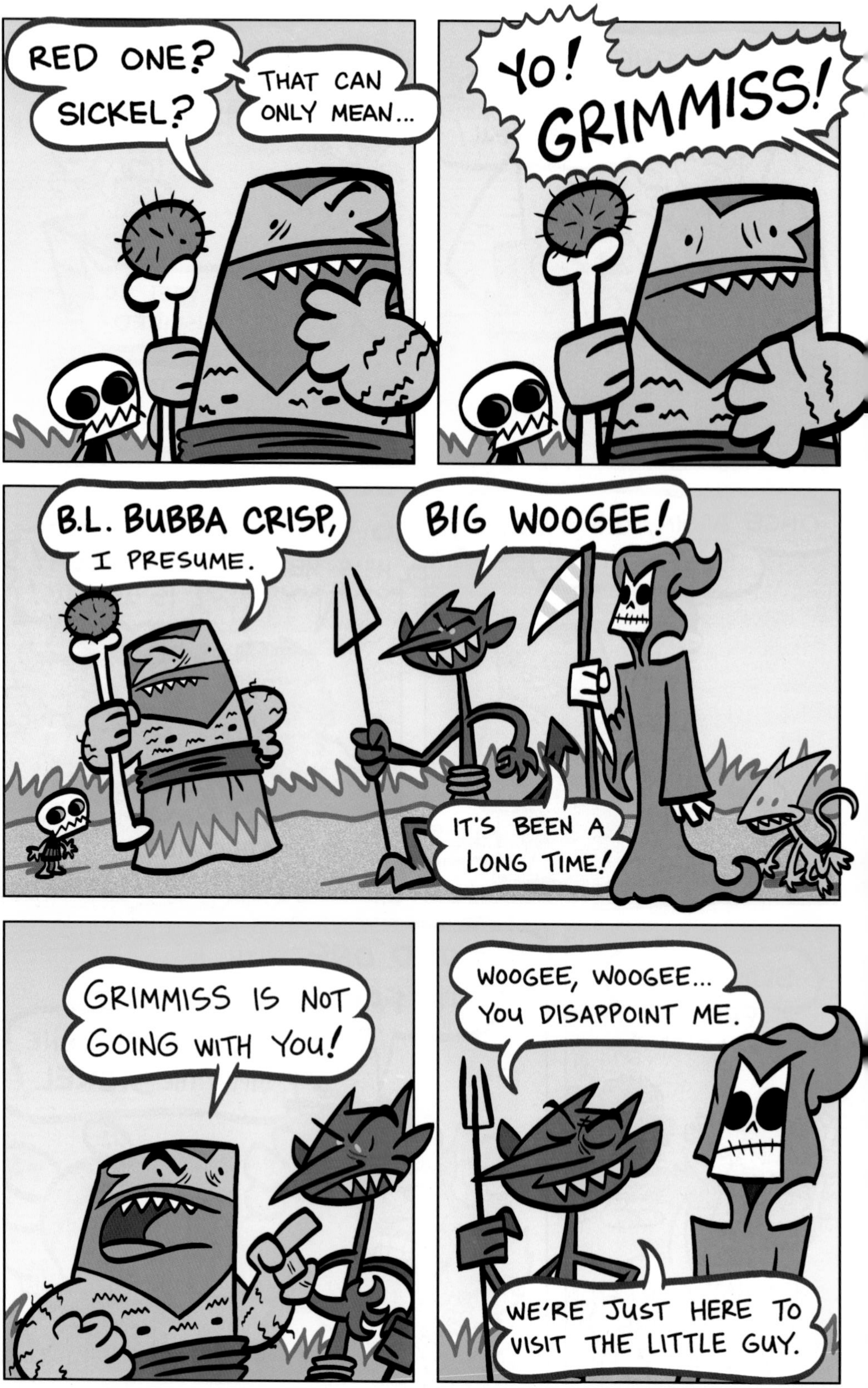
RED ONE? SICKEL?
THAT CAN ONLY MEAN...
YO! GRIMMISS!
B.L. BUBBA CRISP, I PRESUME.
BIG WOOGEE!
IT'S BEEN A LONG TIME!
GRIMMISS IS NOT GOING WITH YOU!
WOOGEE, WOOGEE... YOU DISAPPOINT ME.
WE'RE JUST HERE TO VISIT THE LITTLE GUY.

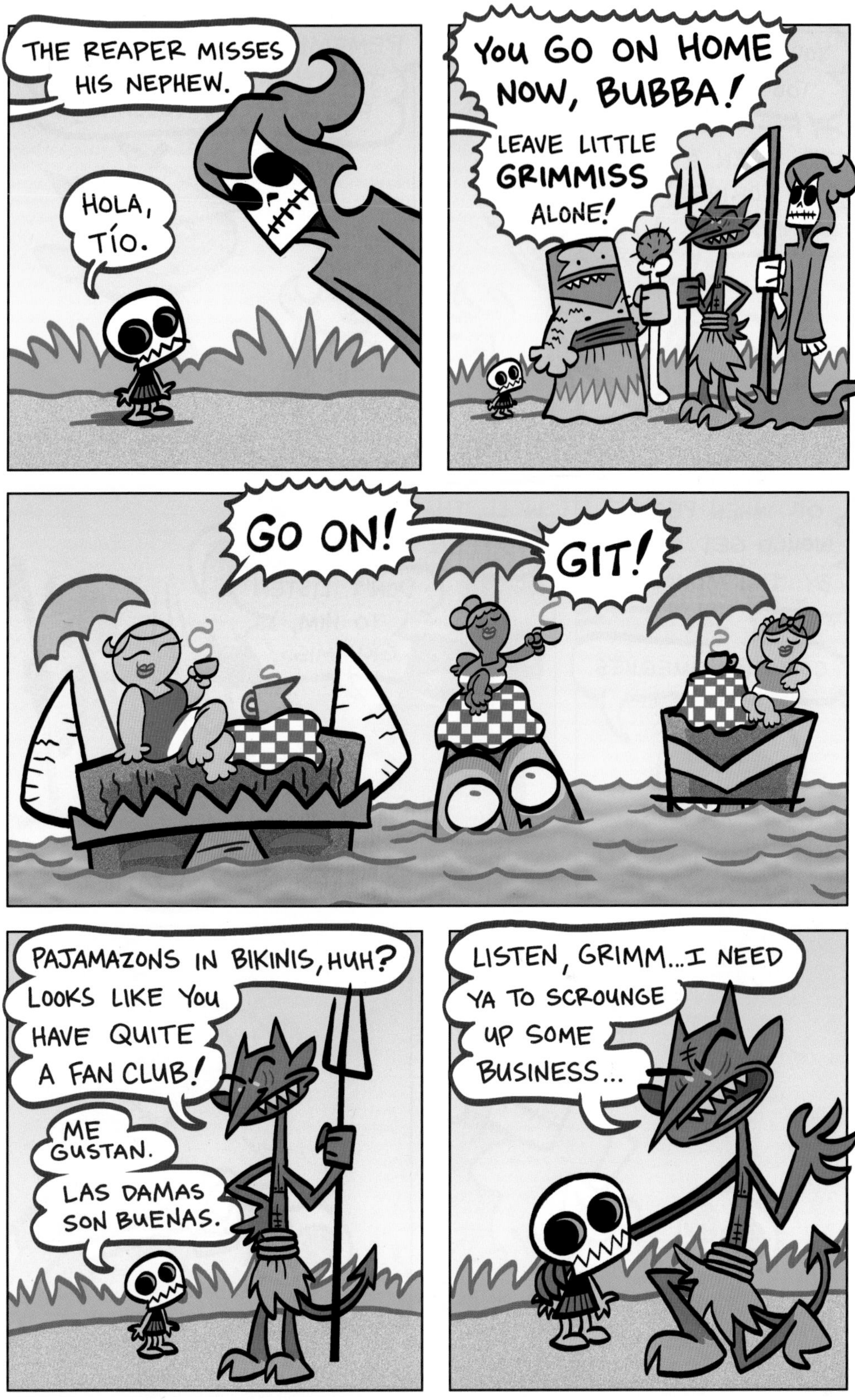
THE REAPER MISSES HIS NEPHEW.
HOLA, TÍO.
YOU GO ON HOME NOW, BUBBA!
LEAVE LITTLE GRIMMISS ALONE!
GO ON!
GIT!
PAJAMAZONS IN BIKINIS, HUH? LOOKS LIKE YOU HAVE QUITE A FAN CLUB!
ME GUSTAN.
LAS DAMAS SON BUENAS.
LISTEN, GRIMM...I NEED YA TO SCROUNGE UP SOME BUSINESS...

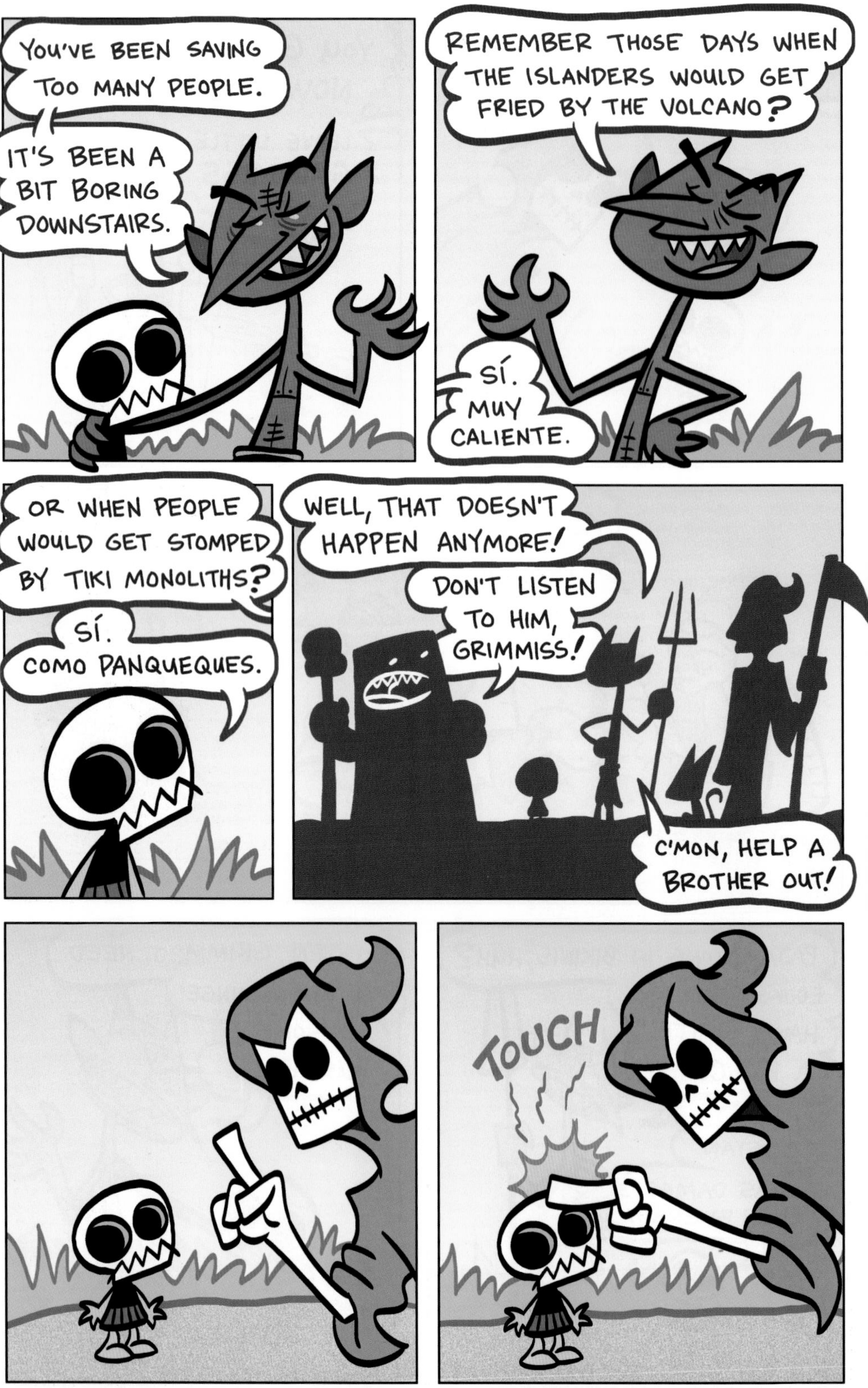
YOU'VE BEEN SAVING TOO MANY PEOPLE.
IT'S BEEN A BIT BORING DOWNSTAIRS.
REMEMBER THOSE DAYS WHEN THE ISLANDERS WOULD GET FRIED BY THE VOLCANO?
SÍ. MUY CALIENTE.
OR WHEN PEOPLE WOULD GET STOMPED BY TIKI MONOLITHS?
SÍ. COMO PANQUEQUES.
WELL, THAT DOESN'T HAPPEN ANYMORE!
DON'T LISTEN TO HIM, GRIMMISS!
C'MON, HELP A BROTHER OUT!
TOUCH

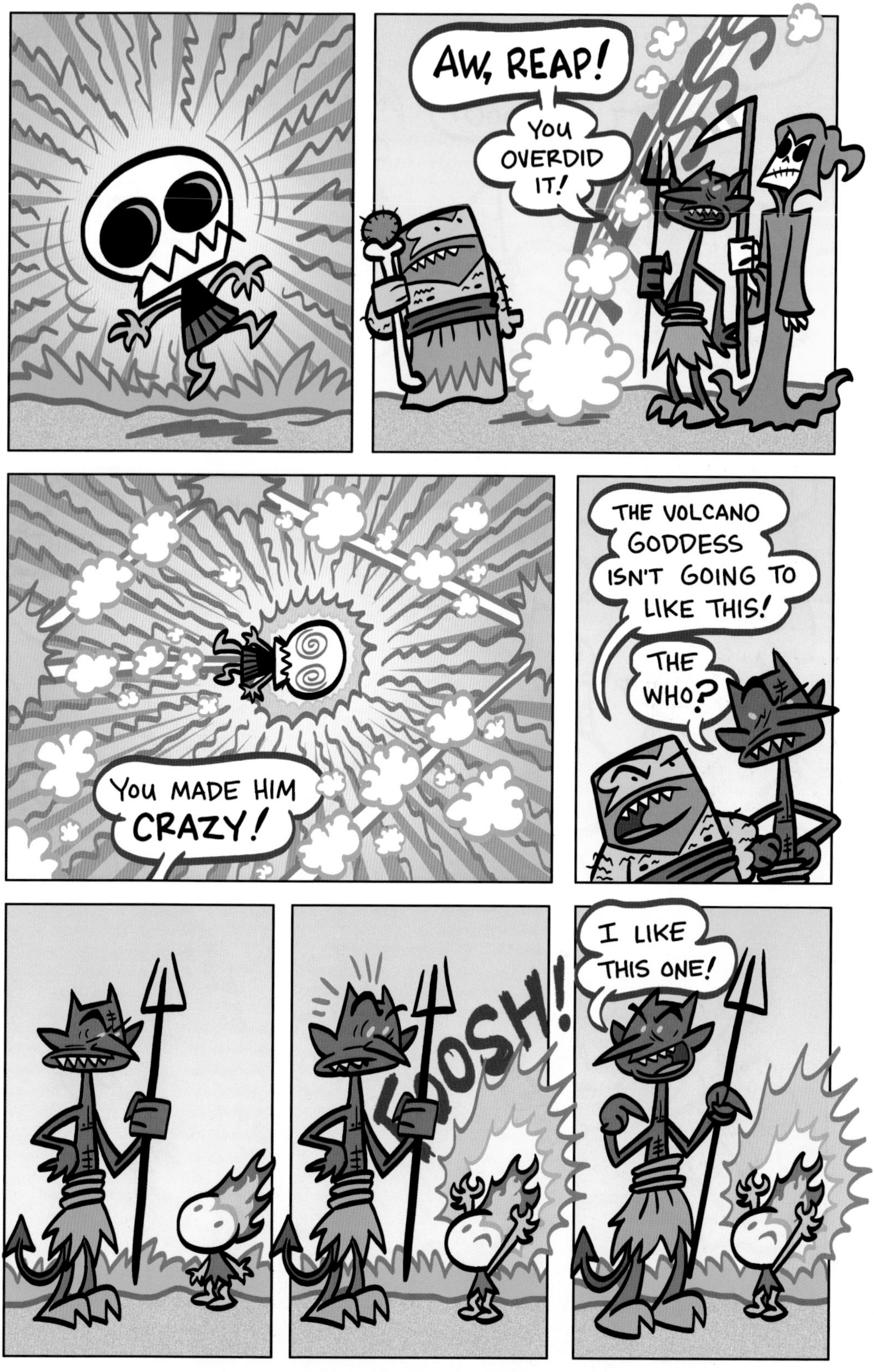
AW, REAP!
YOU OVERDID IT!
YOU MADE HIM CRAZY!
THE VOLCANO GODDESS ISN'T GOING TO LIKE THIS!
THE WHO?
WOOSH!
I LIKE THIS ONE!

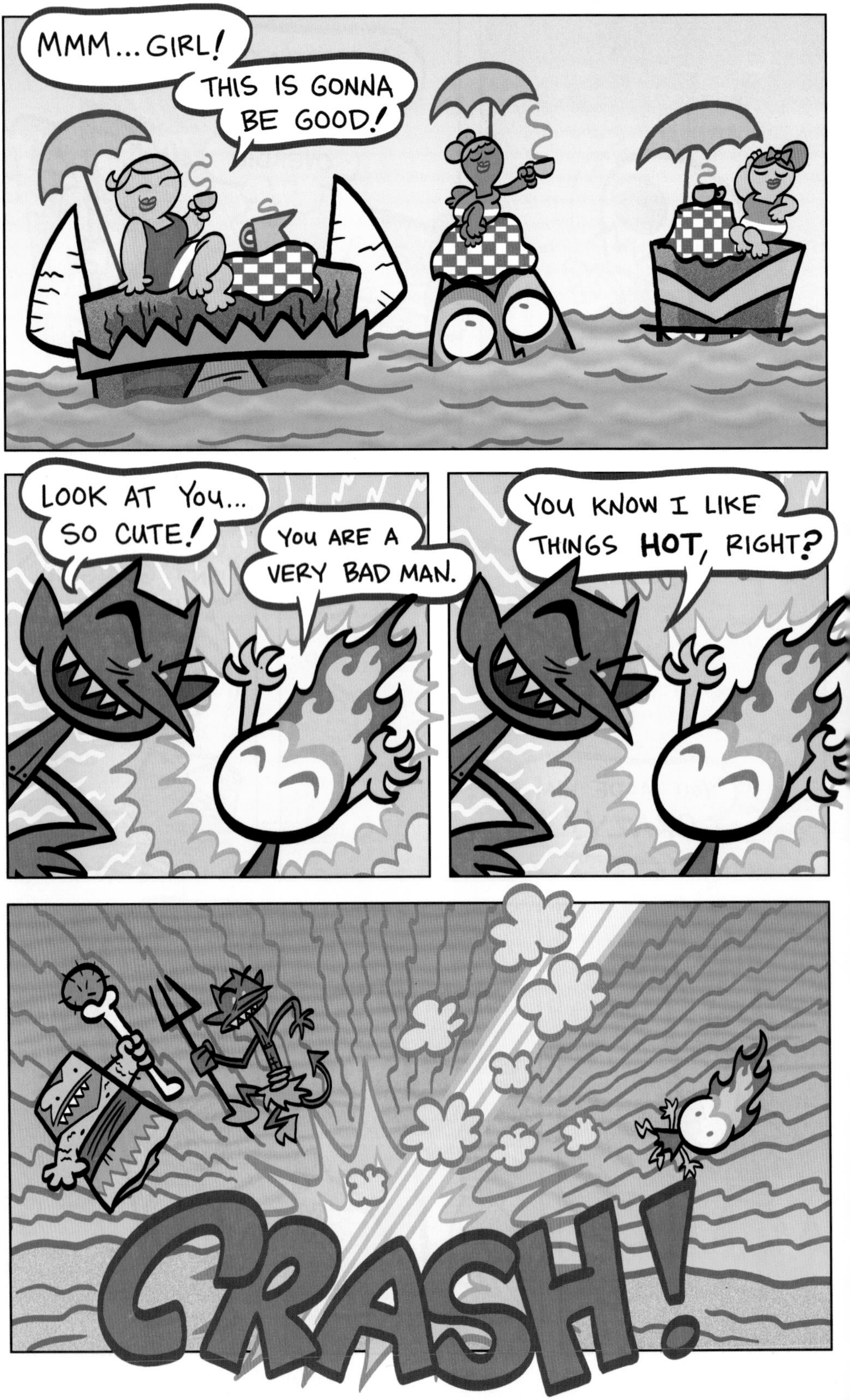
MMM... GIRL!
THIS IS GONNA BE GOOD!
LOOK AT YOU... SO CUTE!
YOU ARE A VERY BAD MAN.
YOU KNOW I LIKE THINGS HOT, RIGHT?
CRASH!

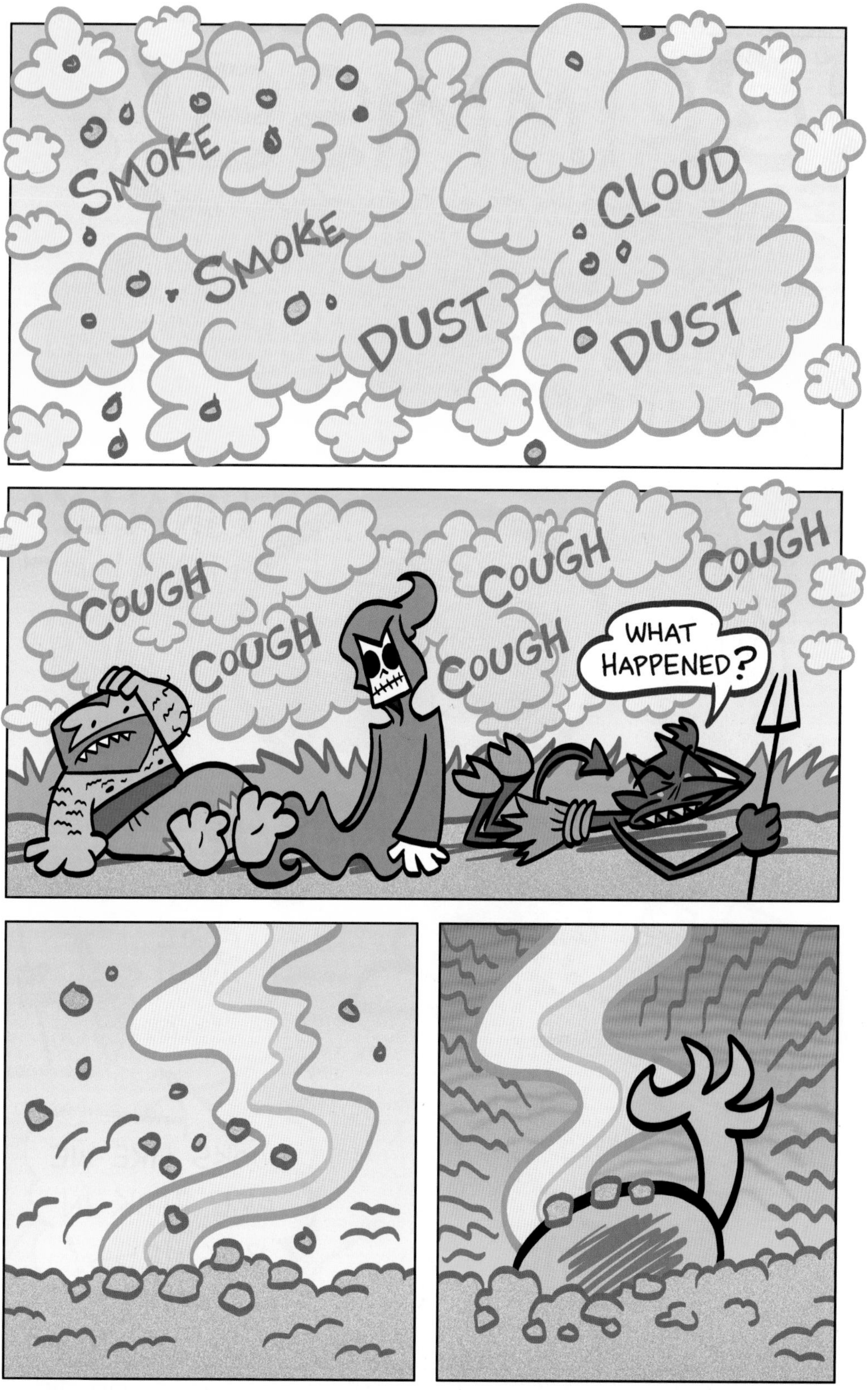
SMOKE
SMOKE
DUST
CLOUD
DUST
COUGH
COUGH
COUGH
COUGH
COUGH
WHAT HAPPENED?

GRIMMISS!
WE'RE DOOMED!!
FINALLY!
LOOKS LIKE WE ARE BACK IN BUSINESS!
EVIL
EVIL
EVIL
EVIL
EVIL
EVIL
EVIL
EVIL
EVIL
EVIL

-EVIL EVIL!

CHAPTER FOUR

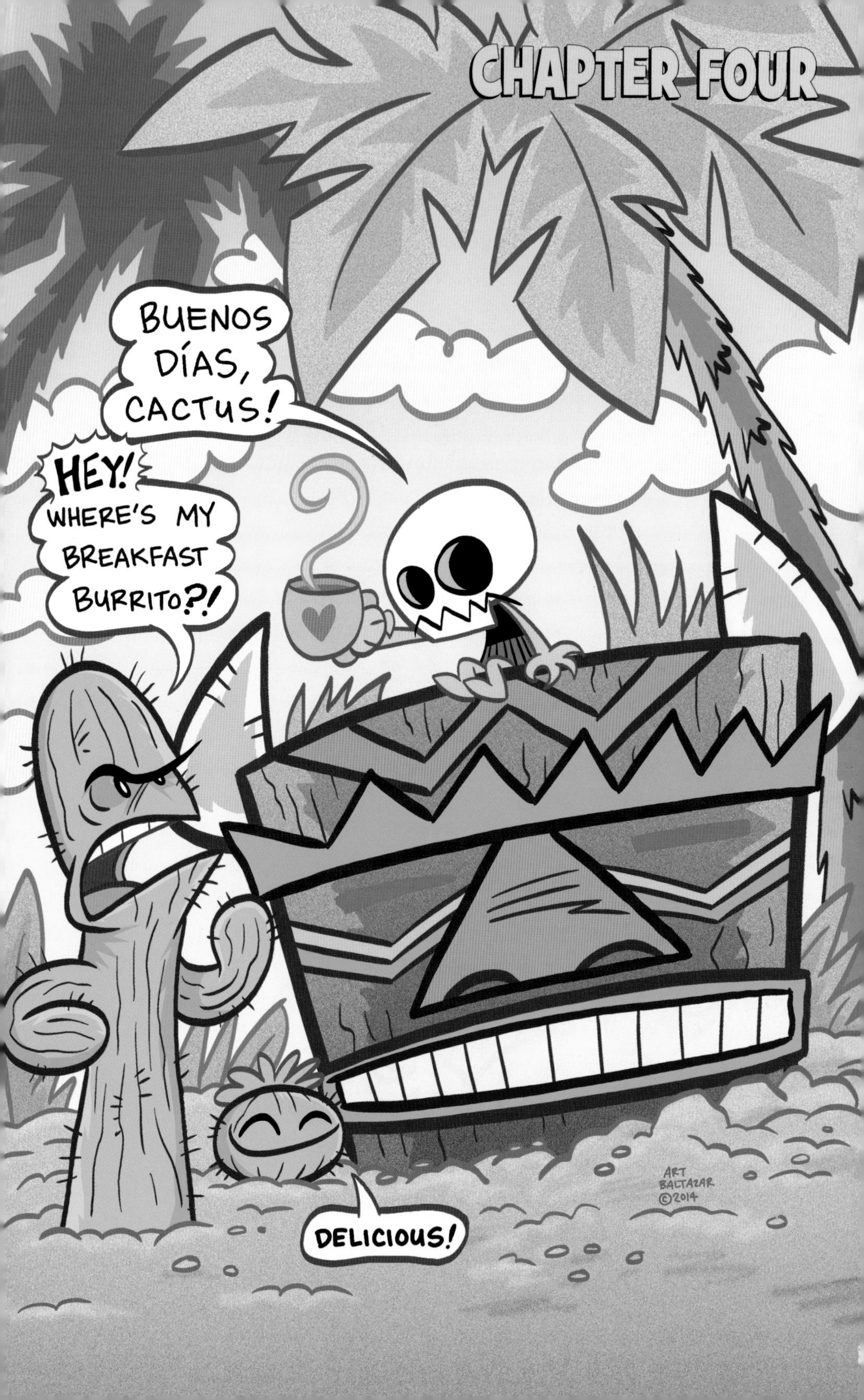

BUENOS DÍAS, CACTUS!
HEY! WHERE'S MY BREAKFAST BURRITO?!
DELICIOUS!
ART BALTAZAR ©2014

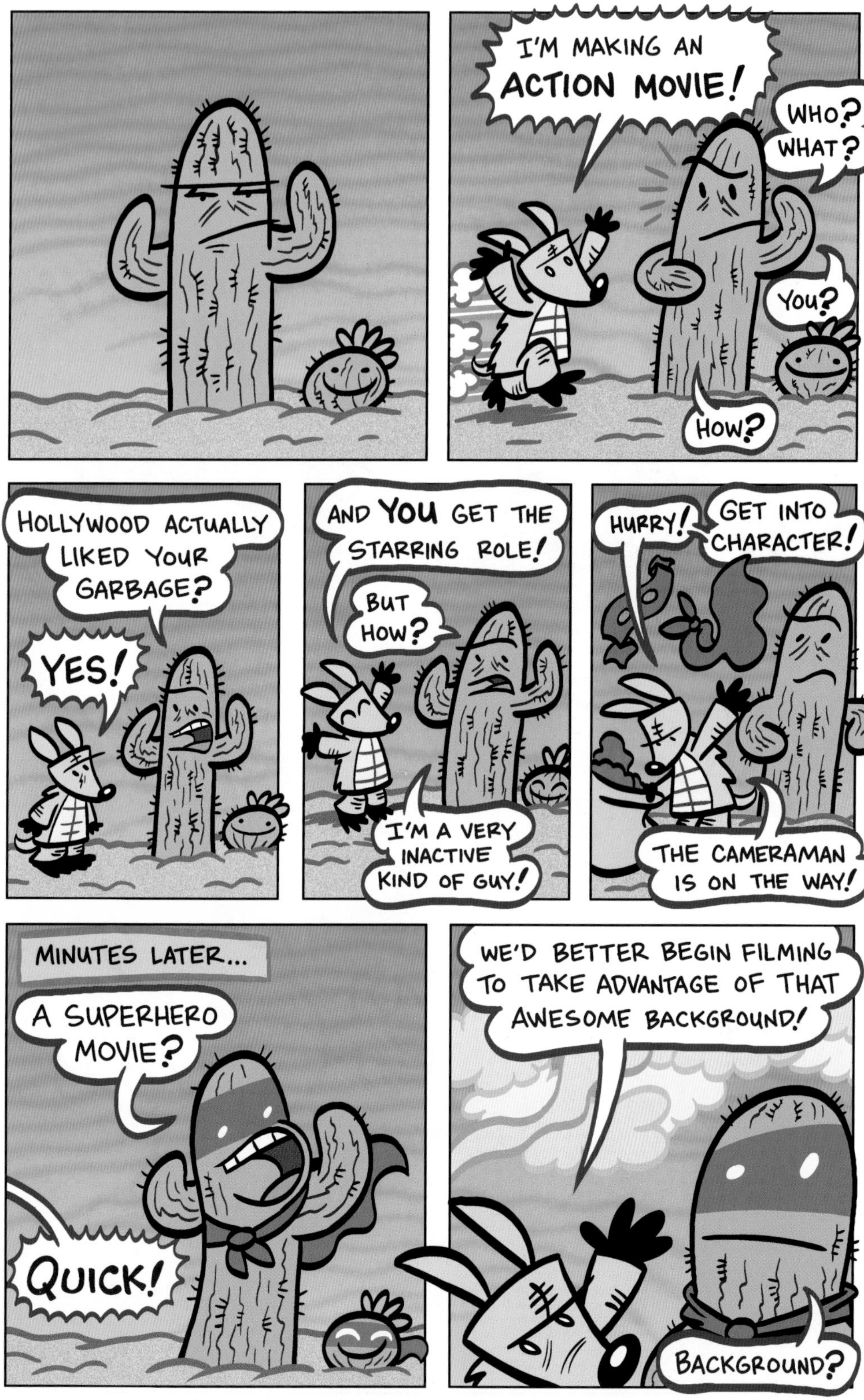
I'M MAKING AN ACTION MOVIE!
WHO? WHAT?
YOU?
HOW?
HOLLYWOOD ACTUALLY LIKED YOUR GARBAGE?
YES!
AND YOU GET THE STARRING ROLE!
BUT HOW?
I'M A VERY INACTIVE KIND OF GUY!
HURRY!
GET INTO CHARACTER!
THE CAMERAMAN IS ON THE WAY!
MINUTES LATER...
A SUPERHERO MOVIE?
QUICK!
WE'D BETTER BEGIN FILMING TO TAKE ADVANTAGE OF THAT AWESOME BACKGROUND!
BACKGROUND?

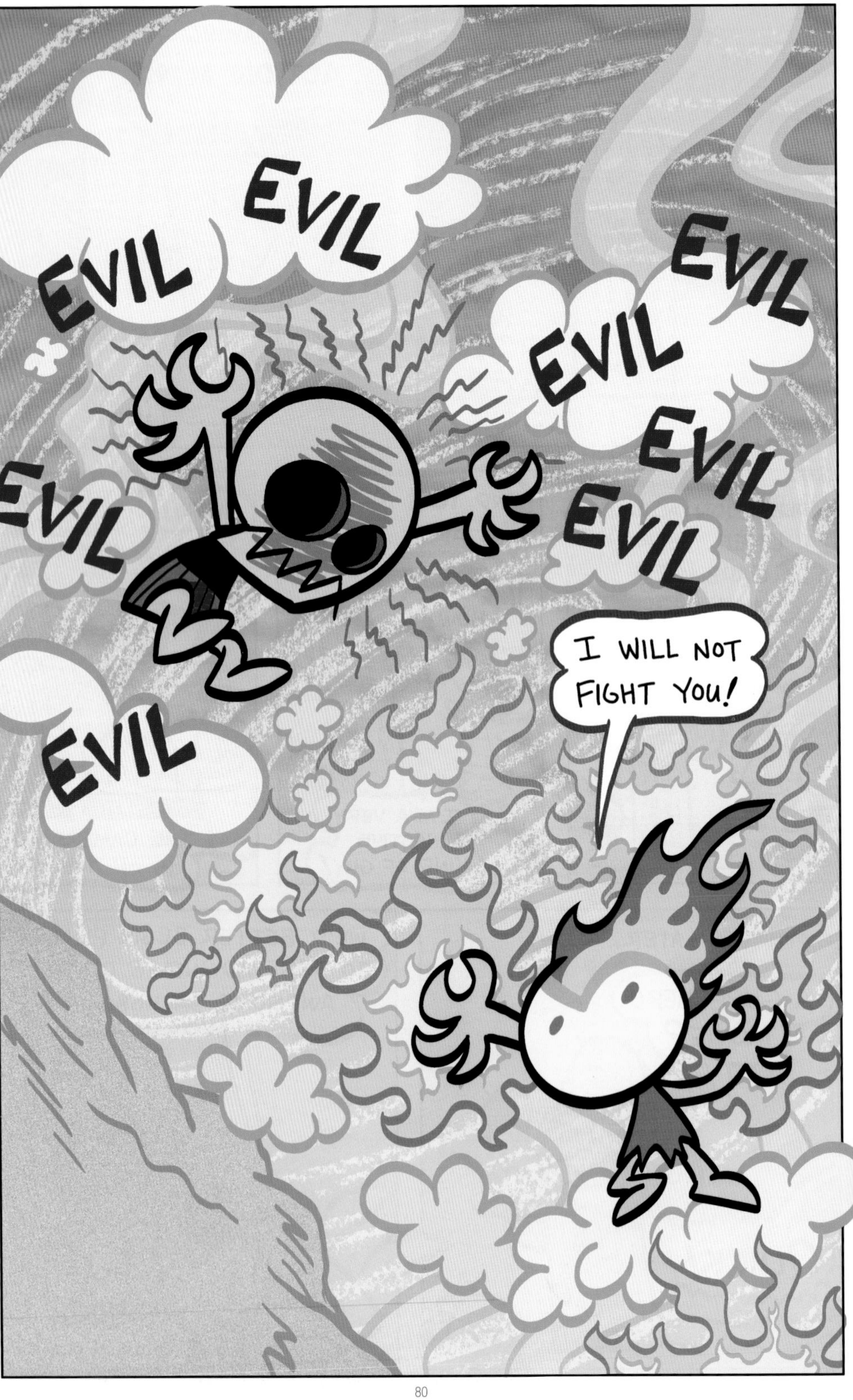
EVIL
EVIL
EVIL
EVIL
EVIL
EVIL
EVIL
EVIL
I WILL NOT FIGHT YOU!

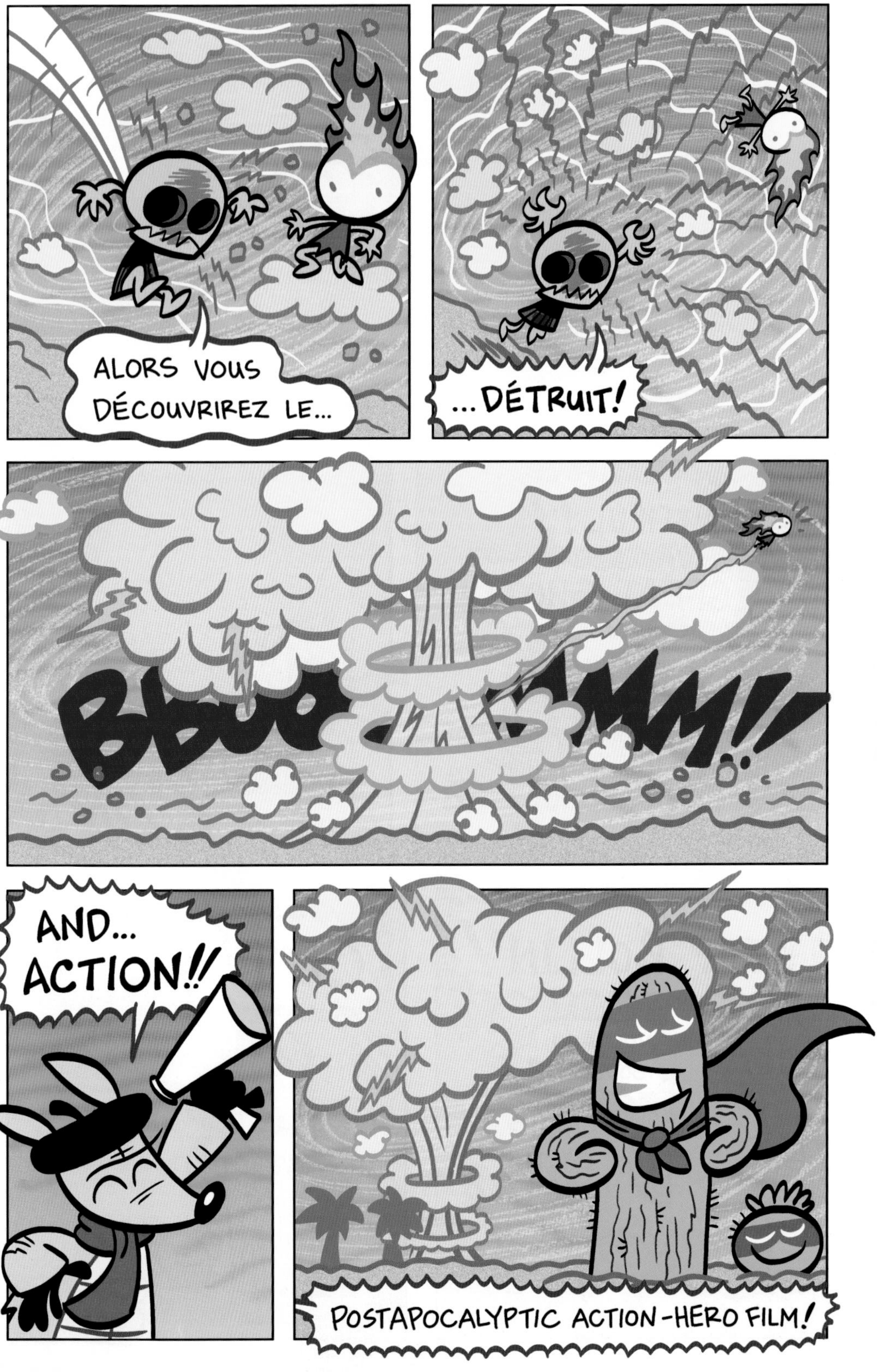
ALORS VOUS DÉCOUVRIREZ LE...
...DÉTRUIT!
AND... ACTION!!
POSTAPOCALYPTIC ACTION-HERO FILM!

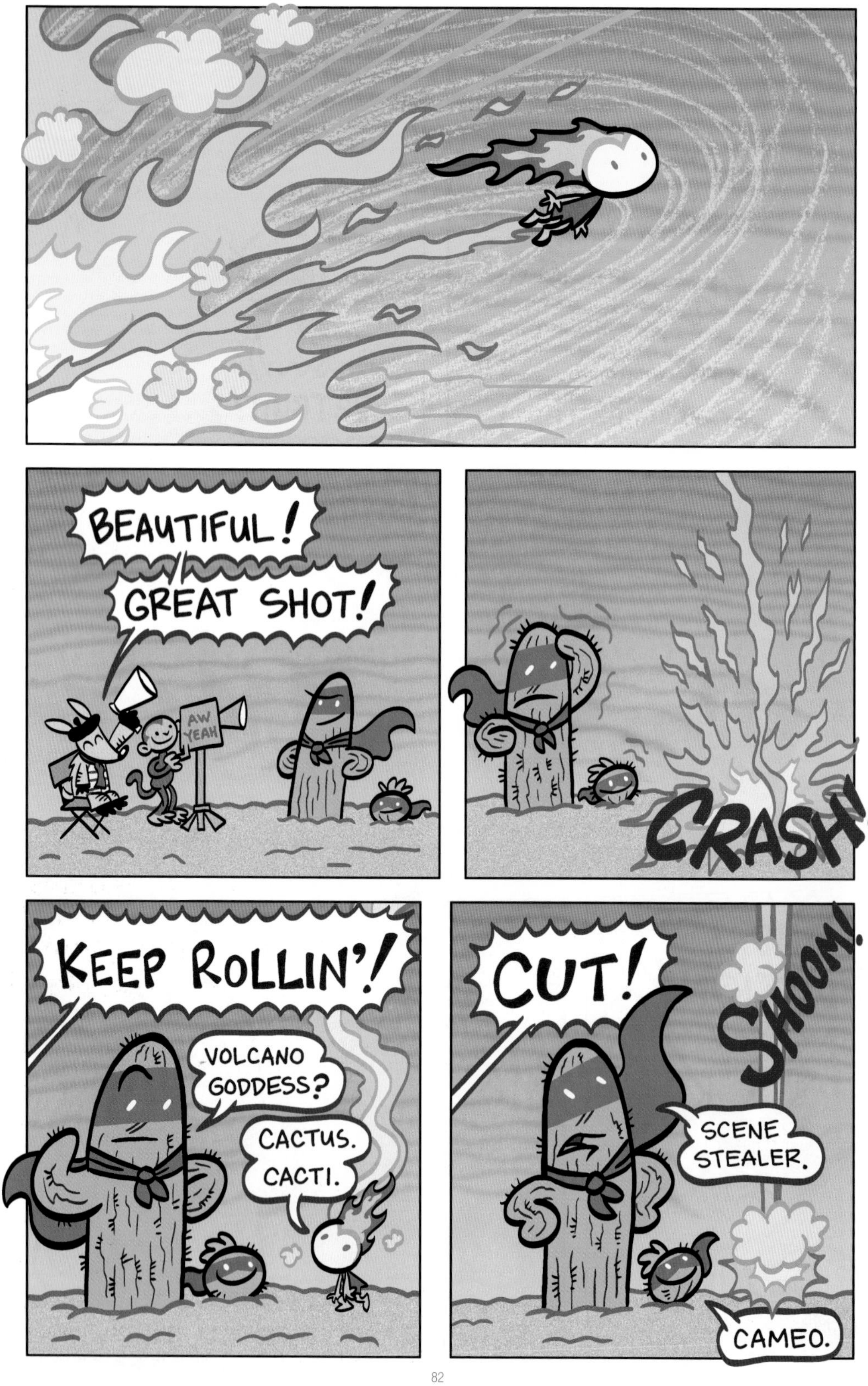
BEAUTIFUL!
GREAT SHOT!
AW YEAH
CRASH!
KEEP ROLLIN'!
VOLCANO GODDESS?
CACTUS. CACTI.
CUT!
SHOOM!
SCENE STEALER.
CAMEO.

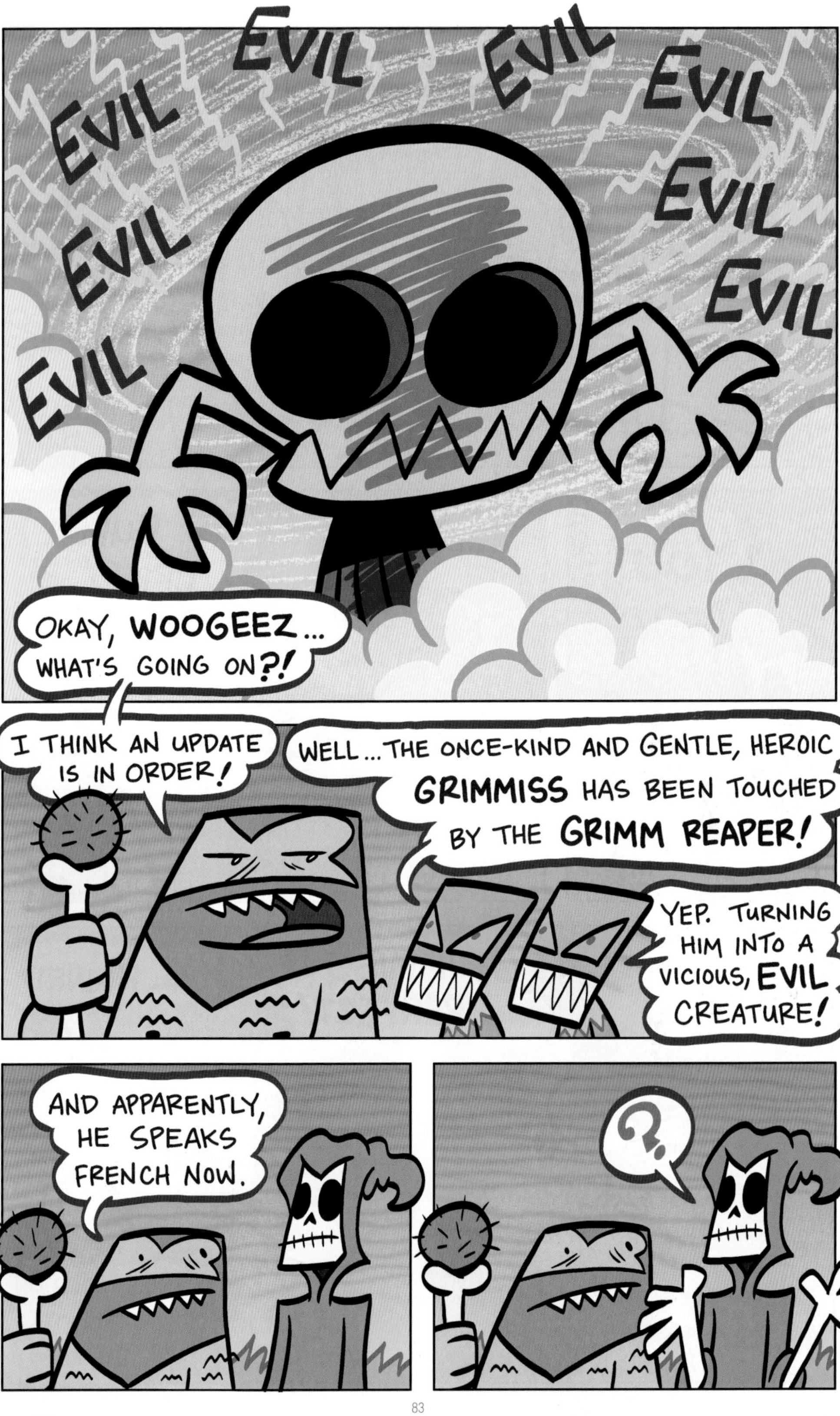
EVIL EVIL EVIL EVIL EVIL EVIL EVIL EVIL
OKAY, WOOGEEZ... WHAT'S GOING ON?!
I THINK AN UPDATE IS IN ORDER!
WELL... THE ONCE-KIND AND GENTLE, HEROIC GRIMMISS HAS BEEN TOUCHED BY THE GRIMM REAPER!
YEP. TURNING HIM INTO A VICIOUS, EVIL CREATURE!
AND APPARENTLY, HE SPEAKS FRENCH NOW.
?

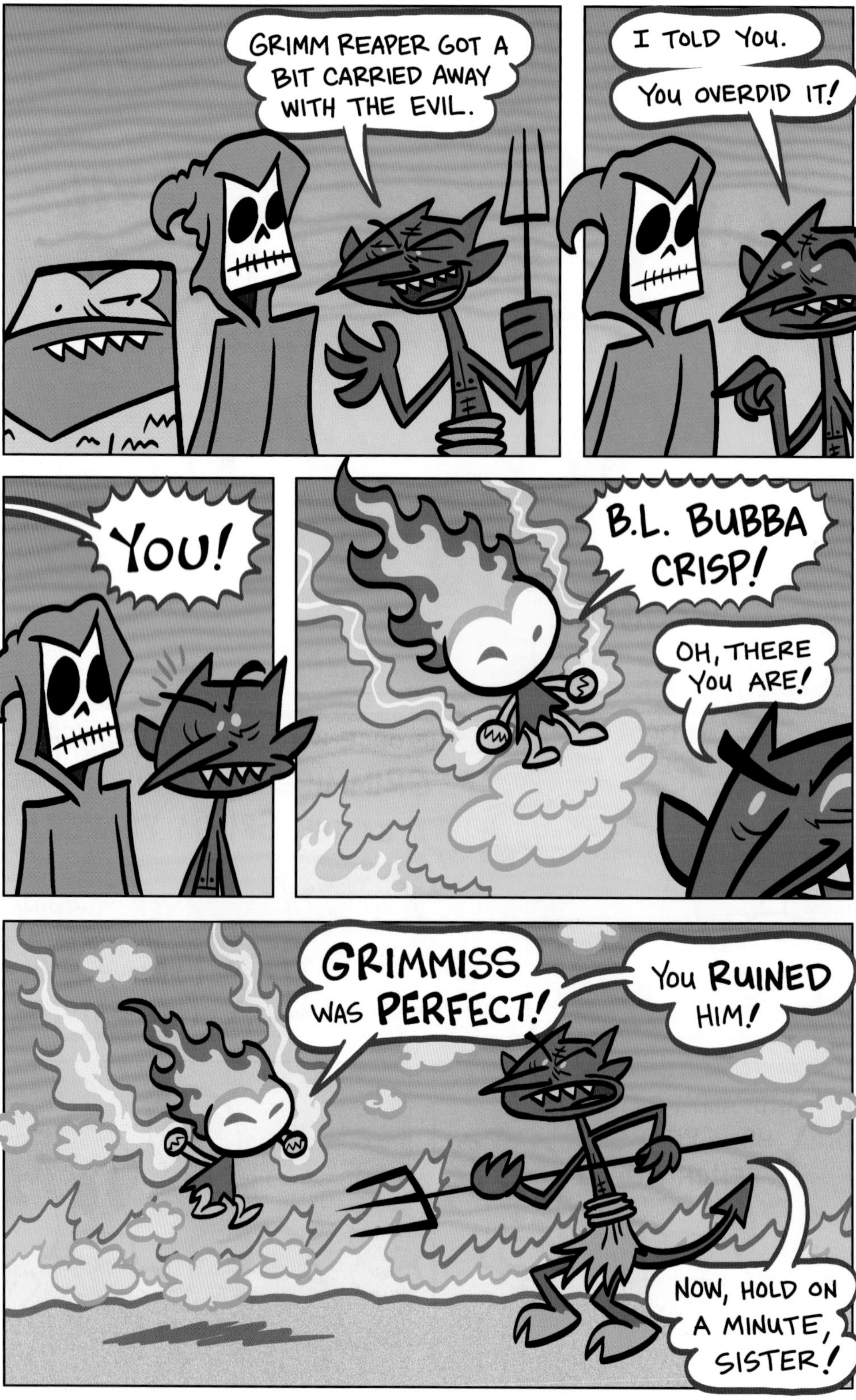
GRIMM REAPER GOT A BIT CARRIED AWAY WITH THE EVIL.
I TOLD YOU.
YOU OVERDID IT!
YOU!
B.L. BUBBA CRISP!
OH, THERE YOU ARE!
GRIMMISS WAS PERFECT!
YOU RUINED HIM!
NOW, HOLD ON A MINUTE, SISTER!

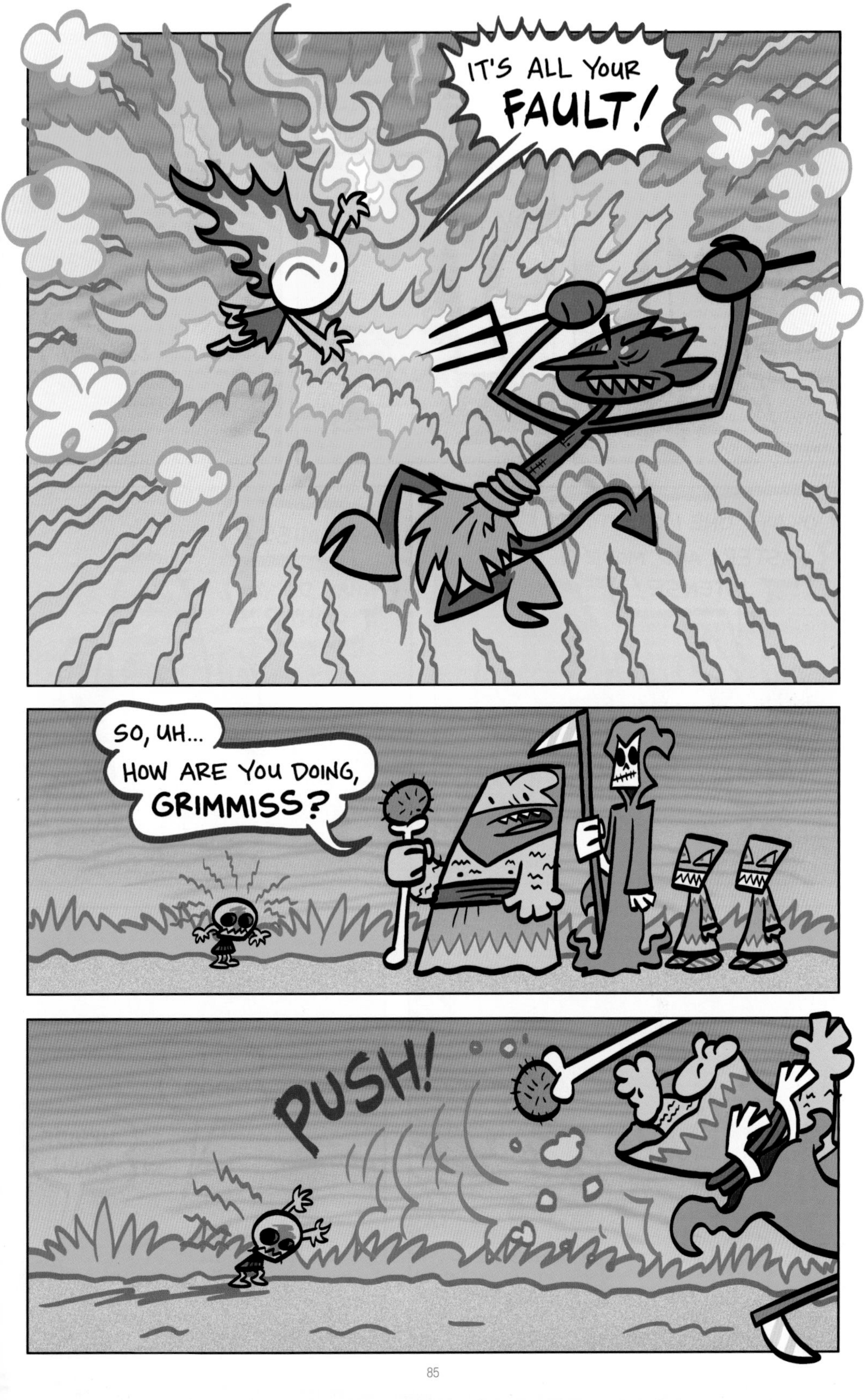
IT'S ALL YOUR FAULT!
SO, UH... HOW ARE YOU DOING, GRIMMISS?
PUSH!

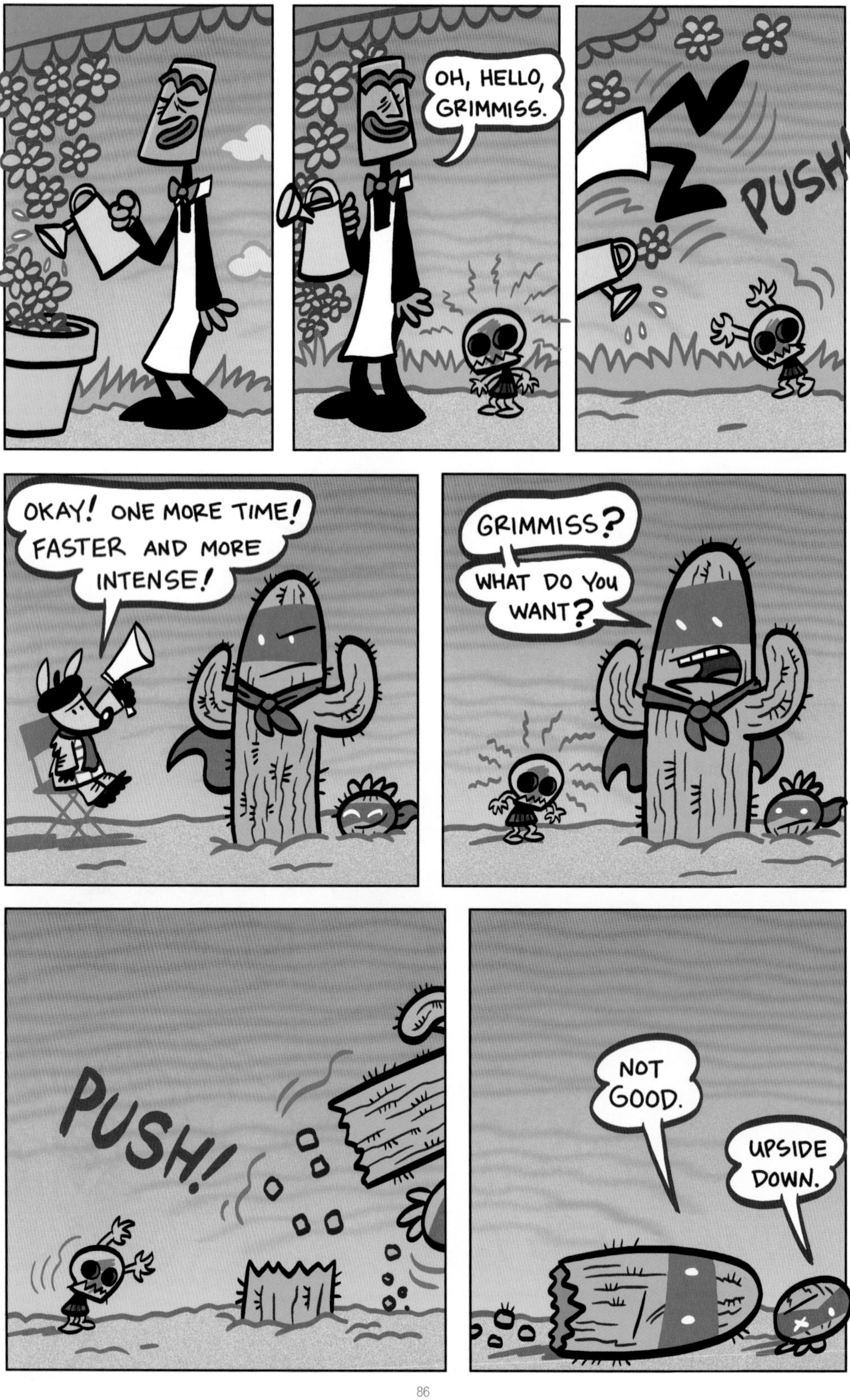
OH, HELLO, GRIMMISS.
PUSH!
OKAY! ONE MORE TIME! FASTER AND MORE INTENSE!
GRIMMISS?
WHAT DO YOU WANT?
PUSH!
NOT GOOD.
UPSIDE DOWN.

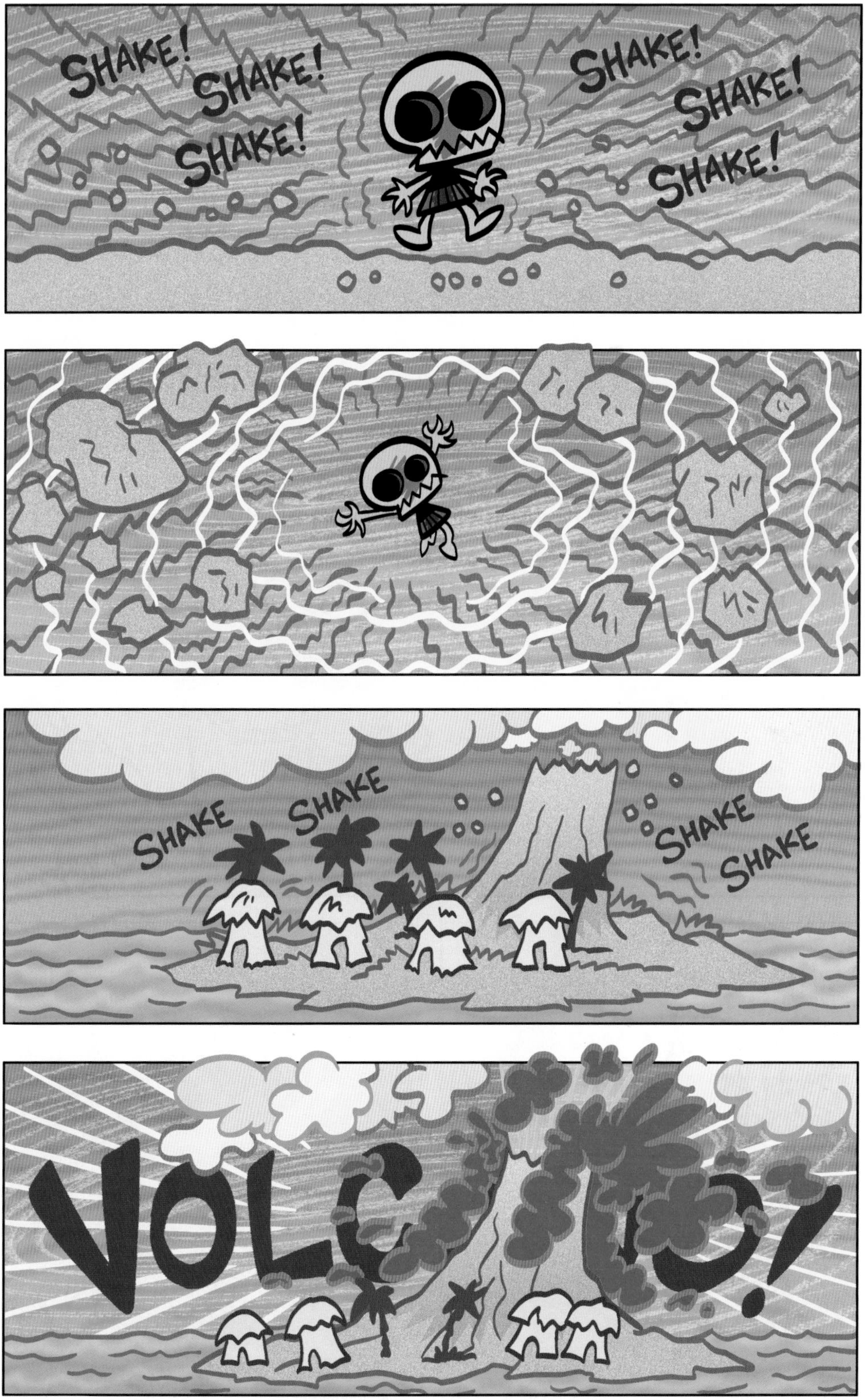
SHAKE!
SHAKE!
SHAKE!
SHAKE!
SHAKE!
SHAKE!
SHAKE
SHAKE
SHAKE
SHAKE
VOLC O!

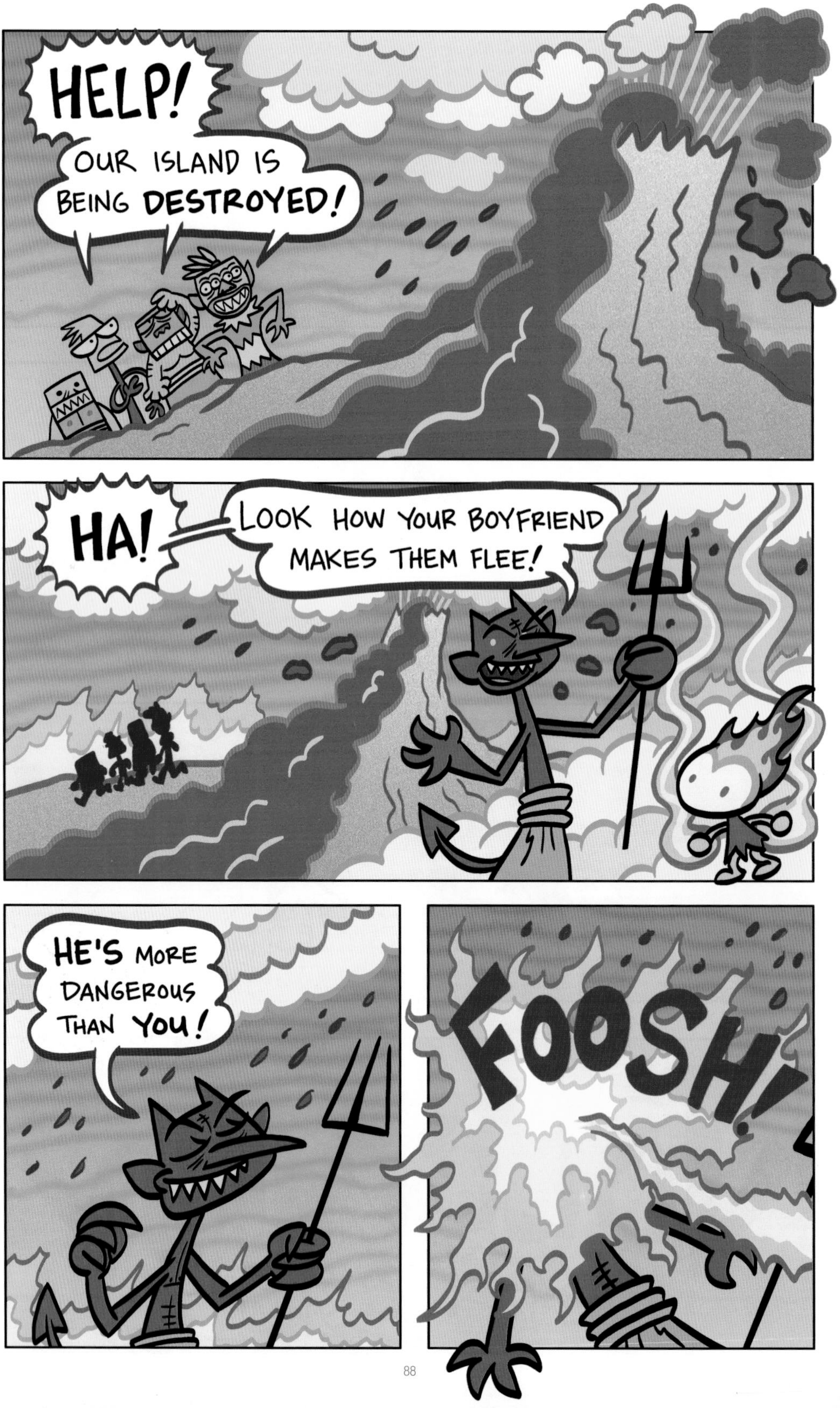
HELP!
OUR ISLAND IS BEING DESTROYED!
HA!
LOOK HOW YOUR BOYFRIEND MAKES THEM FLEE!
HE'S MORE DANGEROUS THAN YOU!
FOOSH!

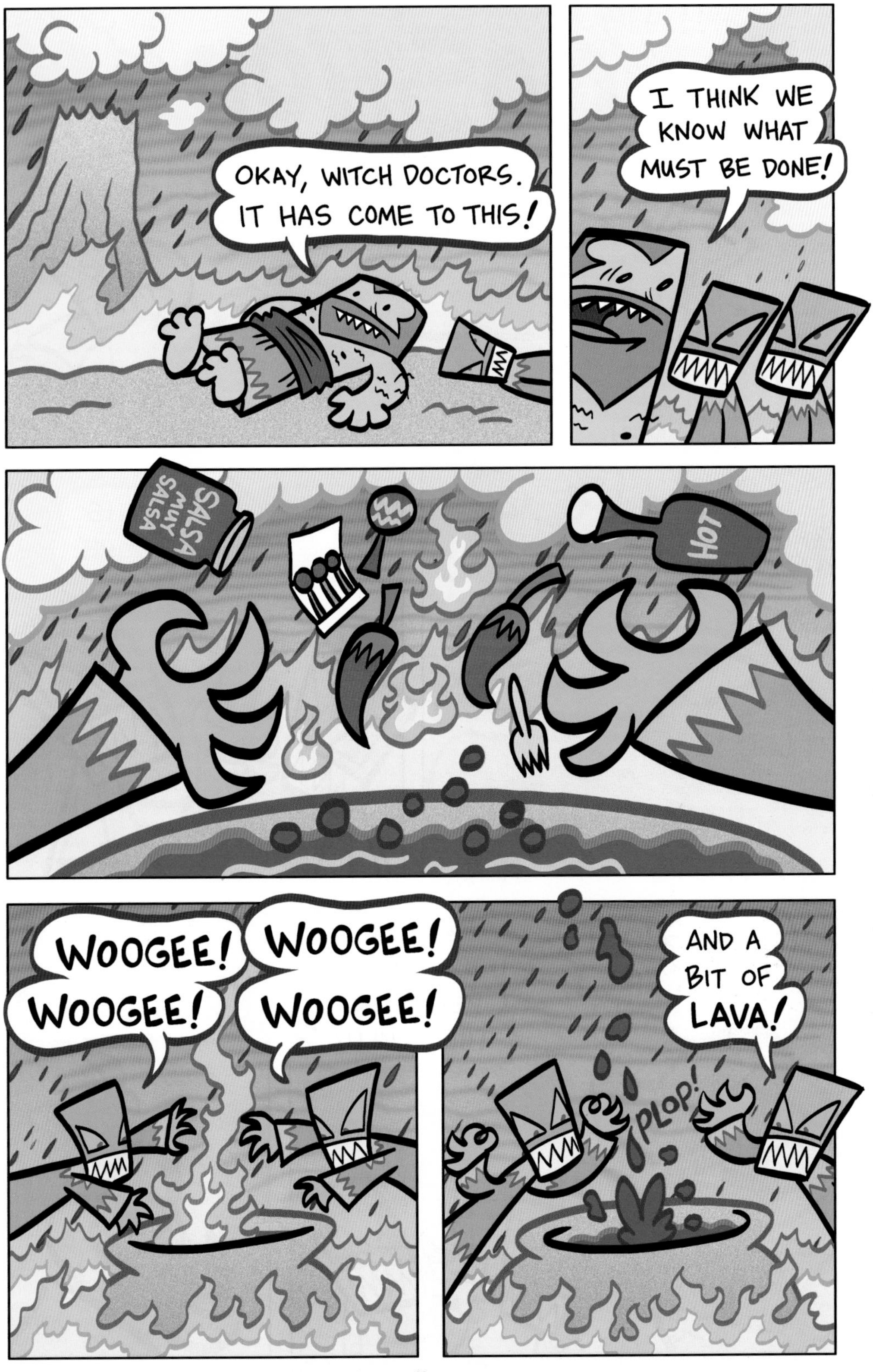
OKAY, WITCH DOCTORS. IT HAS COME TO THIS!
I THINK WE KNOW WHAT MUST BE DONE!
SALSA MUY SALSA
HOT
WOOGEE! WOOGEE!
WOOGEE! WOOGEE!
AND A BIT OF LAVA!
PLOP!

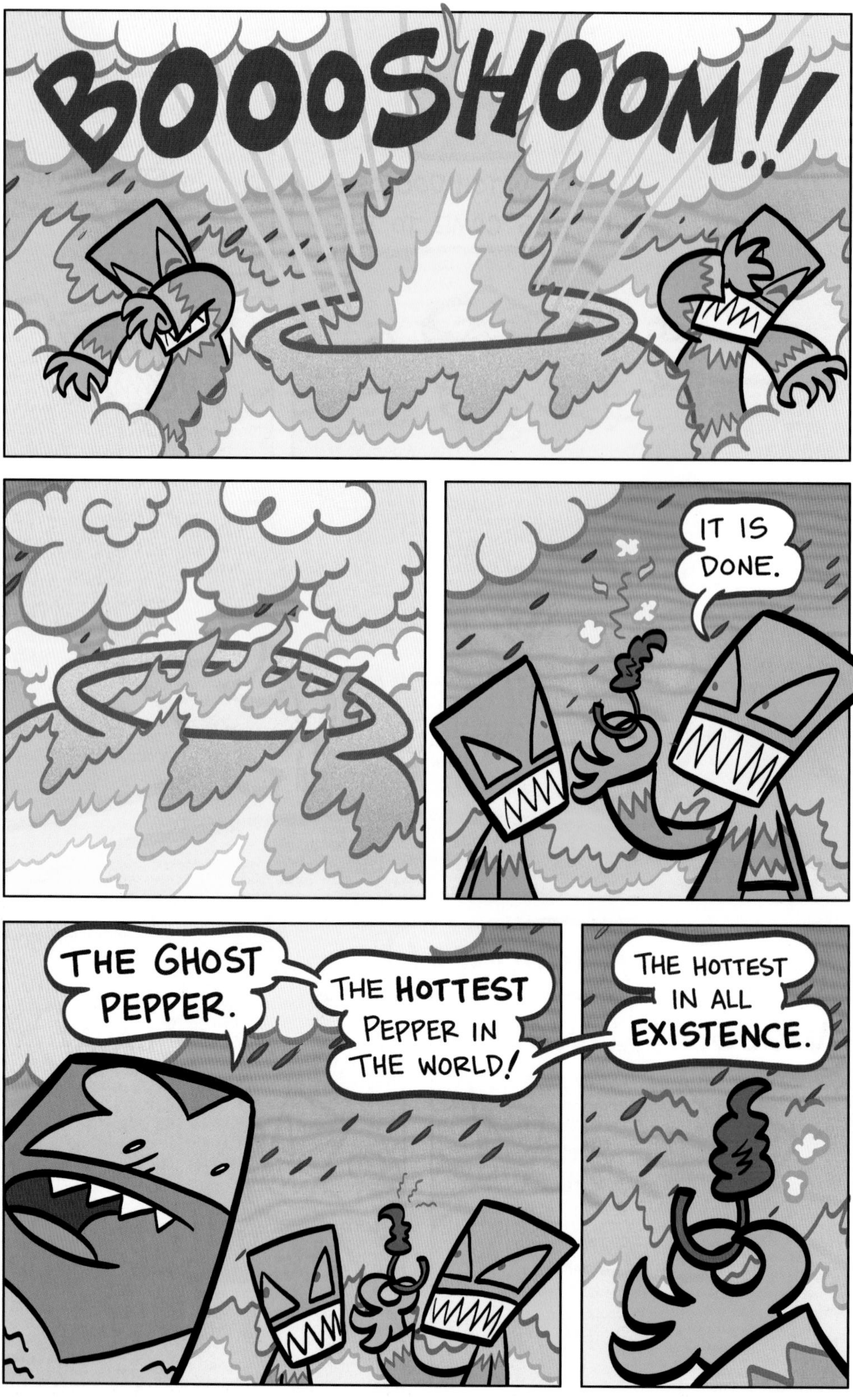
BOOOSHOOM!!
IT IS DONE.
THE GHOST PEPPER.
THE HOTTEST PEPPER IN THE WORLD!
THE HOTTEST IN ALL EXISTENCE.

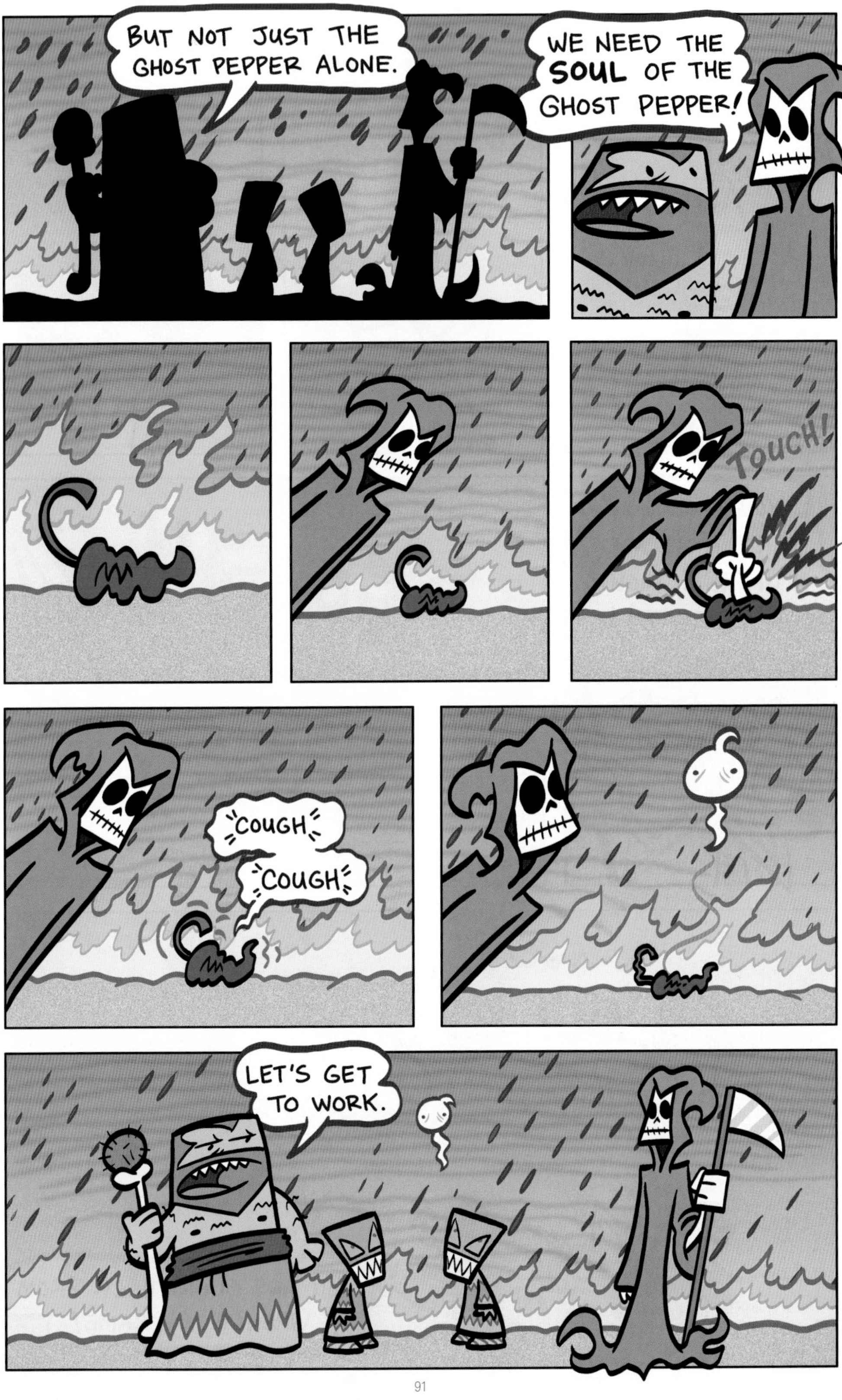
BUT NOT JUST THE GHOST PEPPER ALONE.
WE NEED THE SOUL OF THE GHOST PEPPER!
TOUCH!
COUGH
COUGH
LET'S GET TO WORK.

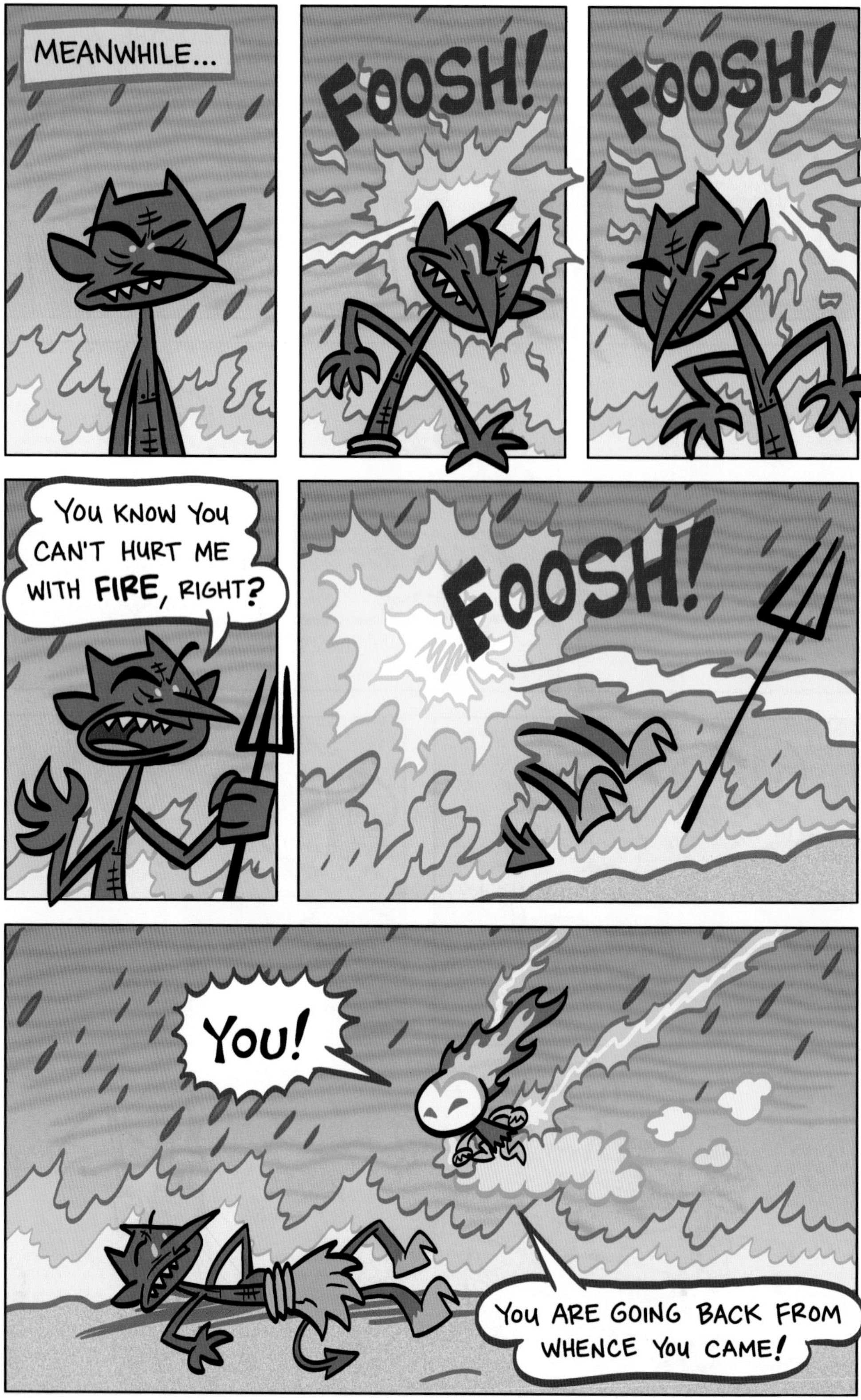
MEANWHILE...
FOOSH!
FOOSH!
YOU KNOW YOU CAN'T HURT ME WITH FIRE, RIGHT?
FOOSH!
YOU!
YOU ARE GOING BACK FROM WHENCE YOU CAME!

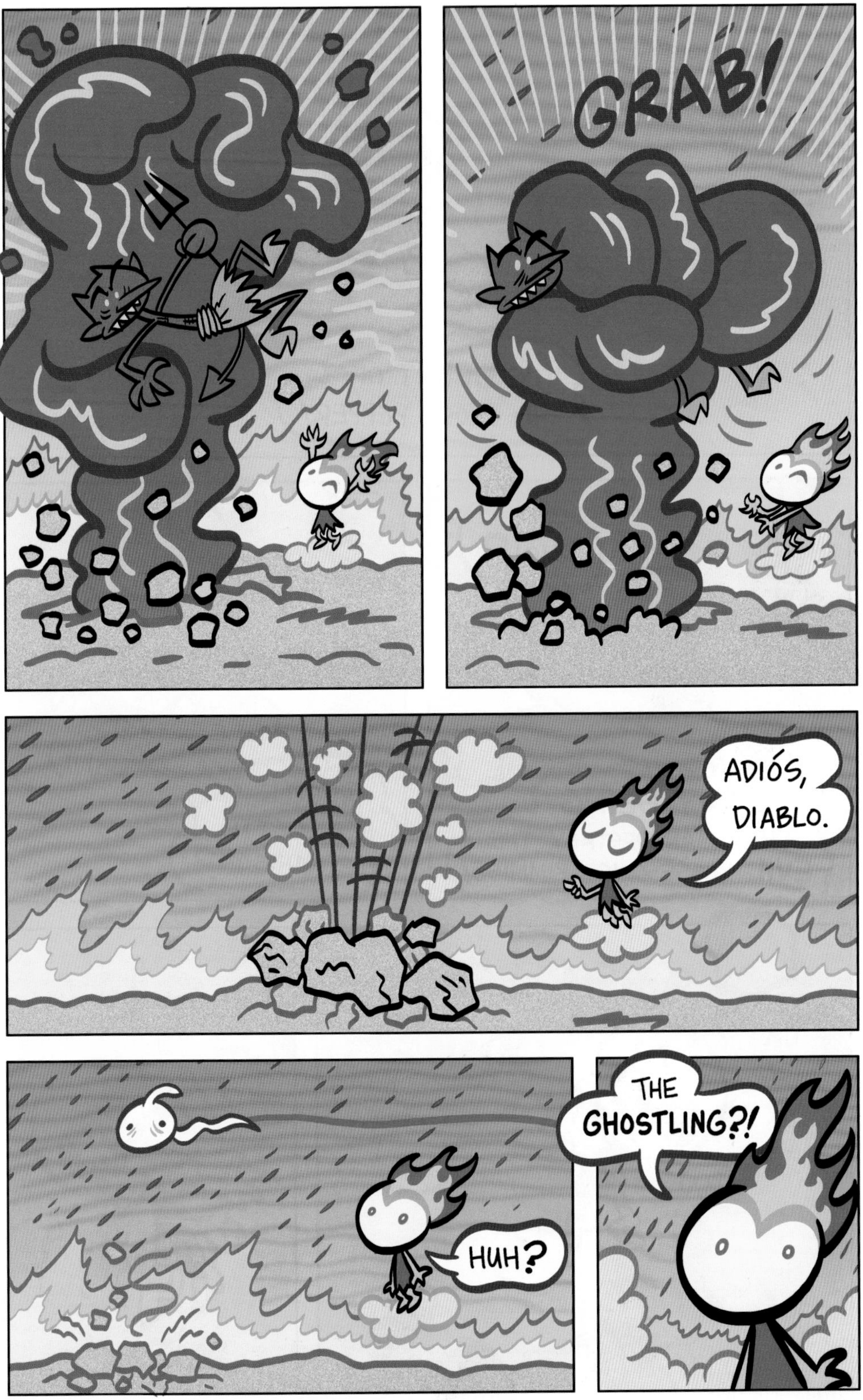
GRAB!
ADIÓS,
DIABLO.
HUH?
THE
GHOSTLING?!

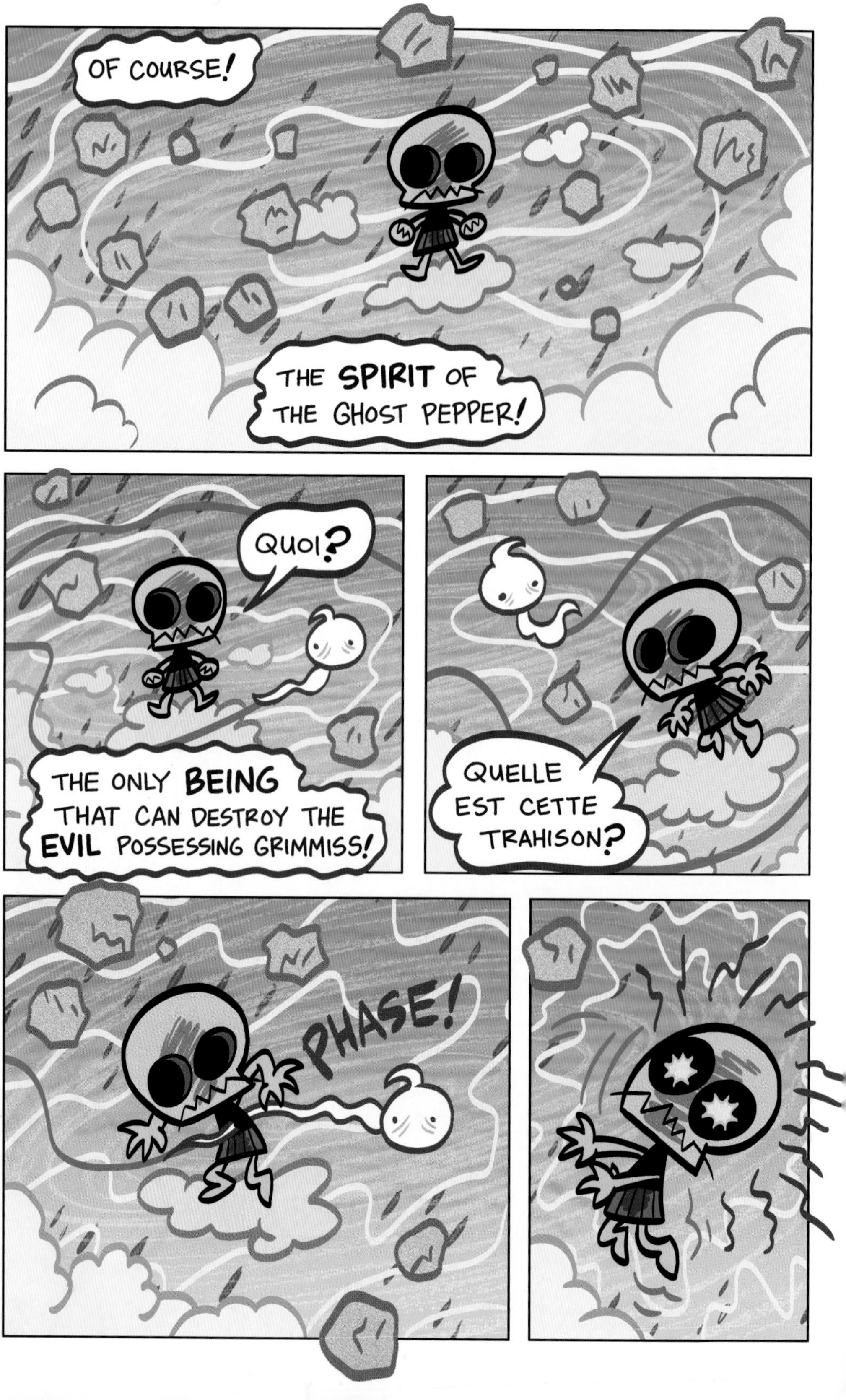
OF COURSE!
THE SPIRIT OF THE GHOST PEPPER!
QUOI?
THE ONLY BEING THAT CAN DESTROY THE EVIL POSSESSING GRIMMISS!
QUELLE EST CETTE TRAHISON?
PHASE!

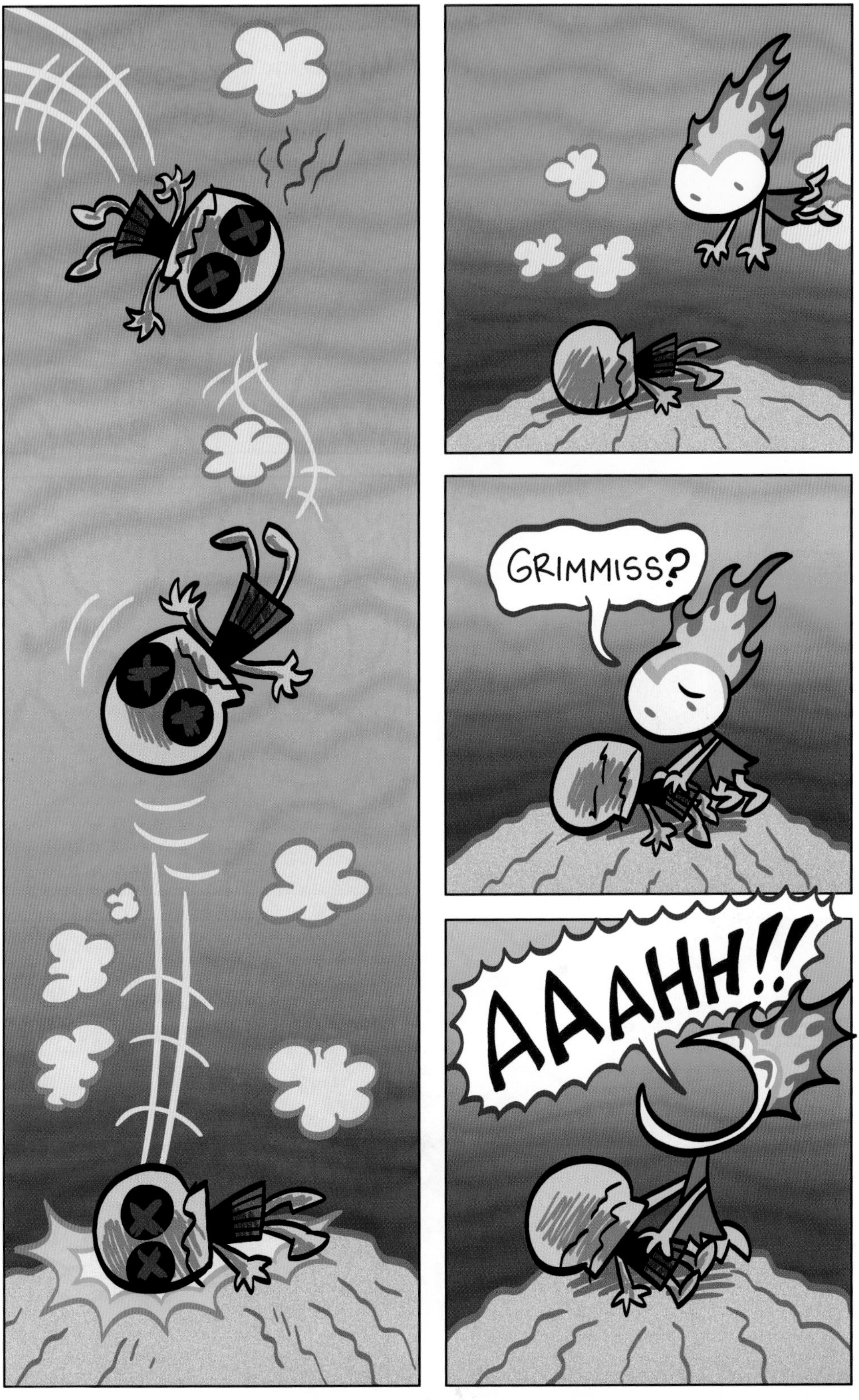
GRIMMISS?
AAAHH!!

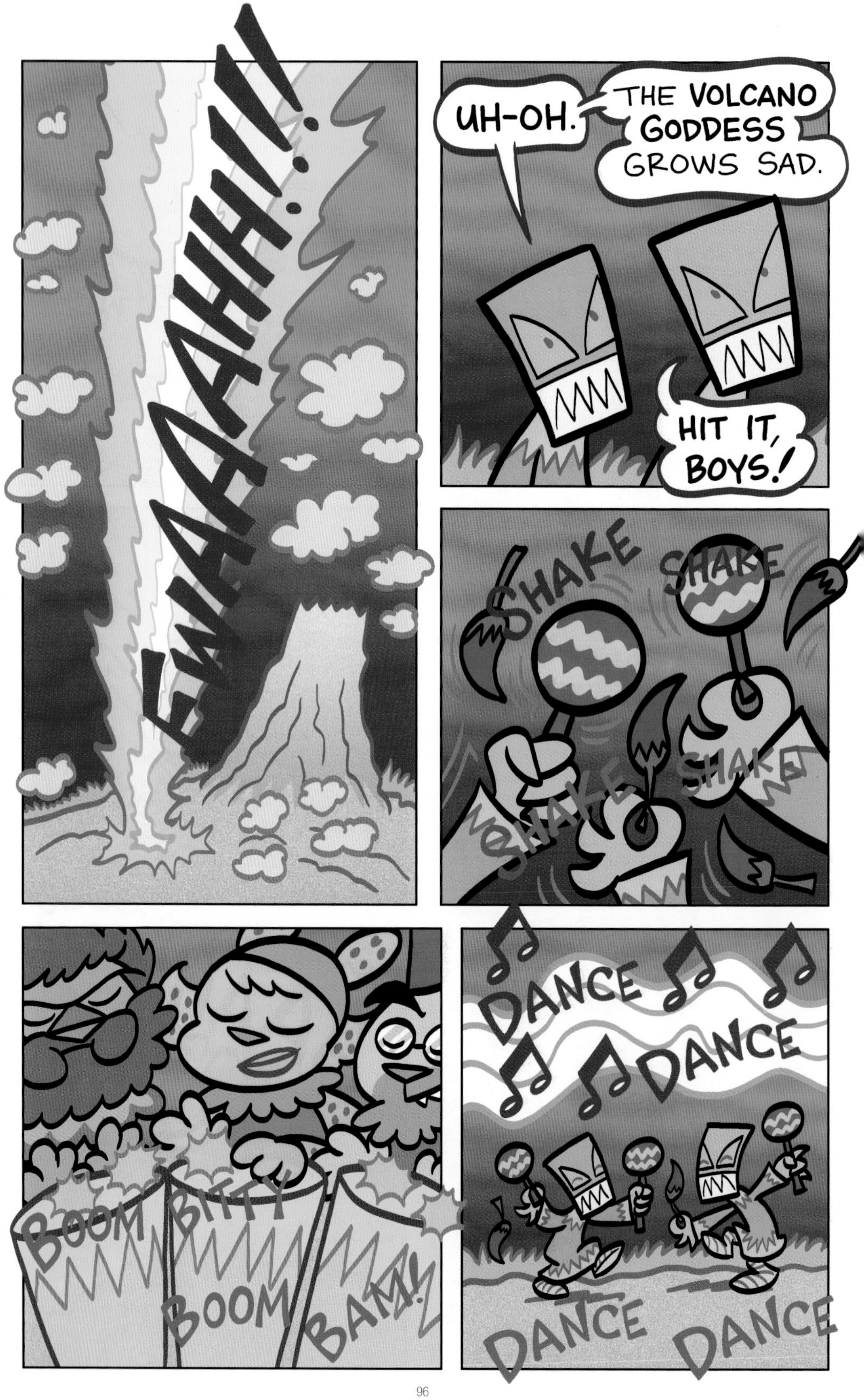
EWAAAHH!!!
UH-OH.
THE VOLCANO GODDESS GROWS SAD.
HIT IT, BOYS!
SHAKE
SHAKE
SHAKE
SHAKE
BOOM
BITTY
BOOM
BAM!
DANCE
DANCE
DANCE
DANCE

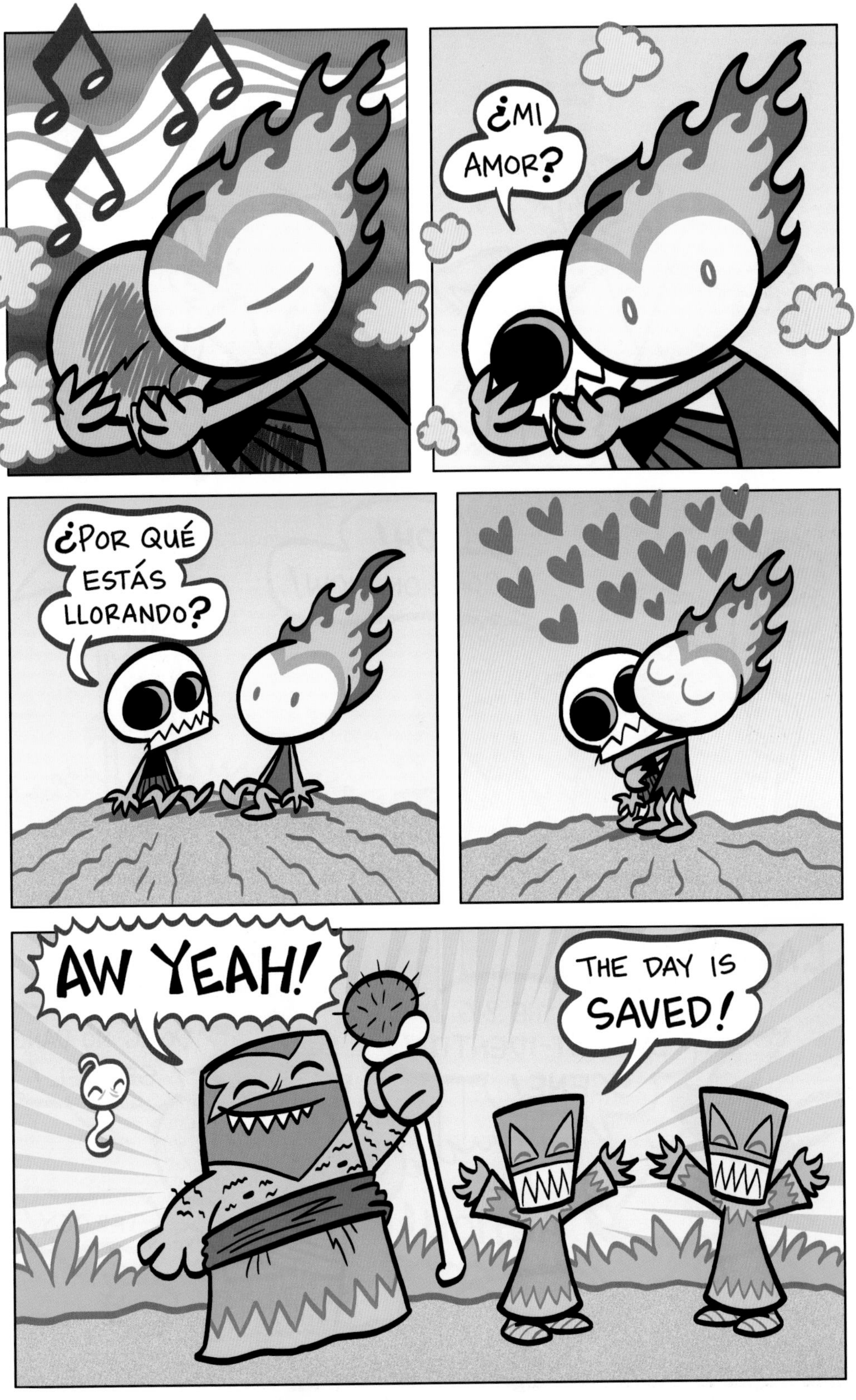
¿MI AMOR?
¿POR QUÉ ESTÁS LLORANDO?
AW YEAH!
THE DAY IS SAVED!

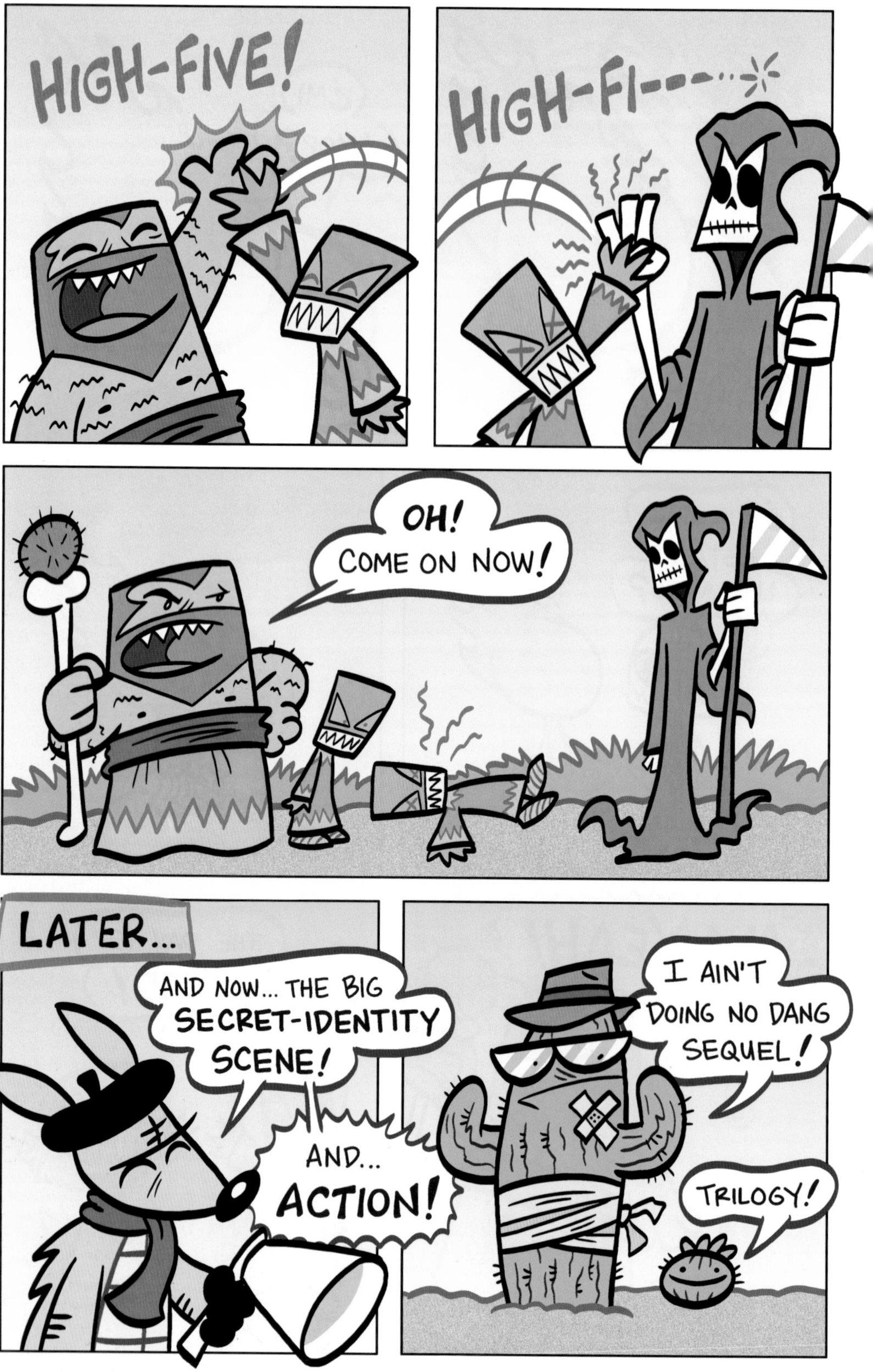
HIGH-FIVE!
HIGH-FI----...
OH! COME ON NOW!
LATER...
AND NOW... THE BIG SECRET-IDENTITY SCENE!
AND... ACTION!
I AIN'T DOING NO DANG SEQUEL!
TRILOGY!

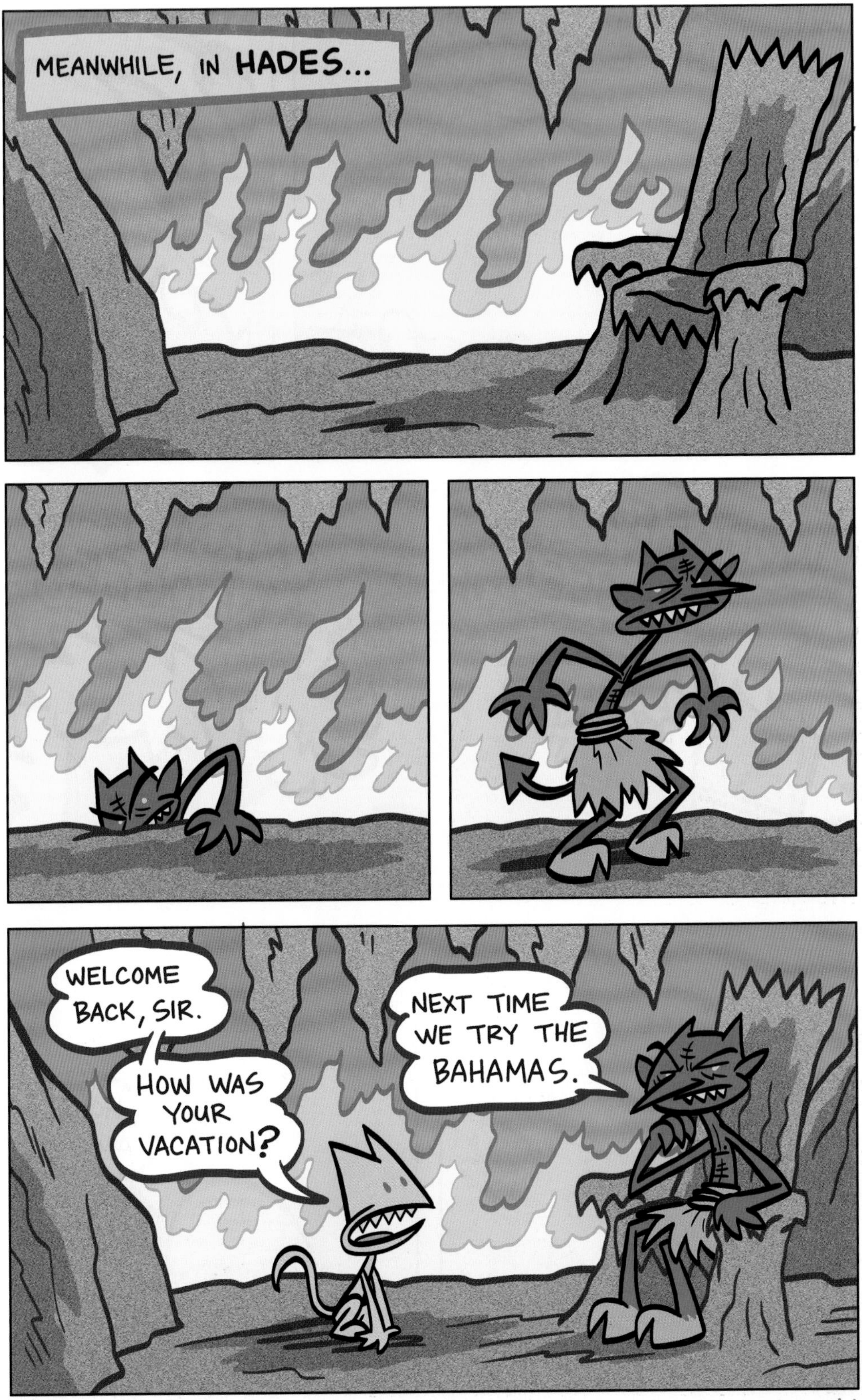
MEANWHILE, IN HADES...
WELCOME BACK, SIR.
HOW WAS YOUR VACATION?
NEXT TIME WE TRY THE BAHAMAS.

—AW YA MON!

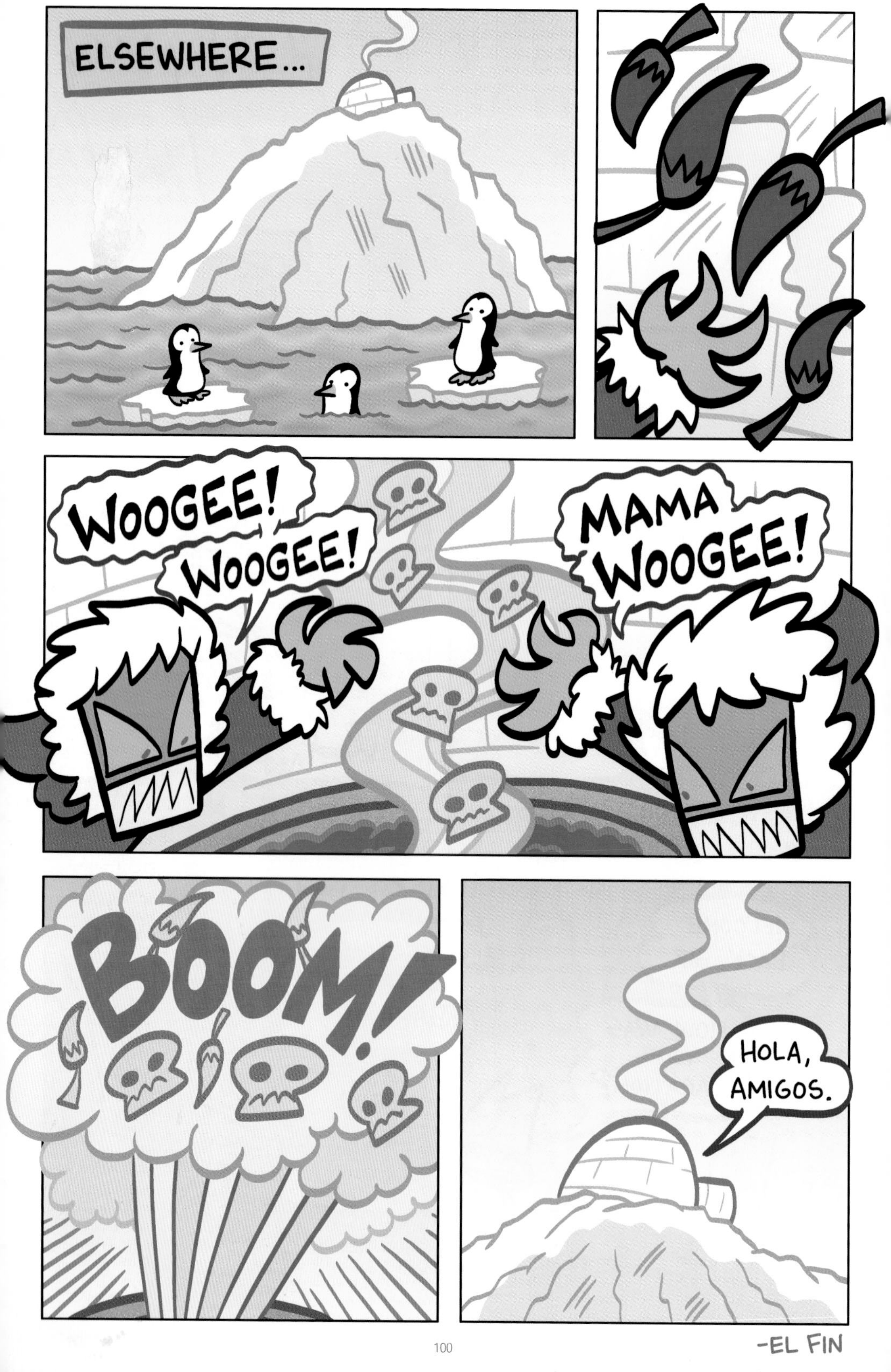
ELSEWHERE...
WOOGEE!
WOOGEE!
MAMA WOOGEE!
BOOM!
HOLA, AMIGOS.
-EL FIN

CHARACTERS!

Here are Art Baltazar's character designs for Grimmiss and his friends and some drawings for Dark Horse's catalog pages. We love them!

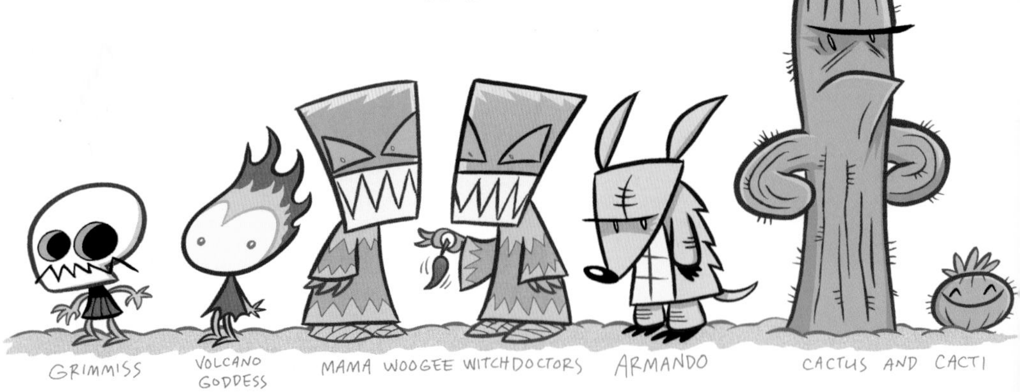
GRIMMISS
VOLCANO GODDESS
MAMA WOOGEE WITCHDOCTORS
ARMANDO
CACTUS AND CACTI

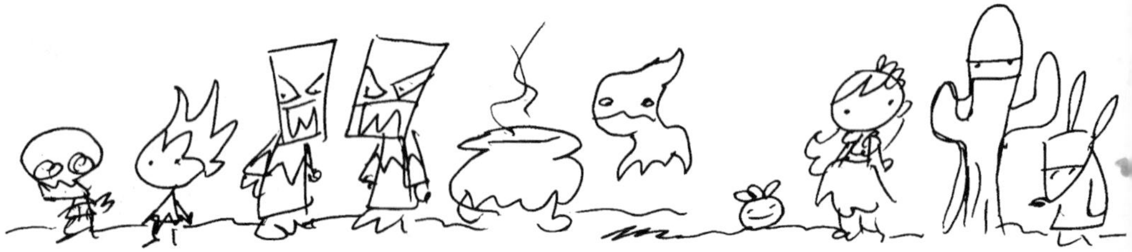

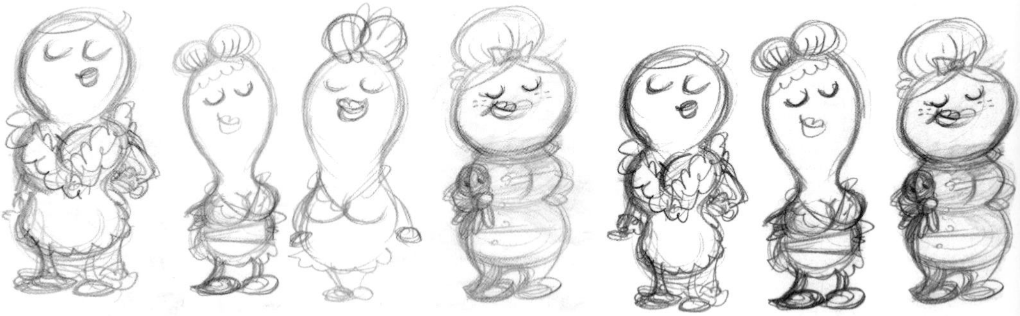

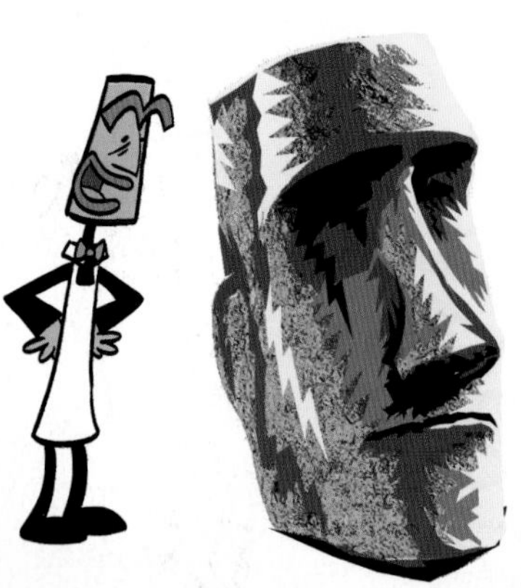

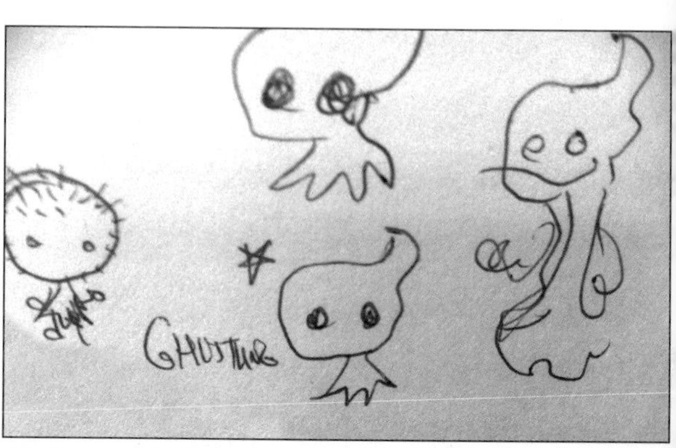

ART BALTAZAR & FRANCO

THE CREATORS OF *Tiny Titans*, *Superman Family Adventures*, and *Aw Yeah Comics!* COME TO DARK HORSE WITH a big bunch OF Rib-tickling, all-ages books!

"Enjoyable work that fits quite nicely into hands of any age or in front of eyes of any child."
—Comic Book Resources

ITTY BITTY HELLBOY
978-1-61655-414-9 | $9.99

ITTY BITTY MASK
978-1-61655-683-9 | $12.99

AW YEAH COMICS! AND . . . ACTION!
978-1-61655-558-0 | $12.99

AW YEAH COMICS! TIME FOR . . . ADVENTURE!
978-1-61655-689-1 | $12.99

GRIMMISS ISLAND
978-1-61655-768-3 | $12.99

ALSO AVAILABLE FROM DARK HORSE!

THE HIT VIDEO GAME CONTINUES ITS COMIC BOOK INVASION!

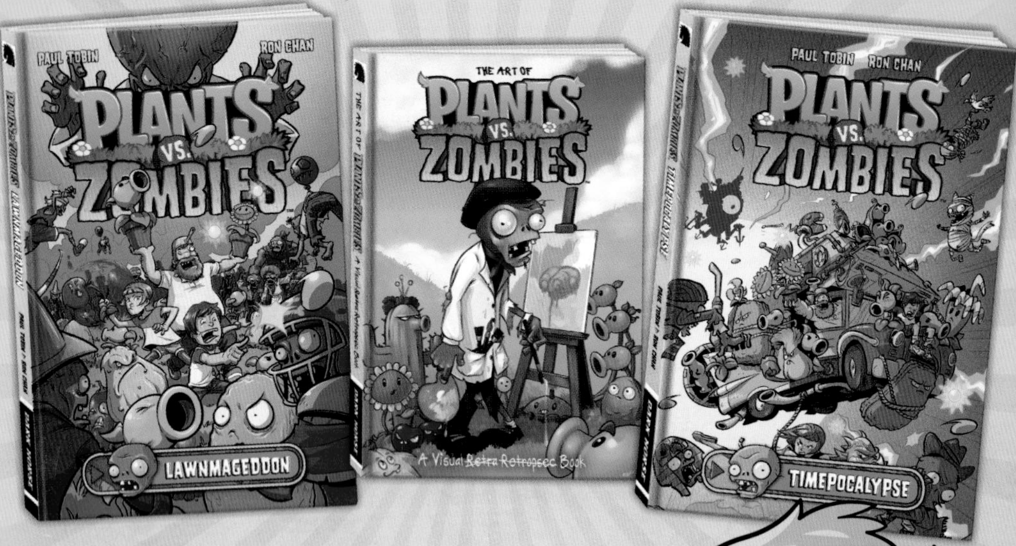
PAUL TOBIN
RON CHAN
PLANTS VS. ZOMBIES
LAWNMAGEDDON
THE ART OF
PLANTS VS. ZOMBIES
PAUL TOBIN
RON CHAN
PLANTS VS. ZOMBIES
TIMEPOCALYPSE

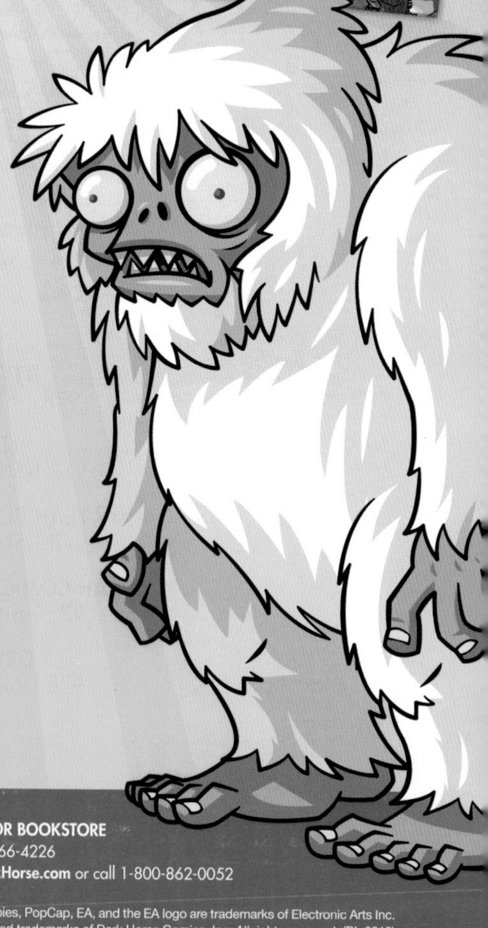

PLANTS VS. ZOMBIES: LAWNMAGEDDON

Crazy Dave—the babbling-yet-brilliant inventor and top-notch neighborhood defender—helps his niece Patrice and young adventurer Nate Timely fend off a zombie invasion that threatens to overrun the peaceful town of Neighborville in *Plants vs. Zombies: Lawnmageddon*! Their only hope is a brave army of chomping, squashing, and pea-shooting plants! A wacky adventure for zombie zappers young and old!

ISBN 978-1-61655-192-6 | $9.99

THE ART OF PLANTS VS. ZOMBIES

Part zombie memoir, part celebration of zombie triumphs, and part anti-plant screed, *The Art of Plants vs. Zombies* is a treasure trove of never-before-seen concept art from PopCap's popular *Plants vs. Zombies* games! A treasure trove of never-before-seen concept art, character sketches, and surprises!

ISBN 978-1-61655-331-9 | $9.99

PLANTS VS. ZOMBIES: TIMEPOCALYPSE

Crazy Dave helps Patrice and Nate Timely fend off Zomboss's latest attack in *Plants vs. Zombies: Timepocalypse*! This new standalone tale will tickle your funny bones and thrill your brains through any timeline!

ISBN 978-1-61655-621-1 | $9.99

DARK HORSE BOOKS
EA
PopCap

AVAILABLE AT YOUR LOCAL COMICS SHOP OR BOOKSTORE
To find a comics shop in your area, call 1-888-266-4226
For more information or to order direct visit **DarkHorse.com** or call 1-800-862-0052